Caribbean Competitors

SIMONA ISLAND, BOOK 2

POPPY
MINNIX

CARIBBEAN COMPETITORS

POPPY MINNIX

CITY OWL
PRESS

CARIBBEAN COMPETITORS
Simona Island, Book 2

CITY OWL PRESS
www.cityowlpress.com

Cover Design by MiblArt. All stock photos licensed appropriately.

Edited by Mary Cain.

For information on subsidiary rights, please contact the publisher at info@cityowlpress.com.

Print Edition ISBN: 978-1-64898-262-0

Digital Edition ISBN: 978-1-64898-263-7

Printed in the United States of America

To hot mess people and the ones who adore them

PRAISE FOR POPPY MINNIX

"Poppy Minnix's vibrant descriptions in *Caribbean Competitors* rush through you, sucking you into the push and pull of Xia and Apollo's relationship until you realize it's three a.m. and you gotta be up in two hours! I loved every minute of this delicious romance and can't wait for more!" – *Codi Gary, author of Things Good Girls Don't Do*

"*Holiday Hotel* should be named Happiness Hotel! I loved this story of Cozi who finds herself and a second chance at love on an impromptu vacation. I highly recommend this story for people who love Happily Ever Afters and Christmas cursing." – *JL Bowman, Author*

"Poppy Minnix brings a fresh breath of air to Greek mythology in *My Song's Curse*. The characters jumped off the page and stole my heart." – *Cassandra Kay, Host of Punchkeys Podcast*

"Putting a new twist on an old story, Poppy Minnix kept me on the edge of my seat." – *Raisa Greywood, Bestselling Author of Demon Lust*

"*Holiday Hotel* is a fun holiday story I'll be reaching for every Christmas going forward. I started smiling on page one, and I swear the smile stayed stuck on my face the entire time I read it. My cheeks hurt. It's that good." – *Imogen Keeper, Author*

"From the steamy flirting to the classic lore, this story's magical from start to finish! Lula's fun voice will captivate you like it does all of humanity." – *Jackie Norling, Author*

"Just like the myth, *My Song's Curse* will lure you in and captivate you. You won't want to stop turning the pages as you root for Alex and Lula's love to endure the odds in this steamy, fun, and flirty romance." – *Lumen Ros, Paranormal and Dark Fantasy Author*

"A wonderful story, in which the paranormal aspect does not overshadow the plot and storytelling. It features compelling characters, lovely description, snappy dialogue, and melt-me steamy moments! A great read!"– *Chloe Holiday, Author*

"*My Song's Curse* was seductive, intoxicating and I was obsessed from just that first page. This was a forbidden love story that wove mythology, friendship and love throughout the pages, and I loved every minute of it. If you enjoy paranormal or adult romance, then you definitely need this book in your life!" – *Star Crossed Book Blog*

THE CASE OF THE SAND INDENTS

*T*he sand is my track. The tree, my finish line.

The alluring rhythm of the pop beats in my earbuds deserves a different type of movement beyond the pounding of my feet, but I can't stop for a dance break. The Moss Monster Meet approaches and with it the dream I've held since I toddled on unsteady baby legs. I'm not unsteady anymore.

Nevertheless, dancing is out of the question. Later at the club or in my kitchen, I can work it until my soul's content. There's a time for everything and now is not—

At the chorus, I slow and spin into salsa steps, swaying hips stretching muscles that were focused on one task alone. Before the verse kicks back in, I launch myself on track. Faster now in this last haul to make up those lost seconds. I've got this so hard. Warrior woman party-of-one coming in hot.

The crowd of ocean waves lined up to my right roars encouragement at my approach while palm leaves flap in the breeze on my left like banners and posters and big silly foam fingers. Each of these final steps works toward the win I will have in a month and five days. My lungs ache, and my muscles threaten to turn to goo, but it's only a threat and I'm not listening.

"Three triathlons," I wheeze into the air. "Two Mossies." I lick my lips. "One more." I am so close to murdering my record. "Just. One. More. Time." I pound past the tree decorated with my old jeans—the ones my thighs outgrew while training for my first triathlon—slap the stop button on my watch and ease up on my sprint. "Six seconds longer?" I huff, then jump out the ache of overtaxed muscles while I shake out my hands. Stupid impossible-to-deny dance break. It's fine. Doesn't matter. I'll win the Mossy anyway. No one else trains like I do.

I stare at the indents on the typically barren sand of Simona Island's western shore. Maybe someone decided to use this as their training ground too. I run beside them for another mile. Slow and steady is my pace, and since I can't seem to deny the music entrancing my soul, I put more jump and sway into my steps. When I return to my starting point, I'm well and truly tired.

I walk the mystery divots, thigh muscles stretching as my breathing slows to normal. It's hard to investigate dry sand prints, but if I'm right, this person's stride is longer than mine.

Maybe I'll have some competition this year. A month isn't a ton of time, but enough for someone to increase their speed and stamina if they're dedicated. So far, none of the residents can beat my times on any of the events. I'd know because I'd hear about it if there was a real challenge.

Visitors will say Simona Island is known for its dedication to preventing overtourism or being one of the best locations to fall deeper in love. Residents praise its ability to be both a small town and a well-stocked paradise. It may be all of those, but it's also the gossip epicenter of the Caribbean. I stay out of it at every opportunity, unless they're talking about my competitors, the race path that remains secret until meet day, or people who have left the island—a person who has left the island.

I swore I saw him at the end of a hallway while I was speeding to the spa to meet a client for their appointment. But when I backtracked, the space was empty. Not even a tall, dark, and handsome shadow. No honey eyes. No easy smile that lifts the right side of his lips a split second before the left catches up. My heart and lungs did all kinds of flippy-floppy things they shouldn't have been doing. A few coworkers were with me and raised eyebrows over how I stared at the spot where I swore he'd been, tilting my head like I couldn't understand why he hadn't teleported from New York to that hallway.

In my daze, I confessed the exact thing I shouldn't have. "I thought I saw Apollo Fischer."

For the rest of the afternoon my coworkers went into whisper mode, which spread like a spritz of patchouli into an unbreathable fog that's never going away. I wished they would have just yelled, "Hear ye, hear ye! Xiamara still constantly thinks about Apollo and continues to get frazzled at the slightest hint of him!" It would have been better than the tension itching up the back of my neck, knowing everyone was talking about me. It made my shoulders raise so high, even Chillax couldn't return them to Earth. And that is my most de-stressing aromatherapy mix.

This island is paradise, and the people are the best this planet offers, but I wish they'd watch reality shows instead of pretending they're in one.

Gossip is the worst. I was the center of conversation for too long when I was little, but I have to admit that when I overhear Apollo's name, I leap onto what's being said as if it's the finish line. Rumors are minimal when it comes to him though; not enough to find out any personal details of his life now. A couple words here and there about how they miss him or that his Ma's been trying to lure him back to work at the Cliffs, but then it's muted whispers and walking away, and I end up falling out of a chair in the dining hall because I'd been leaning so far. Pretty sure half the island heard about that by the time I peeled my red face off the floor.

"Bleh." I stop, turn toward the ocean, and stretch my burning muscles. The waves are choppy today, and the overcast haze whispers about an afternoon shower. A deep, three-second inhale brings my thoughts back to business and away from the man I have no reason to think about anymore. I exhale and shake my head. Moss Monster Meet. Training. Work. This is my life.

My goal for this Mossy is to secure the Moss Boss title. I think Mama is ready to give it up. She's held the pearl trophy for two decades, watching from the sidelines, waiting for someone to win three years in a row.

Waiting for me.

My face is sweat-soaked and chilly. I'm tempted to dive into the ocean, but it's temperamental on this side of the island. Instead, I head over to my shiny blue golf cart and put my foot on the white back-facing seat, leaning in, hands on my warm thigh.

After a speedy back and hip stretch, I drive over the crunchy path of shell and stones toward Simona Island's only main road. It's shaped like a crescent moon on the eastern side of the island, curving against the twin mountains and leaving most of the west to small paths through the jungle.

Vic's blue Tacoma roars around the bend and halts with enough force to skid on the gravel, palm fronds slapping at the windshield. Focusing on navigating the narrow path, I keep moving, veering to the side and into ferns and tiny bushes that wallop the underside of the cart with *thunks* and scratches. As we squeeze by each other, I wave, until I realize who's driving.

It's not Vic.

There's no returned smile, only a courteous lift of his haven't-shaved-yet chin like it's required.

My lungs have malfunctioned, burning to expel the breath

I'm holding. It pops out with a squeak and thank God the truck's windows are up. However, the truck slows to a stop, and the driver's eyes lift to mine, his lips tight. That "let's get this over with" face hasn't changed a bit since we were kids.

I smash the pedal and reel out of there as if being chased, but it's the past I'm afraid will catch up to me. It's not adult-like in the least.

There's no way. Well, there has to be a way because that was not Vic, her daughter, nor anyone else who lives on Simona Island. There's no mistaking it. That face is etched so deeply into my memory that I just know it will be my last vision on my deathbed, and then I'll die awkwardly, and it will be all his fault.

Apollo. I shake my head and snort. "I knew it."

The bumps in the road send my ass off the seat and tell me to slow the hell down or end up there. The truck's taillights disappear past a thick line of bushes.

The part of me that misses him and what we used to be rejoices. Then the rational side remembers how I act around him and says, "Oh, Xia. This is the *worst* timing."

2

A BEE TO HONEY

*A*pollo Fischer's last words to me were, "I'm coming back after graduation. Don't make me wait too long, Xiamara Nivar. This island is in our blood, and we belong here. Together."

It was a promise—or maybe a threat, because how he affects me is a nuclear weapon against my sanity. But he didn't return after graduation, did he? Nor the year after, nor the one after that.

Yet he's back now.

Why? I haven't acknowledged that I saw him to anyone; therefore, I have zero confirmation about his local whereabouts. I'm listening to gossip more than I ever have, sneaking down corridors, hiding behind plants, and leaning toward dining hall conversations—careful not to fall on the floor—and there's not a peep, mumble, or sigh about him. Maybe he was only in to visit his mom and sister and wanted to see the western shore. That's probably it. He was saying goodbye to the ocean, then jetting back to his big life in New York that afternoon. Gone, like he wants to be.

"Hey Xia!"

A shrill chirp escapes me, and I smoosh the bulb of the lemon oil dropper between my fingers. The pipette empties into the glass bottle of what should have been a refreshing blend for the lobby that I was going to call Welcome to Paradise. Now it will be named Ruined by Citrus. I really need to get a set-drop micropipette. It would prevent accidental over-saturation moments like this.

"Hmm," Jose says, walking into my closet-sized consultation room and setting his chin on my shoulder to casually observe my failure. "My darling. Did you just...squeak?"

"No," I lie and swirl the concoction before inhaling. Twenty drops instead of three? Yep. That's just lemon now. I bite back curses and force a smile as I dump the contents in the sink and set out a fresh, sterilized bottle from the overhead cabinet, the emulsifier, oils, a funnel, and purified water. "So, my dancy-pants friend, what brings you to my humble consultation room?"

He spins to lean against the counter as I resume measuring. "Would you like to tell me why you've been silently over-thinking and stalking in the shadows for two days?"

I cock my head at him. Saying no will only enhance his curiosity. "PMS?"

His *womp womp* buzzer sound is impressive. "How dare you invoke the uterine goddesses to escape a conversation. Five minutes ago, I heard—" His perfectly groomed black eyebrows slam into a glare. "—*he's* on the island. And I didn't hear it from *you*. I am super insulted right now."

Of course Jose would hear the exact gossip I was seeking. I keep my eyes on the spray bottle as I tip in the emulsion at the optimal agitation angle. "Who?"

Jose drops his head back and groans at the ceiling. "Xia-mara Abigail Nivar. It's me, darling."

It may be him, my work husband and half of my best friend team, but this isn't a night full of mojitos and mancala—which we've dubbed M&M night. This is work, with people walking by the door, and I have to concentrate on this guest-welcoming concoction.

"Jose," I say with determination yet kindness. "I need to make this for the lobby. I can't talk now." Swirling the oil vials to gently mix them, I focus on the task. Not the still-glaring eyes scorching the side of my face or the thousand thoughts of Apollo determined to poke through every second of silence. "Must concentrate." That reminder wasn't for Jose alone.

"Can I watch?"

"Of course. Just don't move. Or talk." There. That should postpone his questions for the time being. I stretch and ball my fingers. Shake them out. Breathe deep and dive into the method of mixing I've perfected over the years. It's my art, my contribution to making this world feel better through emotion-invoking scent.

Four drops of clary sage drip into the emulsion, two of peppermint I distilled last week, three of nutmeg and lemon. Another swirl of the bottle, then funnel in the purest island water. And there. Perfect. Hopefully. Aroma preference is as unique as a fingerprint, so what matters most is how mixes affect the body. This should sink shoulders, ease the stress of travel, while energizing the mind. After this initial welcome to El Escape, guests will be bombarded with a thousand scents on their vacation, from food and walking around outside to the lavender sheets and disinfectants I'd approved after twenty-two samples and too many phone consultations with the supply company.

Threading the spritzer tube into the bottle, I tighten, give it one more swirl, and spray the air. As I study Jose's face, blood rushes behind my ears and my heart pounds faster than when I sprint. He is the best and most terrifying person to test scents with because every emotion is right there in his eyes and the twitch of his lips.

"Well?" I ask.

His nostrils flare with his inhale, and he squints, brows bunching so close into distaste that I almost turn around to dump the contents down the drain. But then he tilts his head and relaxes into a grin. "That's nice. Homey. It reminds me of an old boyfriend." His hand shoots out to block me as I go to toss the mix. "In a good way. Comfortable dinner parties where everyone congregates in the kitchen and talks over each other because the conversation is marvelous. I like it. Brilliant work, Xia."

The muscles in my neck unlock, and I keep swirling the bottle. Is that good enough though? I did go food-scent heavy, but those create the sharpest memories. Maybe that works, because long after someone has left, they'll be making a meal and it will remind them of Simona Island and the amazing time they had here on their ideal honeymoon or while reestablishing their love with an anniversary vacation. It happens every day here—they should remember it fondly and often.

I nod. "So, I should test it up front?"

He fingertip-claps and bounces. "Absolutely." His arm looped through mine, he drags me toward the door. "And on the way, you can express your feelings about *him* being back in town. I've never met him, you know. It's going to be so interesting, because every time his name is brought up, you play vocal freeze tag. Like you'll be running and someone shouts—"

I slap my hand over his mouth because he's the least quiet person ever, and when he says "someone shouts," he mimics them with deafening gusto. Apollo would hear his name all the way over at the Cliffs and wander this direction. No thanks.

The surprise in Jose's wide eyes registers, and I fight a grimace. I usually appreciate his extremeness. He's going to want answers for this display of muting him. Dropping my hand, I pinch his cheek and smile. "Sorry, but these walls have ears, as do the residents on the other side of the island, and I don't need rumors to spread."

"Mmhmm." He twists his lips to the side. "Are you calling me loud?"

"Of course not." I huff and bump his hip as we walk down the hall. "Just because your projection rivals a jet engine does not make you *loud*. It's a boon, really. You never need to bring along a megaphone, so that's super great."

He makes an insulted squeak and I laugh.

"Well, at least you're acting a bit more like yourself. Even if at my expense." He flicks one of my curls as we turn into the hallway, making our way to the hotel lobby. "But seriously. Are you okay? Is it terribly weird?"

I shake my head, grin in place. "No, of course not. I mean, it's been seven years since we last spoke. I don't know him anymore, and he's just visiting his mom and sister. They're a close-knit family." Which does not explain his extended absence.

"Yeah." Jose scrunches his face. "You're probably right. Although, he's been here a week, and some say he's planning on staying for more than a month."

"A month!" My shout matches Jose's amplification ability. I clear my throat. "A long vacation then."

What's he doing here? He's not building the life he claimed he wanted. He clearly changed his mind about that. He's been living in New York for-freaking-ever. Him being here permanently is not a possibility. Not anymore.

A loud as Jose is, he keeps his voice low and leans conspiratorially toward me. "Some are wondering if he's going to work for his mom."

"It's what he went to school for." His parents fought over if Apollo would partner at the Cliffs with Vic or pilot like his dad. I don't know if he or I had a worse time with parental assumptions. He disappointed Vic and chose his dad and New

York. And I disappointed everyone by becoming an aroma-chologist.

"But apparently, Vic insists he's only visiting and has given up hope that he will work the Cliffs with her." Jose grins wide, but then we turn the corner into the lobby and there's Apollo, leaning on the front desk, talking to whoever is behind the counter. I can't tell, because I drop to the ground and shimmy myself backward, right out of the room. He's here. Why is he here?

I'm a speedy turtle in reverse, while Jose just watches me, standing like a fool in plain sight.

"Come on," I whisper-yell, waving as if the manic motion would drag him closer. "Get out of there."

Jose glances toward the desk and then back to me, pointing to his feet. *Here*, he mouths.

"Jose!"

He blinks at me, then finally...*finally* moves out of the room and holds his hand out for me. I'm on the floor, crouched like I'm in a war zone, heart racing and holding the spritzer to my chest, finger on the trigger to ready my weapon. That's right—I shall spritz them to death with welcoming spray. I think my warrior woman card is officially revoked, and I am highly regretful. This is so silly. He's just a man. A hot man I grew up with and know everything about, except for the mysterious years he was completely separate from me and didn't care one lick that I was wondering about every aspect of the life he was living without me.

I take Jose's hand, and he helps me up. I can't stop myself from backing down the hallway and sneaking into the room behind the lobby. The one with the cameras. By the grace of the universe, it's vacant.

And there's Apollo in grayscale on the monitor, arms crossed, an unfamiliar look on his face. Maybe he's different now. Intense and sexy and unamused. His curls are in twists, and he's filled out his shirt but is still lean. I wipe at the bead of sweat creeping down my neck.

"So," Jose says, making me jolt upright. "This is *the* Apollo."

I'm so very busted. I want to fan my face or maybe spray myself with this blend, but I don't need energizing. My blood is humming. "Yeah. It's...been a while."

"No." The word is long and low, drowning the meaning in sarcasm. "What were you like when he was here all the time?"

Taming down the monster inside me that wants to explode my hair into flames and shoot laser beams from my eyes, I take a deep breath and turn to Jose. "I was fine. Why?" Why did I ask why? That reopens a conversation that should not be happening.

Jose clucks his tongue and shakes his head like maybe I don't get what he's asking. But I do. I'd just rather pretend I didn't so I can keep lying to myself. He turns back to the monitor and hums a sound that has "interesting" written all over it.

This is terrible. The worst, actually.

"He's glorious." Jose leans in to study, and for no good reason whatsoever it makes me want to cover the screen with both hands and hiss. "High cheekbones. I bet he could throw a mean runway scowl. Is that a tattoo above his elbow?"

I lean closer. It is. He has a tattoo. It's geometric and starts at the indent between brachialis and biceps, weaving under the sleeve of his polo. "Seems like it." My mouth waters, and then I choke on my spit and cough.

"Exciting." Jose taps the monitor. "His eyebrows are...rugged though."

I snort. "You and your eyebrow fetish."

"They're so important, Xiamara. It enhances the *entire* face." He signals to his own with wide, circular motions.

"So you've said." I fight a grin, relaxing the slightest bit. Apollo's eyebrows are thick and straight-up sultry.

"Though I'm not sure I could have handled it if those were equally fetching. Swoon. All the swoon, baby." Jose puts the back of his hand against his forehead and sinks with a moan. "Yes, please. Do him, then tell me all about it."

"Jose!"

Footsteps sound in the hallway, and a familiar female voice says, "We need a backup plan."

"Don't I know it." Is that Mama? And Vic, Apollo's mother?

Mama speeds by but turns her head and slams on the brakes.

Vic keeps going, apparently not used to my mother's directional whimsy.

"Xia? What are you do—"

"Nothing. Everything is fine." I dash toward her, grabbing Jose on the way and try to block her from seeing who I was spying on, but Vic is staring hard, arms crossed and the slightest of smirks on her face. No time. I hold up the sprayer. "I made this. For the lobby. It's called Welcome to Paradise. Lemon for memory, peppermint to energize, clary sage will balance hormones, and it's an aphrodisiac—oh, and there's nutmeg. Good for chilling out anxiety." I sniff. *Helpful.*

Vic still stares, but Mama makes a happy coo and snatches the bottle from me to smell it, then shoves it back in my hand. "Perfect. Let's go test it."

Though all my thoughts say turn left and run, Mama steers me right. Toward the inevitable. She can't tell I'm freaking out, or more likely she doesn't care and continues to drag me along with a lock-tight grip on my wrist. I follow, unable to process this moment. I need my Serenity Now or Focus, Felicia, or for my legs to go backward, not forward. They're strong, they could, and no one would stop me, but no. They keep going. My cheeks are hot and everything is hot and—

"Hola," Mama sings as she walks into the lobby and spies Apollo. He turns, and the whole world halts like a slap in the face to time. But we're not stopped, because the corner of his lips lifts and a pang hits my chest. It's been seven damn years. I want to smack him, hug him, yell, and laugh. Instead, all my emotions rally and drag themselves from my soul, up my throat, and a few escape in a quiet, pathetic whimper.

Mama drags me along in her wake. "You—" She reaches up on tiptoes to hug a smiling Apollo, bringing him closer to me and making my heart rate sprint.

He's massive. Not his size exactly, but his presence steals the air. Thankfully, I'm holding my breath and standing too far away to get a whiff of him. Does he still smell like mint and cherries? I never registered the scent of him until I'd left Simona and was serving drinks at a bar in Miami. An inhale of the deepest red Luxardo cherries in a top-shelf Old Fashioned made me flip around as if he'd be there, mischievous and missing me, but he wasn't. I snagged one of the cherries, wrapped it in a bar napkin, threw it in my pocket, then inhaled it for hours when I got back to my apartment like a complete weirdo.

Mama kisses his cheek. "I'm so happy to see you. Everyone has missed you. Right?" She elbows me as Vic slides up next to him, with more concern in her eyes than I've seen in a long while. What's that about?

It feels like the hotel is holding its breath for this enticing black man with a jawline that has filled out since I last saw him. And those shoulders. Oh god, his shoulders.

"Hi?" His voice holds more question than statement.

I drag my attention from his throat up to his eyes, thankful my swoon is internal.

Mama's grip falls away, but Apollo's gaze doesn't. Eyes the color of a jar of honey left in a sunbeam on the kitchen counter peer at me through long lashes. They sparkle and shift light in ways that shouldn't be possible. And I'm held fast, unable to move.

"So this is Apollo," Jose pipes in like shattering glass, reminding me I still haven't responded. An egg could fry on my face. "So lovely to meet you, *finally*."

I should thank him for breaking the spell, because while every inch of me wants to punch him, my gaze is now a glare aimed at him and not stuck like a bee to...well, honey. That thought reminds me of Apollo's eyes again, and sure enough, I'm back for more.

"Finally?" Apollo asks, serious face tipping into amusement. "I'm at a disadvantage, as I'm unsure who you are—wait. Don't tell me." He bites his lip and tilts his head, studying Jose. I swear my friend sighs like an infatuated teenage girl. "You're... Jose? Am I right?"

"You are!" Jose shakes his fists in the air as if they're a pair of maracas. "However did you hear about me?"

"Oh no." Apollo leans toward him. "You first. How long does *finally* entail? Who's been chatting me up?"

Of course, I go bug-eyed at the exact moment Apollo puts his attention back on me because obviously I've discussed him with Jose.

Jose links his arm with mine like he can sense I'm going to sprint for an exit. There are five available. Any of them will do. He laughs. "Oh, you know the tourist island lifestyle. If you're local, you're known."

Apollo makes an unreadable, unfamiliar hum. He speaks differently now. His accent and inflection have changed, and I can't remember him ever using the word *entail*, though we were only seventeen when we last spoke.

"Well, I've heard of you through my mom, of course, and a few others who speak highly of you and what you've done as the dance director here."

My friend turns and gives me a half-lidded, marry-this-man-for-me gaze. I return a that-will-never-ever-work glare. He nods and I shake my head.

Apollo coughs what sounds like amusement against his fist, then tucks his hands in his pockets. "I'm glad to finally join the Moss Monster Meet."

"What?" Oh, now my voice works? It's a bit of a squawk, but it's there.

His smile fades to a more somber note, as if he knows he's treading on sacred ground he shouldn't travel. "Yeah. I thought I'd make an attempt this year. Ma tells me you've made a run of it."

My senses tingle, and another surge of heat hits my cheeks. I don't know if it's out of anger or that he's been talking about me, but it's awkward, as is the silence and all the attention aimed at me. I'm a trapped bug they're trying to identify.

Jose squeezes my arm and gives it a little jiggle. "She made record time last year."

Apollo's gaze heats me like opening the dishwasher during the sanitize cycle, steam and everything. Actually, that may be my sweat. It is. I am officially sweating, though standing perfectly still as if I will blend in with the waves of blue tile on the lobby floor. I refuse to look, because I won't chance that he can read me as well as he used to. My choice is to ignore him and survive another day or meet his honey eyes and liquify.

He clears his throat. "And made record time the year before that as well." Ha! I won this intense game of *the wall is more interesting than you*. But then he says, "I thought I'd see if I can keep up. I've always wanted to compete. Maybe I'll even grab a record of my own."

My mouth falls open.

I remember how fast he is, and he's in even better shape than before. He may not have been preparing for these specific events, but he knows what they are, what they've always been. And how he affects me is a massive issue I can't afford. "You're competing?"

His demeanor shifts to puffed-up boastfulness. "Just said I was. Should be fun."

Fun how? Fun like losing because he hasn't been living on the island for five years doing the tasks the Moss Monster Meet calls for? They're obstacles I train and study. I own that competition. Crossing my arms, I take a step back now that my legs are working again. Jose lets me go. I need to check the rule book. I scrunch my nose. No, that's petty. I can beat him on my own, without whining about fair play. He may not be living on the island, but he grew up here, and anyone who went to school on Simona can come back to compete anytime. I think the Mossy board was hoping that some of the kids would return, remember why they loved Simona so much, and stay.

"Is that a problem?" Apollo clasps his hands behind his back, tightening the shirt's fabric across his chest. He looks like he's fighting to say a whole lot more.

"Just visiting?"

There's a pause that makes Vic turn to Apollo as well, but he grins. "Would you have a problem with me staying?"

I stumble but catch myself. "Of course not." That is the biggest of lies. I have a problem standing near him in this lobby for a couple of minutes.

The way his presence has my palms slick, my feet confused, and my tongue incapable of forming words makes him the most daunting obstacle I've ever faced. I dart for the hallway and for freedom from my confusion.

"We'll catch up soon, Xia," Apollo calls out.

I grit my teeth in a fake smile and slip out of sight. Speed walking the hall, I replay his words with each step. He's back. Apollo Fischer has returned to Simona. Does this have anything to do with our past? No. All the years and zero contact between us make it clear he's not here for me.

The clap of quick footsteps has me glancing to see Jose chasing me. "Woman," he whisper-yells.

I slow down so he can catch up.

"That was a choo-choo-kaboom crash site where I was the bystander watching the uncomfortable flames spin higher. Are you ill?" His face scrunches, making me grimace and walk faster again. "Constipated? You can tell me."

"Jose." His name is a groan. "Sure. Yes, I'm ill. I just need a—"

It's then I realize I'm still clutching the new untested spritzer to my chest. I fight to pull myself together because this isn't like me. I'm the winner of the Mossy, the professional who makes incredible scents and stays out of the Simona rumor mill with her cool indifference. I cannot deal with the way Apollo affects me right now.

My job and winning the Mossy come first.

3

THE ISLAND KING

I'm itching to clear my mind of this mess of confusing cobwebs. Even the gorgeous sunrise only gets a glance of my attention. At the shoreline, I step and jump to warm up as my muscles tingle with anxiousness. The waves are choppy this morning, with an occasional one popping high from the sandbar and pounding the beach.

Over the last two days, I've only been able to sneak in mini-workouts: stair sprints, burpees in the office, kettlebell lifts in the storage room. I need the packed sand under my shoes, the jungle, and even the bog. It may smell similar to rotten eggs, which should send me in another direction, but it's an olfactory memory that brings me home.

The west side of the island lacks the tourist area views, and the sandbar and mini-reef make the waves unpredictable and more suited for surfers than loungers. It remains a raw, untouched playground of natural obstacles. A few homes poke from the thick layer of trees—residents with money who enjoy the privacy of living on the remote, jungle side where monkeys and ocelots rule. There's a small herd of wild goats, ancestors of escaped livestock from the 1990s. Sometimes I see them grazing on the rocky face of Montana Calvo.

The big, bouldering mountain was only a tall piece of landscape until the day Apollo wrapped himself around me, grabbed my hand, and used our entwined fingers to trace the features of the balding man with a bulbous nose and twisty grin. I'll never be able to see it as a plain old mountain again. Because of Apollo, tree roots are hands, rocks are fish, and driftwood zombies paint the beach. Sometimes I wish he'd have left me in the dark, because now he's all over this island.

I toss my head to shake thoughts loose, then put my hair into a bun. With earbuds in and a morning energy mix pumping through, I'll get my focus back. I start at a slow rhythmic pace, occasionally punching out or sidestepping a dance move. Antsy muscles protest against tight tendons for the slightest moment. Silly body. It will be singing soon. My feet fall in thuds against wet sand in sync with the music. I stay close to the shoreline so I have to keep watch, strengthening my ankles with dodges and weaves while I play with the fickle ocean.

What is Apollo doing on such a long trip? I assume he's been in New York working at his dad's helicopter transit company because that was the last career news that mom slipped to me. I hope Vic and Demi are okay. I haven't heard any announcements about poor health—not that I would.

Has he been happy all these years? I could have asked Vic about him at any time, but his business is none of mine. Not anymore. Mama only gives me unsolicited teasers: he's visiting soon to see his mom or dating a new person. She puts the information out there with nonchalance and shows restraint she doesn't have, waiting for me to bite.

Tingles light up my neck before a shadow falls beside me, a solid body in my peripheral vision that makes me sidestep with a shriek. I'm going too fast, too close to the edge of the water. I slop into the receding surf halfway up to my calves and swing around to see Apollo standing there wide-eyed, as if I imagined him into presence. "What—"

A wave slams into the back of my knees, tossing me to my hands. A following wave spanks me. I tumble ass over teakettle to the energetic beat still pumping through my earbuds until a sand collision rips them away and gives my shoulder and thigh more exfoliation than the spa's pumice scrub treatment. Because I grew up on an island, I gulped air before letting the sea take me for a spin. Now, I'll wait out the current while I ponder why in all of hell Apollo is here, on a stretch of beach only I visit in the mornings?

The sand prints. My mystery competition.

The tide retracts, and I lift my head to breathe as arms encircle me, hauling me out of stronger-than-me currents. My bun is mostly undone, leaving half my shoulder-length bob plastered over my face, and I sweep it aside, revealing Apollo, frowning. A swirl of searing emotion invades my body. I have Apolloitis. Symptoms: clumsy tongue, feet, and brain, as well as boiling blood that travels south instead of the northern path it should go.

"That was weird." He breaks into a grin as he walks me to dry land cradled in his arms, a damsel in distress rescued by a knight in sandy sneakers. Why can nothing go right when we're in the same vicinity? I squeak an inefficient protest and struggle to get my feet on the ground.

The amusement drops from his features, and his chest rises and falls before he sets me down, leaving an arm looped under mine and around my back. So close. We are so very close. The heat of his skin against my wet clothes makes my blood hum and my nipples tighten. And then the itch settles in. There is an island inside my bra. And nose and—

I wince and pull my phone from the pocket of my soaked leggings. It slides out like it's emerging from sandpaper. This is why we do not play in the western shore's surf. We run through it to calmer waters so we have easy waves to navigate instead of pissed off ones sent as a vendetta against ocean barriers. And we never, ever take electronic devices with us. The screen remains blank as I give it a tap, but Apollo snatches the phone from me and jabs the power button.

"Hey!"

He holds it away from me as I make a dive for it. "No turning it on until it's dry. You live surrounded by seawater, Xi, how can you not know that?" He puts his attention back on the phone, holding it at an angle. A few drops of ocean hit the sand. "Salt water won't do us any favors though. Want me to try to save it?" His nose crinkles, eyes squinting and lips pursing in the way they do when he thinks I'm mad at him, which I am.

My tongue is another source of aggravation, as it's not even attempting to form a sentence around him, but that's on me. Okay, and a little on him, because he changed everything between us and it threw me for the most impossible loop-the-loop ever.

Here goes. I swallow and breathe deep. "H-how?" My teeth chatter, but only twenty percent of that is because I'm soaked in the morning breeze.

He shrugs a shoulder. "Take it apart, rinse, dry, reassemble, and pray."

I put my hands on my hips. It's an old phone. I can't imagine it'd live through a wave immersion, but I'm not good at backing things up, and I have recipe notes on the digital notepad. The correct ratio of orange to lemongrass for Vivacitrisity will enhance energy but not overwhelm. I groan.

"Okay." It comes out as a quiet mumble.

"Hm?" His grin is more teasing than inquisitive.

I study my soggy running shoes. If I knew I was taking a dip today, I'd have worn my triathlon sneakers. "Yes, please." When I squirm, the grit in every nook reminds me that my clothes, no matter how tight, are holding sand. "I need to..." I thumb over my shoulder and step toward the waves.

"You're not trying to escape by sea, are you?" Apollo asks, dropping my phone in the pocket of his shorts.

"Off to find my earbuds." I fight a grin as his eyes go round, his head moving back inches with his confusion. What the ocean steals stays there. He knows that. I hate that I littered though.

"That's, uh, not a good—"

"I'm just rinsing off. Turn around." When he does, I study the waves, step into the warm water at the right time, and keep my front facing the empty horizon in case of peeks, which is something he'd do—or would have done long ago. I dip to reach under my tank top and lift the bottom of my sports bra, returning the sand dune within back to the sea. A shimmy and a couple of readjusts to the jiggly bits, and my skin is happier. I tug out my hair tie and force my soaked strands back into a tight bun. A mere waistband flip fixes the grit in my pants. This will do for now. If this happened in the Moss Monster Meet, I'd keep going.

I face the shore and, yeah, he's still there, biteable backside facing me, hands on narrow hips. He's got the same structure, but with a man upgrade, and I'm curious. The waves behave as I make my way closer.

"You de-sanded?" he asks.

"Mm-hmm."

When he turns back to me his gaze caresses my lips and slides down. The chill from the breeze does nothing to stop the heat from rolling over me. Why can't I be cool around him? Literally. He's probably just checking for sand and injuries, and here I am squirming.

"So," I say. "Are you...jogging?"

"Nope. I'm standing here talking to you." Despite the playful words, he doesn't appear amused. His clenching jaw acts like it's my fault he showed up here, but I attempt to seem bored, uninterested, annoyed even. He scratches his neck. "Sorry for scaring you. I thought you were ignoring me."

"I had in earbuds."

"I realized that about a half-second before the wave slammed into you. It was impressive. You—" He circles his hand in the air. "—rolled, but gracefully. A solid seven on the wipeout scale."

We used to play spies, twelve years old, hiding in the attic of the clubhouse at the Cliffs, watching first-day tourists get walloped by hurricane season waves that only appear picturesque and enticing for frolicking. We would rate their tumbles from a low one, a simple clumsy sidestep, to a ten, a lost battle with ferocious currents that left them sand coated and clawing at the shore before the sea dragged them out and employees had to intervene.

Those were our comfortable, friendly days.

I smooth my hair, making sure it's behaving. "Felt like an eight. Eight-point-five."

He gives a snort and tightens his lips as he kicks a hole in the sand with a wet sneaker. "Headed back home or...?"

Or what? "Why would I do that?" Work is in a couple of hours. I need to run, sandy and soaked be damned. I hustle to Blobfish Rock and sit on it to drain out my shoes.

Apollo sits right behind me, startling me. This is too familiar. I'm tempted to lean against him as I used to, back to side, my head on his shoulder and his resting on mine like a perfectly fitting puzzle, but we've changed too much in body and mind.

"You are jumpy."

Only around him. "You are silent. And you aren't running." My shoe squelches when I jam my foot in, but I take off, passing him.

I find my rhythm quickly, muscles not too angry about

fighting with the ocean floor. Do not look back, Xia. Don't. I grit my teeth and peek, like an idiot. Apollo isn't far behind, and his lips raise. I stumble and swing my head forward to pay attention. It was a divot in the sand. Had to be.

"I'm close to catching up with you," he calls out. "Do not leap into the sea. I think it may be after you. It wants more than your earbuds." He falls in line with me, sneakers squishing.

Finding the perfect tension of damp but not packed sand, I speed up. "Your shoes are wet."

"I needed to perform a shoreline rescue. It happens. So... aromachology? How's that?"

He's not even breathing heavy. Just casual conversation as we run, not jog, the shore. "I love it," I say, attempting to hide panting. "Finding the right scent mix for people is rewarding." How is he keeping exact pace and still looking fine? "And you're flying helicopters?"

"Yeah. It's fun. I've met a lot of interesting personalities, that's for sure."

Huh. "So you're doing the same thing your dad was doing when he was here?"

He's quiet long enough for me to glance at him and his pursed lips. "For now. I heard you do several things at the spa."

Well, now I'm extra curious. "I do. Massage, aromachology, and training for the Mossy."

"Is that a job title? Moss Monster Meet trainee?"

Nodding, I lick my dry lips. "May as well be this time of year."

"Think I'm ready?" He increases his pace a step before me.

I narrow my eyes and kick off into a sprint. "No."

He laughs, but then I hear his pounding feet behind me. We're getting near the jeans-palm mile marker. I pass by it and slow. Apollo is right beside me, not breathing any heavier than I am.

"You're a runner," I say, walking in a circle with my hands on my hips.

"Every day."

"It's harder in sand."

He licks his lips and blows out a long breath. "That's why I run on the beach at least twice a week."

"Shut your face, you do not." My eyes widen. That was old me coming through. Easygoing, chatty me who thrived on the safety of believing Apollo saw me as a friend, and a friend only. Learning I was wrong on that was a direct hit to my center of gravity. I began stumbling over my words and my feet while he remained his suave, good-smelling self.

"I do too. This may be hard to believe, but Long *Island* is surrounded by water." He flicks his eyebrows. "It actually has beaches with sand and an ocean and kayaking."

"Have you been training for the Mossy?" Is that why he's here? It's a dream of every native.

"We were born on Simona Island, Xia. When have we ever not trained for the Mossy? We grew up balancing toys on plates as we pretended to win the Beach Tray Dash."

"And making our parents drop their rings in the bathtub for the waterfall retrieval."

"Exactly that, yes. But I haven't been formally training. It means a lot to you, doesn't it?"

"Yes. Mama has had that trophy for decades." I swing my arms, nervous energy returning. "So you're here for an extended vacation and to run the Mossy."

He follows my slow jog, silent for a long stretch. "It's where I've wanted to be for a while."

I bite the inside of my cheek and refuse to look at him.

Apollo gives me a gentle push toward the waves. "I bet you an Island King that I make it to the parking area before you."

"You're on." My response is an automatic slipup, though the legendary banana cream custard with a spiced caramel-crisp crown is well worth another sprint. He takes off, and my muscles flex into action, then we're hauling ass down the beach. Hellfire, he is so fast. Arms pumping, form almost perfect. I'd work on his left calf and ankle to correct that slight dorsiflexion. It's stunting his stride. He pulls away. I shouldn't be staring at the hard lines of his thighs and backside. Focus. There is no benefit to being last. Not even a stellar view.

Breathing comes in controlled, deep breaths, and when I'm positive there's no winning this, he slows. Apparently, my stamina is better.

Then I see why. A line of horses and riders stand still, watching us from the treeline next to the parking area. Vic is on her chestnut horse, Hermes, as is my main competition Monique on Malbec the Mustang, and...no. Kingston is here on his prized Andalusian. As lead bartender at the Cliffs, he's the gossip pulse that only rivals my mother, but at least Mama doesn't talk about me.

I trip, going airborne in a slow-motion dive that I wish was on fast-forward. Maybe then I wouldn't see the widening eyes, then the scrunching noses, and after that the baring of the oh-shit grimace of the onlookers who should not be witnessing the soon-to-be Moss Boss headed toward an inevitable sand sandwich. Can't stop gravity. Dammit.

At least I roll. It's not pretty, but nothing is hurt but my pitiful pride, which gives me the finger and digs a hole to hide in for eternity.

Then, Apollo is there, crouching and cupping my cheek as if this indent I've made is my final resting spot. Farewell to thee, Xiamara, who was not meant for the gravitational pull of this planet and the impact of best-friend-turned-crush-turned-competition giving last rites with his lust-inspiring fingers.

"You won." I fight not covering my face with both hands and shimmying myself deeper into the sand.

"Xia," Apollo coos. "You hurt?"

I sit up and brush myself off. Apollo offers a hand, but I shoo him away and grin wide, straining the muscles in my cheeks. My nose and limbs tingle for oxygen. "Of course not. Just—" I signal toward the clean, empty sand and stand on wobbly legs. "Tripped on a divot. Sand, you know?" I wave at the others. Kingston's phone is in his hand. I swear if he took a photo or is already texting, I will...well, I don't know, because Apollo has my wrist between his fingers and I may swoon to death, but it will be dreadful, the wrath I will bring down on Kingston.

Vic and Hermes trot over. Like the angel she is, Vic pretends I didn't just eat it while doing what I do best. "Nice run, you two."

I almost huff but hold it back and grin. "Thanks. He's fast."

"He is." Her voice went slow and deep on her words. Disapproval?

Apollo drops my wrist and looks downright angry. Why should he be?

Vic moves Hermes toward me in his bowed-head gait until he nuzzles his fuzzy lips against my palm, his big brown eyes half-closing as he nickers out a warm puff of horsey air.

"You both did well," Vic says. "How do you feel?"

Scared, annoyed, and embarrassed even more now that she's asking how I *feel*. "Like I just ran four miles and sprinted one right after. How are you feeling?"

"Hopeful," she says while eyeing the ocean. "It's a rough start, but I bet it's going to settle into a glorious day."

Apollo pats Hermes, then loops a finger in the noseband of his bridle and turns him.

Vic's amused chuckle has me out of the loop of conversation. "See you at dinner, son. Happy day, Xi-Xi."

As soon as she's herding the others back through the jungle's trail path, Apollo faces me. "When do you have time for an Uncle Alfred's Custard trip?"

Never. I latch my fingers together and cup the top of my head, widening my ribcage to get more air. "Tomorrow afternoon?"

"I'll be busy until early evening. Late night?" His voice isn't the mellow, rolling melody it used to be. It's tight and to the point: a New Yorker in a hurry and frustrated at the meandering tourists blocking the sidewalks. "Nothing better than a ten p.m. custard run."

I shake my head. "They close at six during the week now. Artie says he's too old and needs his beauty sleep."

Apollo rumbles a laugh that jingles my insides. "That sounds like him. This weekend then?"

"I'm free," pops out of my mouth before I think about it.

"Well, then," he says, inching closer. Too close. So close that I'm a fluttery moth astonished by a full moon in the middle of the night, except the moon is a fiery sun and I'm going to burst into flames. "It's a date."

4

NEEDS MORE CAMPHOR

*I*t had to be a joke. Dating me is the worst idea and he knows it. Not that I'd even date him. But it's not a date. It's a debt collection.

I force myself to interact with my coworkers as if Apollo-entering-the-Mossy-anxiety doesn't exist, and because my masochistic side needs to hear if everyone knows I can't stay on my feet anymore. While there's no mention of me or Apollo, there are side-eyes aplenty. To distract myself from my worst nightmare that I'm positive is now reality, I prep smack talk for the Cliffs employees. 'Tis the season to get sassy.

I step into the spa lobby, which looks more like a sleek lounge. I helped choose the design for this space and wanted it to be the opposite of the typical minimalist, bright-white spas, a contrast to the electric blue and sunshine of El Escape Azul. The floor is black marble with gold veining. All surfaces are sultry shades of deep charcoal, fancied with gilded embellishments. Even the shelves that house glass vials and bottles of aromatherapy, skin, and nail products glint against dim lighting. I add earthy scents such as salt and stone to all the moody room aromatics along with grounding frankincense and cedarwood.

Stella pops around the corner a second later like the psychic spa manager that she is, her caramel bob sharp against her round face, two slight wrinkles forming at the outer corners of her dark eyes and spreading. Today, paired with a grim wince, those wrinkles are an entire mood. "You stressed, lovey?"

So much. I wave a hand through the air. "I'm fine."

Stepping behind me, she tests the tension in my neck. "Oof. You are worked up." Her lean into my pressure points makes me sag. "The body doesn't fib. Hold the counter." I do, and she presses knuckles into my lower back. "Are you sore?" she asks in a silky whisper reserved for stressed clients.

I groan in response as the acupressure eases my muscles. "Can I book a jabby appointment with you?" She's brilliant at acupuncture, and I'm going to need every trick to regain some equilibrium before this "date."

"Let's make time tomorrow if our schedules match. It's been busy."

We divert guests who want to vacation the week of the Moss Monster Meet to the surrounding timeframe. Because we're a private island, we make our own rules, and my favorite is shutting down tourism for nine days to reset our businesses and catch up on tasks that would otherwise disturb clients, then party with the Mossy and a bonfire.

"It's going to be worse next week," I say.

"Is it ever." Stella moves into a percussive technique over my left shoulder blade. I must hold tension there. "And you're on a lighter schedule." Her tone isn't reprimanding. It's a statement because everyone here knows this means so much to me.

"I have a competition to win."

"You do." There's a grin in her voice. "Which is why you have to remain upright."

My muscles tense right back up. "What?"

"No more falling." She clucks her tongue and works harder against my rigid stance, even down to the hip I rolled against. "Relax, Xiamara. You are going to run that race and win it all. I just know you are."

I hate this island and its gossipy ways. Fine. That was a lie. I don't hate it. Simona is my home and the people are well-intentioned, mostly. But really?

She gives a final pat to my back and heads to the computer. "I have two boxes of your products to ship out today."

"Oh!" That is the distraction I need. "I'll pack them up." The presentation needs to be just right for when the client opens them. It should smell like El Escape Azul and return them instantly to the memories of their vacation.

Stella pats my arm. "They're already packed, but I faced them the right direction—"

"Used the glue dots?" I really should have done it.

"I did. And two spritzes of Escape on the paper filler." She holds a finger up as I open my mouth. "And placed the card in the correct spot with the wax seal. It was gorgeous, Xia. I promise."

"Thank you." It sounds perfect and I'm positive it is. But that doesn't stop me from wondering if I can sneak into the back room where packages await pickup and peek inside. I should see them, smell them, to know that they're how they need to be, but that fills me with guilt. Stella is dedicated to making every aspect of the spa flawless. She did it correctly. Probably.

She smiles and opens the calendar, then reaches for her mug of tea.

Despite the quiet ambient spa music piping out of the room speakers, my thoughts whir and flit against the astronomically loud click of Stella's mouse and the slight squeal of my right nostril with every breath that seems to be echoing off marble. I can't hold back. What is everyone saying? "How did you know I fell?" And even more importantly, how I fell.

Her mug pauses an inch from her lips. "A video on the group page. The one only residents can join." She takes a sip as I tamp down my inner rage. Not only did Kingston film a sneaky video of my shame, he posted the damn thing to social media. He's the worst. Stella sets her mug down and puts her hand on my arm. "It's nothing bad. No one is saying anything, just..." She flashes me a tiny, apologetic grin. "Want me to take care of it?"

"Are you going to hack all the technology and make it disappear?"

She crosses her thin arms and lifts her dainty chin. "I could." She couldn't, but she's sweet to indulge that dream.

I smile, but I'm positive the upper half of my face looks revenge ready. "It's fine." It's not, but if I freak out, I'll draw more attention to it. "Do we have client appointments?"

She eyes me warily, twisting her lips to the side, then gives my arm a squeeze and picks up her mug. "Not for a few."

I nod and head toward the rows of products on the shelves, turning the ones that are slightly off-center so the labels are perfectly aligned.

"So...how is it having Apollo in town for a nice chunk of time? You two were close before college, weren't you?"

Tingles creep over the back of my neck, and I scratch at the sensation. We can bring back the silence now. Making a small affirmative hum, I uncap the tester of Chillax and inhale, prepping myself for the recon I'm about to do. "We—"

"Hi." The familiar deep voice strikes my body like lightning.

I jerk, and the bottle slips from my fingers. A squealy "Eeeee" comes from me as the room slows. I swipe with my superior reflexes, smacking the open vial to my other hand, which starts a volley between the two. Bat, spin, tap, twist. Oil splashes my skin. After five rounds back and forth, the floor is the victor.

I'd be angry, but my serotonin levels rise from the fragrance of chamomile and lavender, vanilla, and tiniest hint of clary sage.

But the air isn't just thick with scent; it's heavy, pressurized with a tingling presence that was on my neck moments ago. I was too busy inserting myself into the island gossip to notice. Got the message, universe: mind my own business, keep to my goals, and avoid Apollo.

"Smells nice," Apollo says from the doorway, arms crossed. "Are you okay, Xi? You seem to be..." My skin sets fire along the path his eyes take. He brushes his fingers over his lips. "On edge."

He stares at my hips as if questioning what's there, which makes sense with the curves I didn't have when he was here. Possibly because of the effects of chemo, I bloomed late—right after Apollo left. Having my body noticed and appreciated took some getting used to, but now, with Apollo's studious gaze, I wonder what thoughts are circling behind those heated honey eyes.

Stella passes me a ball of paper towels, a trashcan, and a spritzer of general cleaner. I give her my best *everything is fine* blink. Putting my attention on the shattered vial and oozing oil helps me refocus.

"That for me?" she says, crossing to Apollo and taking a bag from him. He doesn't even have a chance to respond before she's heading to the hallway. "I need to drop this off at the front desk." Beaming, she heads out the door. I want to yell for her to come back. Tell her she's abandoning me, and we don't do that here, but that would reveal that my heart is flopping around my chest like a caged bird. I can't face him alone in this small, highly scented place.

"Um." I stare at the pile of oily glass as I struggle with how to get him out the door. "Do you want—like—need anything before you go? Um." Something he'd like but not? *Make normal but brief spa conversation, Xia.* "I created a new massage oil blend." *Oh god.* Why did I say that? He's going to think a whole plethora of things he shouldn't about rubbing down bodies. His body. *My* body. The summer's thickest heat slides over my hips like lover's hands and presses between my thighs.

"Maybe. What does it smell like?"

I shakily drop collected glass shards into the trash. There's no escape here. "Like, uh, wood—cedarwood. Grapefruit. It's called the Rejuvenation blend. It's nice. People think so." My nose crinkles.

"Meh. Not sold on the cedarwood."

The tightening of my fingers stops the trembling. Cedarwood mellows out the entire formula. It took me two months to perfect that recipe. I dump the intact bottom of the vial and the stopper into the trash. Maybe I should add a microdrop of patchouli to the Chillax blend, since it doesn't appear to remedy irrational, pride-fueled rage. "It matches the grapefruit and mutes the cinnamon. But the touch of camphor..." I lower my voice to a mumble. "...would be nice right about now." I added the camphor to take desire out of the equation. The anti-aphrodisiac calms people and lets them focus on inner reflection instead of the needs of their nether regions.

"What was that?"

"Nothing."

Sperrys enter my field of vision, and Apollo tugs at the knees of his cornflower chinos and squats. Rich umber fingers with clean, short nails come close, halting every movement of my body except my organs, which flutter. He taps my chin once, then twice, and lifts until I face sun-touched honey.

Everything tightens and not in a good way. I'm taken back to the last time he touched me like this, the puff of mint before...I murmur an incoherent non-word and crush my lids shut, not willing to confront his reaction. I only open them when his soft chuckle rolls over me.

"Um." He tilts his head, close enough to lean in. "What was that?"

I shake my head and lick my dry lips, but his fingers remain. "Nothing. Anything else? It's not the weekend." No need to see me before our *date,* right?

"No, it's not." His finger remains on my chin, sweeping the curve and sending an army of chills down my neck and curving around my ears. I lean into his touch. I'm taken deeper into the past, back to the beach seven years ago. The haze of too many sips from his sister's *borrowed* flask. The fuzzy towel we lay on to watch the stars, but ended up watching each other instead and discussing constellations, books, and life. His unexpected touch, and the moment I thought we were soulmates because nothing could be so perfect. Then realizing that we were the least perfect couple in the world. I stiffen like we're in that moment again, and his fingers fall away.

"Need help?" The question is quiet and, if I'm correct, clipped. He takes the spritzer bottle beside my knee and aims it at the floor when I pinch the last bit of glass in a paper towel. I nod and he spritzes, then brings it up to his nose. "Make this too?"

I swipe as if my sole purpose is this floor's cleanliness. "No, because of cleaning regulations, but—" My mouth clamps shut seemingly on its own. He doesn't need to know that I worked with their development team to create the right concoction because I'm obsessed with scent. That seems braggy. Or an overshare. Or rambling about myself like I used to.

His exhale is so impatient that, yeah, I'm adding some other notes to Chillax. "But what?" His words are still soft but monotone. As if they bored his tongue on the way out.

He asked. I can't not respond, front roll, and sprint out the door, though I've mapped my exact path. I study the sparse glitter of glass caught in the wet paper towel. "This is lucky number twenty-three on the quest of decently scented regulation cleaning products." I stop there.

"I bet you felt bad returning crap-scented regulation cleaning products." His lips twitch with the slightest smile.

I did, so I didn't send them back. "Other areas needed them. The pool staff doesn't care if the outdoor towel holder smells like what someone thought a pinecone smells like."

We stand up together, and he looks over my shoulder. Rustling brings my head up. Jamie, our muscly masseur, is traveling down the hall like he's in a speed-walk race to the back office.

And my excuse to disappear has arrived. "Hey, big guy, I'm coming." I turn to Apollo, though my face is flushed hot. "We have to prep for painting during the client break."

His close presence causes my grin to drop.

"Jamie? Really? Doesn't El Escape have an employee fraternization rule?" Old Apollo would have shoved me sideways and told me to stop flirting in his loudest voice.

No, but why is he asking? "No."

His scowl deepens, but he takes a step closer. "He's all wrong for you." His words are so quiet, maybe I heard something else, like a slurred "His sarong's free-oo," but no, I didn't.

Does he seriously think he can walk in after being gone for seven years and tell me who I'm supposed to be with? "And you know who's right?"

His jaw tightens further, and the tingles on my neck amplify so much, I lift my chin further to ease the sensation. And there we live in our bubble of tension.

Apollo yields. Steps back and turns his head in the direction of the man who's not good for me. Which he's right about. Jamie and I disagree on everything from product descriptions to massage techniques to what foods are best for fitness. He's the annoying older brother I never wanted.

And Apollo is...he's the one I didn't know I wanted, then wanted so much, then wanted to forget but never could.

With heated cheeks, I pivot, stumble on my weak knees before internally screaming at them to get their mind in the game and make my way to the shelves where I will continue turning every label to a perfect angle and not break anything else.

"Wait," he says, fishing in his pocket. His tone has shifted to apologetic. "I have your phone."

That halts my escape. "You do? Is it very dead?"

"Actually, it's quite alive, and I charged it for you." I nod, holding my palm out, but he keeps it closer to his body than I'm willing to stretch toward. I'm not sure I appreciate this peace offering he's teasing me with. "Demi watched over my shoulder and gave unhelpful tips."

Demeter is the only child of Vic and Enzo who hasn't left Simona Island to work for her dad. I see her around sometimes, but it's been a while. "How are she and Athena?"

Apollo turns the phone in his hand as if it's a coin, long fingers sliding over the surface until it has no choice but to tip and roll against his palm. Are the lines across his skin the same, or have they changed too? I used to trace them when we were kids, fascinated by the pink roadmap, until he'd close his fingers and trap me. "They're good," he says. "Well, except Athena is having an unpleasant first trimester and Demi is mad at you."

I'm confused, shocked, and have a thousand questions. Most important things first. "Athena's pregnant?" When he nods, I hold my fingertips to my smile. "She will be an amazing mom."

He tips his head back and forth. "She'll rule them with the intensity of a drill sergeant. She certainly had enough practice with us, didn't she?"

I smirk. "Maybe with you. She used to sneak me cookies when you ran off without me."

Athena not only knew how to bandage a skinned knee but sang and danced with the radio and braided my hair while we shared snacks. She gave me a taste of what siblings are like and was the best consolation prize for the energy Apollo stole from the room when he wasn't there.

"What?" His jaw drops in the most delightful way. I've always enjoyed his reactions. "Oh, I'm going to talk to her about that. I used to get blamed for eating all the sweets in the house. How did I not know that?"

I lean against the counter and cross my arms. "Because you were off playing cricket with the boys. And I would be..." I trail off. Pouting at being left behind.

My stomach sinks at the way his eyes divert to my phone, which he's still idly spinning. "I thought you'd follow."

There's tension in the air between us again. It feels like we're fighting, but I can't pinpoint what about. My walls of defense shoot skyward. "Sometimes, I didn't want to try so hard." Heat spills into my cheeks, and I look toward the doorway, praying for Stella, or a client, or a parade of monkeys to interrupt.

"You..." The growl in his voice brings my attention to him. "You never needed to try with me."

I did though. And I still failed. I waft my hand through the air and smile. "It's fine."

He squeezes my phone and holds it out. It's clean, slick metal is now warm from his fingers. I swipe my finger over the surface to see if something I had on there was offensive. Four slashes appear. I hold the screen to him. "What's this?"

He leans, and his gaze intensifies so much I nearly step closer to poke him in the chest like I used to do, nose to nose, stare to stare. But I don't trust myself around him. "It's your passcode menu. Always passcode your phone, Xia."

"Why? It's always with me."

The particular shift of his features drops me into a memory. Us playing mancala, and I'd make a wrong move. He would win. That's his face right now because he's moves ahead of me, but there's no competition here, unless we're talking about the Mossy, and he can't win that with my phone.

His eyebrow rises, like, *Wanna bet?* "Until you leave it on a counter," he says, slow and menacing. "Or someone swipes it from your bag."

"I'm on Simona Island, not in New York."

He moves closer. "There are guests from all over the world here on the daily. I'm sure you've left it on the desk at some point. Then whoever has possession of it has access to not only your email but social media accounts, photos, and so on, and so on." He rolls his hand through the air, stirring up my anxiety. "And so on."

Oh my god. The photos? My email? I have after-run sweaty selfies that I wouldn't post in a million years but send to the other half of my best friend team so Roxanne can make gagging sounds at me and tell me she can smell me from Florida. And what if he saw a too-recent email from a certain online store confirming my purchase of "Big Jack" and a bottle of lube? Those are the last things I want Apollo to see. I chew my lip hard. "What's the code?"

"Eleven, twenty-two."

I put in the numbers and the moment I hit the two, I see it. "Your birthday."

He shrugs and looks toward the open French doors and hallway beyond. "And you're getting a case for your phone."

"A what now?"

"A protective case." He steps back, running his thumb over the knuckles of his fist. "A strong one able to withstand the power of my *hello*s." He signals to the trashcan containing broken bottle shards, giving a playful pout that confuses me more, then rolls his eyes and shoves his hands in his pockets. "Need me to pick one out for you?"

"I can do it." The background on the screen is a picture of a glaring Demi and Apollo, both of them pointing their fingers in a reprimand. I turn my phone to Apollo with raised eyebrows.

At least his nose scrunch when he thinks he's in trouble hasn't changed. "Just testing the camera."

"Uh-huh." I nibble at my grin as I look at the photo. Why haven't I gotten together with Demi recently? Oh. Because she reminds me of Apollo.

"I hope to see the new case this weekend." He's at the doorway, half-in, half-out like an indecisive cat.

This weekend. I can't skirt out of our...*date*. No, not date. A bet. It was a bet. "Um, Friday or Saturday?"

"Friday," he says, as if angry at the day. "I have to train Saturday."

My hackles rise. I'll be training as well in the afternoons. Running, the waterfall, and kayaking with Nico on Sunday. The owner of El Escape has become my trainer for saving tourists in the fastest, safest way.

Apollo steps to leave but lingers and peeks back at me. "Phone case. If you don't have one, I'm going to make a bet with you that I get to pick it out. I'll win whatever it is, and you will have the most sparkly, orange case the world has ever known."

I mentally uppercut the grimace trying to hijack my expression. "Orange isn't so bad." It's actually the worst. Just terrible. The color of pylons, kids' hospital rooms, and the walls of the old hotel that still splatters against the blue throughout El Escape to show respect to the lost building. A nice mustard would have been better. Or lime. Teal. And...*sparkles*? Oh, hell no.

"Have a good day, Xia." And he's gone.

The room is colder, darker. Still beautiful and sultry, but a lifeless, marble box lacking sparks or sun or honey.

5

NEW RULES

I check Mama's message again from the parking lot of the Cliffs. *Important Moss Monster Meet Announcement. Come to the Paradise Room at the Cliffs at 2 pm Thursday.*

We've never had a meeting for the Mossy before. For thirty-five years, contestants have just signed up, arrived on the day, and ran the course. More goes on behind the scenes as they slightly alter the exact path each year and mark off certain areas so enthusiastic onlookers don't get trampled, but all that is super-secret business.

Which may be why Mama hasn't responded at all to my messages asking about the announcement. She and a handful of others make up the Mossy board.

I have two minutes to get inside. I'm not late to anything, but if I go in there, I will see Apollo, and I have a hard enough time putting one foot in front of the other without giving him the chance to speak to me.

So I wait, cart parked as close to a bush as possible, and watch the clock, jerking when the digital eight pops into a nine. A tap on the windshield makes me scream.

Apollo tilts his head, navigates spiky leaves and holds out a hand. "You're going to be late."

"I'm not the only one." I stare at his extended palm, then slip my shaking fingers into his steady, warm ones. Tingles dance from the contact point, sending a wave of chill bumps up my arm. Once I'm up, he drops my hand and I'm left struggling to find words.

"Let's go." He grips my shoulders and pushes me toward the clubhouse.

Somehow, I remain on my feet and remember what I was going to ask. "Do you know what this meeting is about?"

He steps beside me and opens the glass door by its diagonal brass handle. "Do *you*?"

I glare up at him but fight with the tilt of my lips. "I wouldn't have asked if I did."

"Oh," he says with a genuine smile that makes my knees wobbly. At least he hasn't lost his brattiness completely. I loved that about him. It always gave me an excuse to poke and prod him for answers that he'd sometimes give and sometimes withhold until I jumped on him with tickly fingers. I can't do that anymore though. He tilts his head toward the building. "Ticktock."

We jog over the clay tile of the lobby and past the woven chairs with fern-patterned cushions, then Apollo swings open the meeting room door. I dart in and freeze, because I'm walking into a Moss Monster Meeting with my rivals, coworkers, and mother...with Apollo.

To add fuel to the fire in my cheeks, he runs into me, catching me around the waist before I can fall. And now, not only am I arriving with him, he's plastered to my backside, and I'm clinging onto his arm like a huggy koala on a tree branch. Maybe if I faint, it will distract them. *Faint, body, faint!*

It does not. I whimper.

And Apollo laughs. "Hello, everyone. I found this one

wandering the parking lot. Let's hope she's better at navigating this year's course." I flick his hand and he lets me go, but I have to admit I miss the closeness and the twitches of his chest from his amusement.

Laughter in the room slides my humiliation into a softer light, and I force a smile. "He's only trying to make himself feel better for being the last one to the meeting."

"Just like he'll be the last one over the finish line," Monique finishes for me.

The group's reaction is delightful inhales through bared teeth and many "ohs." Nico's girlfriend, Cozette, waves, standing beside the few El Escape competitors, bouncing on her toes. Relaxing, I return the gesture and find one of the two available seats—and because the universe is a mischievous beast, Apollo takes the other next to me. I keep myself as small as possible to prevent touching so I can focus.

The adventure twins are here—tour guides for the Cliffs, both fussing with their identically cut black hair. There's the sour catering manager, Frank, who glares each time I look his way. Ten others, two who are new to the contest, and of course, Monique sits next to Demi, who wiggles her fingers at me and then casually twirls her hand around to flick off her brother, making me laugh so sharply, I cover my mouth.

"Xia?" Mama sits on a table in the front of the room between Vic and Miss Ruth. The seventy-year-old wedding coordinator's bright lipstick makes everything surrounding her seem grayscale, and she's wearing massive bejeweled glasses today. Cozette joins them, as does Kingston, who I resist glaring at. So this is the Mossy board of directors.

"Mm?" I answer, biting my lips together.

"Start us out by explaining the Moss Monster Meet."

Oh no.

There are hoots and calls of encouragement from the room because this is what I do every year all over Simona Island. A month before, I rally enthusiasm by reminding everyone of the upcoming event. Except Apollo wasn't here for that. There's no getting out of it without looking like something is wrong.

Apollo leans toward me. "I want to hear this."

I laugh, hoping it's somewhat normal, though that's the last thing I feel, and remain sitting. Because if I move, I'll probably take the table and Apollo with me, and then we'll be in a heap on the floor, all entwined arms and legs and...I should concentrate.

"If I must." I breathe deep.

"Oh, here she goes," Monique says, rubbing her hands together.

My announcer voice can be loud when I want it to. "There is officially one month and four days until the thirty-sixth annual Moss Monster Meet!" I rainbow my hand through the air. "The grueling adventure competition made up of five challenges—"

"She'll be incorrigible until this is over," Frank murmurs.

"—*That's right*, five challenges will send participants from the rival hospitality companies on beautiful Simona Island into ba-ba-ba-beast mode to win the title of Moss Monster Champion." I cup my mouth with both hands and do a crowd roar, loud enough to be heard over the laughs and half-hearted clapping.

Cozette punches the air. "I cannot flippin' wait."

I fight shrinking into my seat. Mama grins wide, glancing between me and Apollo. I refuse to acknowledge his overwhelming presence, though he is an emotion furnace on my left. I'm acting normal-ish, and seeing his eyes, knowing what he thinks because I understand his face so well, will make things worse.

"So..." I widen my eyes at her. "Why are we here?"

Her smile flips to fake. I have the same one. I'm a young clone of my mother from our loose, brown spirals that frizz without a palmful of product to our pointy chins and our thin, dainty feet. Even the muscles of our thighs have the same curve above our matching knees. Her hair now has sparkles of silver, and her tan skin is freckled from years without sunscreen—something I use daily—but when we hold pictures side by side of us at the same age, we match like a pair of handmade socks. I gained an extra two inches of height and my eye color from my dad. If Apollo has the tint of dark honey, I have bog moss—yellow-green muddled with a bit of dirt.

"We have an announcement that may come as a shock to you," Vic says beside her, giving my mother a tight smile.

My chest feels like an ice block just moved in. They're not cancelling the Mossy, are they? I'm so close. They can't do that, it's tradition.

"Though some of you have mentioned it in the past." Mama fidgets her fingers. Another blatant tell of her nervousness.

I cross my arms. They better not.

Vic claps her hands. "This year's Moss Monster Meet will be run...in teams!"

"What?" blasts out of my mouth.

Mama gives me a brief mom-glare warning.

"Teams," Vic repeats. "Of two. Partners to rouse teambuilding. We're a tight-knit community, and we operate like family, but that doesn't always show during Moss Monster season, now does it?"

There are laughs from around the room, but not from me. I am definitely not laughing.

"Cozette." I cross my arms. "Was this your idea?" She's an event planner and one hundred percent pro-teambuilding.

Her face makes a cute deer in headlights look, emphasized by her big brown eyes and lips shaping an O. "No! I don't think." She shrugs, giving a bared-teeth grimace. "It certainly sounds like something I'd want to do, doesn't it? But—" She holds up a finger. "I do not mess with tradition. So when it was brought up, there was a board vote, and we decided unanimously that this is a fantabulous idea."

Miss Ruth pats Cozette's arm. "That is true. Time for a bit of change, yes?" She permeates warmth toward me, making me want to pull my knees up to my chest and hug them. "We need to strengthen our bonds."

I harrumph at the wedding coordinator's words. She bonds people all the time with her perfect ceremonies on this perfect island. Of course, she wants everyone closer. *Oh.* I slowly shift further away from Apollo. She's not thinking about us, is she? Because if she's looking for another couple to marry, she can grab Cozette and Nico, or Monique and Demi. Apollo and I were friends, but on a romance scale—with ten being compatible, and one being a catastrophe—we're a negative five.

She raises a penciled-on eyebrow as if reading my mind. "Considering all the drama surrounding the events over the last couple of years."

Okay, that's fair.

The Moss Monster Meet brings out at least one top-notch line of gossip that will span the year. Last time, it was the lifeguard who missed the start because she had a very late—and athletic—meetup with two arcade workers at El Escape Azul. The hotel staff still reference that day as "the troublemaking triple tryst." I, however, was disappointed. I think she'd have been fun to beat. It may have been close.

The year before that, it was said the playful rivalry between two interns wasn't playful. I honestly couldn't tell from the smack talk—we all get into it—but then it came to blows at the waterfall during the Ring Retrieval event, and one tried to drown the other. It was a complete shock to the island, and now interns can't participate unless they've worked longer than a year. That's cut down on entries and, unfortunately, banter between the resorts during the Mossy. Now we only exchange barbs with those we know well.

But they think taking on a partner will help with that?

"Can you explain how the events will work?" Apollo leans forward, elbows on his knees.

Mama nods. "The Beach Tray Dash, Wave Rescue, Lost Tourist Search, Waterfall Ring Retrieval, and Golf Cart Tour will be completed with your partner."

"Will they be in that order?" Monique asks.

"Good try," Mama says. "You don't need to know that part, now do you?"

"Well—"

"Shh." Vic clamps her hand like a duck snapping its bill closed, but she's smiling.

Mama makes a dramatic throat-clear, pausing to listen for any other interruptions. There are none. "In the Beach Tray Dash, one partner lifts and passes the tray off to the other, then runs to the end, waits, then passes again, and puts down. Scoring remains the same: deductions for spillage, not following the new rules, tripping up other contestants. Got it?"

Sounds of agreement make a round through the room.

Mama continues. In the Wave Rescue, one navigates the kayak while the other rescues the victim, then they work together to pull them to safety. As that's my weakest event, I begrudgingly admit that having another person to get them onto the deck would be helpful. But the rest? Partners will run as a unit to find the lost tourist, which is the worst idea. Someone tagging along is only going to slow me down. During the Ring Retrieval, one partner calls guidance for the other, which makes no sense since I'll be underwater searching for rings. In the Golf Cart Tour, one drives while the other plays tour guide. Where's the challenge in that?

When Mama falls quiet, the room breaks out into murmurs and laughter. Are they actually happy about this? The whole idea makes me rub at the tightness in my throat.

"What about the Moss Boss title?" I drop my hand and ball

my fingers, crossing my arms again. "How is that going to work with a partner?"

Little wrinkles of concern finally form around Mama's eyes at this entire sham. "The title will still go to the individual who wins three consecutive years." Her lips tighten as if she's preparing me for bad news. I've seen that look before during the hardest moments of my life.

You have cancer, Xia.

We don't want you to go to the States.

We're selling El Escape, but everything is going to be okay.

Is it though, Mama? Her chest rises and falls in an impressive sigh. "They just have to win as a team."

My teeth ache from my clamped jaw. So my win is at the mercy of a partner. I turn to eye Monique, but she's high-fiving Farid. The just-turned-twenty-year-old has been a beach lifeguard at the Cliffs since he was fifteen. Is he better than I am? Demi's focus is on me. She's frowning, mimicking my stance with crossed arms. Her gaze flicks next to me, narrowing before she stands, also gives Farid a high-five, and walks out of the room.

I cave and look left. Apollo's elbows are on his knees, hands clasped, and there's an intent question in his honey eyes.

I can't do this.

I stand, hopefully not too abruptly, and make my way to the door, forcing a smile I don't think I've ever felt less like giving. "Gotta get back to work. Bye all."

Waving at muted farewells, I duck out, speed walk to my cart, and haul ass out of the parking lot before anyone else comes out of the building. After I auto-drive myself to El Escape, I drop my forehead to the steering wheel.

I want to win. On my own.

6

HE SAID DATE

J've skipped running two days in a row. Thursday because it was raining with a thousand battering drops as only the tropics experience, and today because I was afraid of crossing paths with Apollo. I'm worried about the Mossy.

All my first choices are taken: Monique and an agile house-keeper, also Farid. Too bad my neighbor isn't joining. Apollo would be head of the list if he didn't make my body do things like scurrying into the ocean and preventing a clear thought. Who knows where I'd end up if I had to see him constantly until race day. Still, I'd end up carrying a few people piggyback if I were to pair with them. That will not work for a win. I need to figure out a different approach to this problem and find a partner who doesn't turn me into a walking disaster zone.

Instead of doing what I should—choosing a partner—I've scoured my phone for everything he could have seen while it was in his possession, and yeah, I should have had a passcode. There's nothing preventing me from becoming mayor of Simona Island or anything, but when I imagine Apollo coming across my recent backside-in-a-cheeky-bikini photo that I should have deleted, my face heats like a distillation flask over a wide-open burner. I like my body. It's strong and resilient, but I wasn't going for a sexy photo op. I was doing a cheek check to see if the bottoms were too skimpy, and they *were*. Just...*boom!* Butt shot. No magic filter. No moody lip pout. No modesty. At. All.

Since I already massacred my vow to not let Apollo distract me, I add to my list of infractions and internet-stalk him. His friend request notification made me pace for an hour before I accepted it. I tap through every picture and update, peeking over my shoulder as if someone has invaded my home to watch me obsess over this man.

There are a few photos of him with sleek and stylish New York people. He appears to fit city and island life like a sexy chameleon, and I'm left wondering what Simona means to him. Are we a nostalgic memory or a painful regret? My vicious, wounded side hopes it's the latter. Especially when I look at those magazine ad models and want to both be them and scratch their eyes out. Not because I'm jealous—that would be impossible—but because they were close to him in body and I never was. They had more of him—the older, adult version.

They're draped against him, tucked under his arm like they reside there, joker grins pointed at me as they say, "You missed out on this."

I burn those thoughts to the ground while internally screaming, *I played flashlight tag in a freaking jungle with him and know his middle name. Do you? Huh? Do you?* But that is not my place nor my business. Except he invited me in. And confused me more than ever.

One of his last posts is a picture out the airplane window with the caption, "I'll miss you, New York, but I miss her so much more."

My heart thrums a wicked beat as I stare at his words. Who is this *her*? A tiny, hopeful voice says, "Could be you," but I smash that hope to dust because the notion is ludicrous. I bet he's talking about a much-needed visit to see his mom. Or maybe it's someone in New York.

The comments don't help calm me down. They span from "we will miss you too" and "come back soon" to Demi's "Bringing the drama since right now" and a cute brunette who asked, "Hey, um, who's her?" I'd like that confirmed too, stranger, but he didn't reply.

How am I going to survive while occupying the same fourteen square miles for the next month? We went forever without a word after a lifetime of knowing each other. This new era of awkward can't last. I won't let it.

My phone buzzes in the late afternoon as I'm checking off inventory.

Don't break anything. I'm walking in.

I slam down my checklist, making everyone in the lobby jump, and bolt down the hall toward the back door. When I fling it open, Apollo is standing there, leaning against the wall in mesh shorts and a t-shirt.

Scrolling through his phone, he lifts his you're-so-busted gaze. "You weren't running for it, were you?"

"No," I bark, breathy and sharp, whipping my head around to observe the hall. I glance back at Jamie, who's working at the computer and staring at me, give him an everything-is-peachy grin, then shut the door. "I was checking for packages." I was definitely running for it. Too much, too soon, too unnavigable. And far, far too hot. Those shorts are one miniscule leap from sexy sweatpants. Just thin mesh and elastic, so easily dragged over hips and firm thighs.

"Oh," he says, snapping me back to attention. "Too bad. I wanted to know if you could go for a run with me before dinner. You, literally running, would have been destiny."

A snort escapes before I can clamp it down. Our ship of destiny crashed and sank into murky depths long ago.

He straightens, pushing off the wall and prowling closer. "What is it?"

I drag my eyes from how his shirt fits his chest and pretend the gray paint can cleanse the image of him from my retinas. What did he say before all that destiny garbage? Oh. Running together. Why? "I can't. I have a client. Massage. Inside." I snatch my bottom lip under my teeth but an "At five" slips out. "And six." Shut up, stupid mouth of mine.

He smiles. "Okay. I'll see you at eight. Does that give you enough time?"

"I thought you wanted to go later?"

His almost-grin is pure mischief and urges me to step close and tuck my nose into his shirt. I've missed his playfulness. "Didn't you say lights go off at ten? Would you prefer an Island King after dark? I mean—" He tilts his head and leans as if planning to capture my lips, and my breath halts in my lungs. "It could be fun to be in the dark with you. Talking. A toutbon —" I'm not even sure what that means, but I melt when he speaks Haitian Creole. "For real—" Wait. That's what that means? A for real what? And why am I leaning closer? "Date—"

And I run. Directly into the door when I spin to escape. The thud of my cheek and shoulder against thick frosted glass echoes down the hall. With a groan I slap the handle and crush my eyelids shut so I won't see his reaction, even though the familiar expression on his seventeen-year-old face is burned into memory. The *what in the hell is wrong with you, Xia,* look. All squinting eyes and tilted head.

As soon as the handle latches behind me, I catch Jamie's nosy intrigue, his eyebrows reaching toward the ceiling. "Did you just run into the door?"

"Just...bumped into it." I bite back a whimper. "It's...fine. I'm fine."

"You're pale."

"All good. How's your day?" I put my hands on my hips, then drop them because that feels odd. Why would Apollo suggest that my bet fulfillment could be something more? Was it to embarrass me and make this night more tortuous? I can do enough of that on my own, thank you very much. There's a knock against the glass behind me and even my spleen cringes. Anyone from the hallway would see the shadow of my head through the frosted pane.

Jamie purses his lips, eyes squinted. "Uh—"

"Open up, Xi. You were never good at hide-and-go-seek."

Jamie rubs a finger against his top lip as if trying to hold it in place to keep from laughing.

I pretend I'm not dying right now and throw the door open. "I was too. I was hidden for over an hour once."

Apollo grins, standing next to the wide-eyed delivery man.

I laugh and wince simultaneously. "Hi, Karl."

"Ms. Nivar." His one-dip nod is his signature greeting to everyone he delivers to. Formal name, sharp head nod, every day of every year. The only things that change are the lines on his face and the gray in his hair. And because our only conversations are about him or me, with no mention of what anyone else on the island is doing, my shoulders ease down. He hands me a box.

Apollo picks up another and steps closer.

I step back.

He moves again, backing me into the office. At least we're not alone this time.

Except we are. The room is vacated, barstool still spinning, calendar up on the abandoned computer. I wait for a bottle of polish remover to roll across the floor like a western tumbleweed, but it never does. That's disappointing. It would create a diversion.

I hug the box to my front while Apollo places the other on the desk, glances at the slowing barstool with something resembling speculation, and turns to me. "I knew where you were the whole time. Behind the well, creeping around the stone while I circled."

"You didn't know until you found me. Why wouldn't you have just called me out?"

Mancala-win sparkles in his eyes again. What is happening? My grip on the box grows tighter, and the glint simmers.

He takes a slow step closer, and his intensity tumbles into jesting. "I was saving the best for last."

My lips twitch. "Liar."

His lips part, and he tongues his inner cheek. This man is thinking hard. But then he nods, huffs a tight laugh, and turns. "Eight. I'll pick you up at your house."

"No, I'll—"

And he's out the door faster than I could have moved.

"Eight" rings down the hall.

I dive into boxes, trying not to hear the hands of the clock slowly ticking. *Tick. Tick. Tick.*

By seven-thirty, I step from the shower, put my hair in a towel, and stare at my reflection through the lavender-scented steam. He'd said *date*. For another torture session that has become a daily activity since he showed up in El Azul's lobby, I try to picture a friendship with Apollo now that we're adults. Me, a wreck in his presence, and him, cool and beautiful as ever, making me aware that my foolishness is not an internal dilemma. No. It's out there for all to see.

Maybe someday, we can be friends. Him returning to Simona again to visit with his family, significant other, and kids. I growl. Okay, so maybe we can't be friends either.

I disagree with my wardrobe, fight with my hair, and fuss

over shoes, as if that would matter. There is no solution here. No fix, no escape.

There's a knock at two minutes to eight. My heart is going to flap its way out of my mouth and fly away as soon as I open the door. I do it anyway. Who needs a heart?

His vintage Frankenstein t-shirt half-tucked into linen pants with rolled cuffs makes me smile. This isn't date attire. I like both his tropic-chic and city-cool style.

After his gaze sweeps from my sandaled toes to mid-length striped skirt and crop top to my messy bun hair, increasing my internal temperature with every inch he studies, he pivots. "Let's go."

That's it?

He turns halfway down my path, walking backward with his hands in his pockets, pebbles crunching under flip-flops. "I haven't had Uncle Artie's for two years. How sad is that?"

I follow on wobbly legs. "You were here two years ago?"

The passenger door of his mom's blue pickup opens with a rusty creak. "Visited for New Year's and Ancestry Day. So a year and a half since I've been home, except that I stopped in for a day last November to bring Demi pizza."

"Pizza?" I ask. "That's a long trip for food."

He stretches his neck like he does when he's nervous, then gives a tight smile. "You've had New York pizza, right?"

"I have." But for Demi? They've had their ups and downs through the years, Apollo being the spotlight stealer that he is and his youngest sister letting him know each of his flaws whether true or not. "I'm not sure I'd travel with it."

He hangs on the corner of the open door, arm perched over the top rim. "It's her favorite NYC thing." Maybe I'm reading him wrong because we've both changed so much, but I'm picking up a sadness to his words, a reluctance that says there's more to this.

"What happened?" When his eyebrows furrow, I continue. "Why did you bring her pizza from New York?"

He shrugs a shoulder and glances to the side as if checking that we're alone. Which we are because I've already done about fifteen area checks. "It was when she broke up with Eden for good."

I wince. That had been a volatile relationship that ended with a fire and a restraining order. Even I had stayed in the gossip circle for that update, then dropped off a big basket of comforting scented goods when she moved into her condo for a half housewarming, half starting-over present.

"I bet that meant a lot to her." I squeeze his fingers before I can think beyond how sweet he was to do that, but then drop his hand quickly and settle on the fabric seat. It smells like Vic and fake vanilla. Sure enough, a beige cutout picture of vanilla beans hangs from the rearview mirror. I should make car sachets. "Is that why you've returned for an extended vacation?" I keep coming back to his post about missing New York. "To check on Demi and your mom?"

"Part of it." He closes the door, quietly though.

He slides into the driver's side. "Seatbelt. Unless you need help with it?"

I fasten it so fast, he chuckles, leaving the tension from our conversation outside. He clicks his while pressing the acceleration. Guess he didn't lose his lead foot. Actually, I think it's worse.

"There are no cars here," he says. "It's so odd."

I point at the full driveways, though they're mostly a variety of golf carts. "Um." I'm proud of my almost word because the fake vanilla scent is being replaced by a hint of the past. Cherry.

"Those are golf carts. Say it with me. Golf—"

I gently punch his solid shoulder, then jerk my hand back and link my fingers in my lap. We are no longer kids, or on playful brawling terms.

"If I wasn't driving this truck." His side-eye is more intense than I could have ever imagined, and I fidget with the hem of my shirt to hide the squirm of my hips. I want to ask. I really, really want to say, "Oh yeah, Apollo? What would you do?" But I don't. I stare out the window like I don't care one bit.

The boxy houses of Simona are the colors of kids' toys, saturated by the setting sun. Primary blue and red with cream shutters and boxes of flowers. Pastel yellow, green, and pink contrast against the electric tones of every piece of trim and equally bright doors. Some yards are sand with sparse grasses, some pebbled with footed bowls sprouting massive leaves. One is deep-green sod with trimmed boxwoods and a marble, three-tiered fountain with a cherub at the top.

I glance out of the corner of my eye at Apollo. This must be such a difference to concrete and skyscrapers. What does his NYC apartment look like? Tiny with an open design where a bed with rumpled sheets sits off to the side, between a big window and a kitchen even smaller than mine? Or maybe he's in a bedroom at his dad's house. Does his space smell like him but mixed with the city? I bet I could make the perfect diffuser blend to highlight his scent.

I toy with the idea of asking him what his life is like now in the city, but he clears his throat and asks, "How's your dad?"

"Now that he's retired, he has an espresso and a book within a foot of him at all times. How's yours?"

He turns onto the main road toward town. The houses blip by faster.

"He's very happy where he's at, and his accent is strong as it's ever been." He flits his hand around a bunch as he pronounces a nonsensical word mix of accented dialect, most with an additional s and plenty of dramatic flair. As I cover my mouth to keep from cackling, he pulls into the gravel lot of Uncle Artie's and parks between two golf carts. The tin-roofed, brown A-frame shop hasn't changed in forty years, from its sliding order window to its orange neon sign.

"Shall we?" He asks but waits as if he's giving me an out. Is he?

I can't go back on a bet. That is not how the game is played no matter how tempting. The door handle squeaks when I lift it and I'm out, eyes on the crowd under the neon glow of the Uncle Artie's sign. There are a lot of people here. I clear my throat and study the multicolored gravel, making sure my feet continue moving.

I step beside him, arms crossed tightly against my ribs like an iron shield, which I promptly drop, because these are my people, and I must. Act. Normal.

Focusing on everything that is not Apollo helps. The sugar, sweat, and herbaceous scent is uniquely Uncle Artie's lot, and the sounds of a regular Friday night make this surreal moment of having Apollo back on the island a bit more palatable.

To our left, a makeshift band of guitars play harmonies while a hand drum keeps pace along with a knee-high little one rocking a guiro like she was born for the instrument's ratcheting rhythm. Singing pops up from a yellow table, then breaks into laughter, then song again. An older couple dances, eyes locked as if they exist only for each other's gaze. Around them, friends and families sway to the strummed salsa, some serious, some offbeat and uncaring as if their main purpose is stoking the others' giggles.

As we continue toward the line, we pass ten teenagers sitting atop a teal picnic table, conversation as loud and big as the sparkly future ahead of them. Too bad none of them are old enough to run the Mossy. I grin wide and wave, pitching out a couple fast questions about a trip to South America the school is putting together.

"Wait," Apollo says, shoving his hands in his pockets. "You all get to go to South America? We never went on a field trip."

Because we didn't have Nico the secretive billionaire and his determination to create a new generation who want to save the planet, starting with this island.

Kids' heads bob in sync. Alani, the most curious girl I've ever met, says, "It's a funded eco-program to learn about the impact of deforestation and lack of recycle programming in rural areas."

"Xiamara!" a table yells, then heads turn one by one, and we are officially in the spotlight. It's the same greeting I always get when I come here, but it feels far different with Apollo beside me. Even more so with him seeming to hide behind me. That's a role-reversal I wasn't expecting.

"Hey, friends." Waving, I step into motion to move this show along as I get callbacks and field small talk about the Mossy. It doesn't seem to have spread to the entire island that there will be partners, which is a relief, because I'm not sure what to say yet. I have no partner so...

"Long time no see," a British accent bellows through the crowd formed at the double window. All eyes that weren't already gawking turn toward us, and Apollo's pinky finger brushes mine. Is he nervous?

I peer up at him and nudge his hand. "What's wrong?"

His lips purse, then he gives me a squinty grin and smooths the hair on the back of his head. "I'm not sure why I thought I'd know everyone. There's a lot of new people."

"Of course, there are. You haven't been here for seven years." Alright, that came out snippy. Apollo's tight grin slips away, but then one specific squeal makes me grimace.

7

SERIOUSLY THOUGH, CHILLAX

*J*ose sprints from the line and halts in front of me, arms crossed. "You're avoiding me."

"I'm not." That's a lie. I've been slinking around El Escape's shadows instead of barging in to visit. This is the exact situation I should bounce off him, but I don't know what to say to anyone except Roxanne, because she's not here and can't see me acting foolish. I've barricaded my words a like a hermit in a hidey hole while I deal with my thoughts, which have been flitting between work, the Mossy, and Apollo.

"Hi, Apollo." Jose sighs and turns to me. "Woman! Where have you been. Wait—" His hand settles on my crossed arms, and he sends a wide-eyed glance at Apollo, then me, back and forth as he assembles the wrong puzzle. *Oh shit.*

I give tiny sharp shakes to my head.

"Are you—"

"NO!" Hopefully, my laugh isn't as maniacal as it feels. Nothing to see here, people. "No," I repeat much more quietly, and without even stealing a peek at the simmering energy beside me. I don't want to know his reaction. "I lost a bet and owe Apollo an Island King."

"Oh, the loss. Yeah." Jose's eyes crunch up in pure sympathy, and my stomach drops. That video has to go. Then he shakes himself and pops on his chipper-dancer face. "And now you're partnering?"

"No." I stare him down, attempting to bombard his brain-waves. *Later. Later, Jose. Seriously, freaking later.*

Apollo crosses his arms and eyes the crowd. Is he part-nering with someone already? Is that why he hasn't brought it up and is giving me zero reaction to this uncomfortable conver-sation? What if he has? He's really fast and could potentially beat me, especially when I can barely stay on my feet when I'm near him. Oh, this is bad.

Little demons dance in Jose's gaze when his "ahem" brings my attention off Apollo, and I wince. "M&M catch-up on Sunday," he says pointedly. "You have Monday morning off, so don't give me anymore of your—"

"Okay," I say and squeeze his arm. "Okay. Deal. But only one mojito. I have to train."

He relaxes and looks at Apollo. Please don't invite him to M&M night. Please don't invite—

"Well then," Jose says. "Happy evening, all. Enjoy your date."

"It was a bet," I grumble.

Jose laughs and drags me to him to tango like we so often do, especially if we need to share something secretive. "Sweet, Xia. Since when do you lose?" He leans while twirling me through quick steps we've taken thousands of times. "You are... blushing? Woman, there is a roomful of tension here, and we are *outside*. You owe me all the explanations. All of them!" In Jose style, he launches me out in a spin...and directly into Apollo, whose fingers slip around my waist where he halts me, facing him.

I get my first real inhale of twenty-five-year-old Apollo Fischer. Cherry just like before, but also mint. Not toothpaste, but a sprig snapped from a dewy morning plant. It's pure, clean pleasure: a shower after a triathlon, fresh and hot, and my legs are gelatinous tentacles with no rhythm or grace. His thumbs circle the crests of my hips, making all my womanly parts tighten with longing, and the only thing that keeps me on my feet is the fear that his touch will disappear if I melt into the pebbled path below. I'm holding onto firm biceps while my thoughts swirl. He's *touching* me, and Simona is watching. *Move closer. Inhale him like a diffuser stick at the Perfumarie.* I can't. He's been here for a split second and what does that mean? Nothing, because his broken promise overshadows any thoughts about us partnering.

There was a day when standing here in his arms would have been the most natural, meaningless motion. Our conversation would have us laughing instead of staring in silence. I'd have shoved at him, and he'd have...I don't know. He could be so random with his attention. Toss me over his shoulder, tickle me, hug me, sweep my legs and lower me, then ask why I was sitting on the ground so everyone could hear. He dips his head until his lips brush my ear. "You've changed." His statement is a rugged rasp that's deep enough to penetrate my spine and send a purr through each cell of my body.

If he stays where he is, I'm going to turn my head an—oh. I can't. I inch away. "How so?" Is that breathy voice mine? *Pull it together, Xia.*

His grip tightens, but then his chest rises and falls, and he turns me toward the short line at the window. "You're more confident. More accepting of people watching you."

"People are watching?" Of course, they are. I'm falling all over myself around him.

"How could they not?"

I crinkle my nose. So, he has noticed my clumsy tendencies in his presence. Still, he doesn't have to rub it in.

Jose is in a conversation with Uncle Artie, but both of them watch us as they chat. Artie grins, and Jose's sculpted eyebrows raise in interest, and he looks like he's about to do a bouncy clap of happiness, though I'm not sure what for. We step behind an older retired couple who live in the north neighborhood. They bob their heads in greeting, and we do the same.

"Did Jose teach you to dance like that?" Apollo crosses his arms, parting us. He left a warm mark on me, and my tingling nerves fight to hold onto it forever.

"Helped," I say. "I—" I blow out a long breath through pursed lips.

"You probably learned in college. Local dance troupe? Or did someone bet you to learn?" His words are soft, but his jaw is tight.

"There was no dancing at massage therapy school." I stare off at the darkening line of trees where El Escape Azul stands tall in the distance, the rooms' massive windows lit in a checkerboard pattern. "I only bet with you."

He's quiet for so long, I'm forced to glance back at him to see what he's thinking, but he holds his plump bottom lip between his teeth in an expression I'm unfamiliar with. "Were you taking lessons from Lady Belladonna before Jose got here, or did he teach you?"

Isn't he being nosy? "The owner of the strip club I worked at offered ballroom training." My words rush out, piercing through the buzz of surrounding chatter with an edge of sass. My stomach balls, but I brush my smiling lips with my fingertips, then grip my skirt as it flutters in the breeze that's finally cooling as the sun sets.

His chest rises and falls with a lengthy breath. "You're joking with me right now."

"I may be." The couple in front of us takes the large-sized paper cup, whip poking over the top along with two wooden spoons, and then we're at the sliding window.

Uncle Artie claps his hands when he sees us, holds up a

finger, then rushes out the door beside the window to drape his tall frame over me, encompassing me in a cloud of sweet cream and ginger tea. He squeezes me with lanky arms that could coil around me twice, then gives Apollo a hug as well. "High time you got yourself back here for a solid span." He grips Apollo's shoulder. "It's a shame you have to return to that city."

Apollo grins wider than I've seen since he returned, all pristine teeth and joy. His eyes crinkle like his mom's do, and it hurts to look at him, he's so beautiful. Always has been. "I happen to like *that city*."

Of course, he does. He did post that he would miss New York.

"I jest. It's a nice place to visit, but your ma is so very happy when you're here." He turns to me. "As is this one, I'm sure. Aren't you?"

My heartbeat races off, but Apollo gives a light shove to my shoulder, knocking me on track. "She's not happy at the moment. I won a bet, and she owes me an Island King."

Uncle Artie claps his hands once and backs to the door. "You two and your games. This one's on me, then she'll owe you another."

I get out the B sound of "But," except he's already back inside. Apollo's profile is smug as Uncle Artie assembles cups of custard, layering in caramel, banana chunks, and whip at his stainless-steel workstation. *Games.* We've always played them. As soon as I returned from that first chemo trip, Apollo made it his duty to learn every card and board game I'd played with the kids I met in the hospital. I hadn't been competitive before, but when Apollo would explain how I could do something better or would pick up the rules and start reading them out loud as if I didn't know how to play, it sparked a war within myself to prove I knew everything, could do anything he could, without his help. He made me bonkers. I wish he still made me bonkers in that familiar way and not in this new uncertain way.

A glance around shows whispers behind cupped palms and looks over shoulders. We're standing in the Simona Island spotlight. Rumors will spread to my mother if they haven't already. I'm shocked she hasn't tracked me down yet and given me the Ilaria degree. I take a subtle step away from Apollo.

He puts his hands in his pockets and bends his head so he's closer to me. "Is it that dreadful being around me?"

"No. I just. I'm—" I crinkle my nose and shrug. My heart is beating faster than when I jog for hours. He ups my temperature to impossible-to-survive degrees. "I don't..." Know how to do this. "I—What do you want with me?" Too direct, too awkward. I fight not to run, but we're surrounded by nosy, familiar people, and while I've embarrassed myself around him plenty of times, I'm not willing to be the woman who not only runs for exercise but also from emotional distress. I'll be damned if it's going to be me the island is talking about until next year.

Apollo's worried eyebrows ease first, and he straightens, mumbling something that sounds like, "What don't I want with you?"

"What was that?"

He seems more interested in the exterior siding than my question. He jerks to attention and points. "Oh look."

"Here you go," Uncle Artie says. Two big Island Kings sit in front of him.

We say our thanks and swear to be back again soon. I snatch one custard and bite the highest arch of the crisp crown made of spiced sugar, give a moan and thumbs-up to Artie, then follow Apollo toward a bright purple table furthest away from the building.

"Good?" he asks as we settle across from each other.

"Always." Dished in the paper bowl before me is the taste of sweet comfort, the smell of childhood afternoons, and memories of every first date.

Apollo pushes the whipped cream aside to preserve the best part and skims the slightest bit of banana custard off the top. His stance shifts, sinking into a rolled-forward relaxation I haven't seen on him since he was much younger. "I make you nervous."

"No." The word is clear and immediate, surprising me because obviously that's a massive lie. "You don't." I shove a big bite of custard in my mouth to give myself a moment to figure out speech around Apollo. I shake my head, tongue still refusing to play it cool or even lukewarm. I hate my reaction to him. How I can't pull myself together and be the person everyone else on Simona Island knows me to be.

"Really?" he asks. "You don't act the same with me. We don't...play." His lips tip up. "As much."

"We're not kids anymore, Apollo." I nearly bite my spoon in half and force myself to calm down, wishing it wouldn't be awkward for me to bring out a vial of Chillax and inhale. Around anyone else I would, but we're already in a territory of weirdness I don't want to be in.

"I am *well aware* of that."

I must be misreading the smolder in his gaze. That can't mean what I think it does, because I believe we're fighting over the one thing we never had—closure. He left, sent a few cryptic messages I didn't know how to respond to, and now he's back and we have no clue what ground we stand on.

Setting my cup down, I link my fingers and lean in, because island residents have sharp hearing. "Well, you're not acting like it."

"No?" He tilts his head, gazes at my lips, then lower. He takes the slowest, sexiest bite of custard. My nipples must be trying to break out of my thin bra to get to him, because the right corner of his mouth twitches. What is he doing? What am I doing? The world is upside-down, topsy—

"How's my Mossy princess, eh?" a male voice interrupts.

Justin is the only man I know under the age of sixty who slicks his hair straight back. He also has a vintage motorcycle but is missing the cigarette pack in his sleeve to complete his greaser style.

I plaster on my fake smile and turn to the man now sitting on our table. "I'm fine. You?"

He winks. "I'd be better if you weren't on a date right now."

"It's not a—"

"I'm Apollo." He stands and holds a hand out. The men shake, Justin's smile never faltering.

"Uh, yeah. It's been a while. I'm Mia's bro."

Apollo's eyes widen, the recognition that he's talking to his ex's brother apparent. There's the slightest wince. "Oh, *Justin*. It really has been a while." He crosses his arms.

"It has. You heard about my sis and Brad, right?" He puts his goo-goo eyes back on me. And this moment just got even more awkward.

"I did hear about that." Though Apollo certainly doesn't look thrilled about it. Probably because he didn't like Brad.

My first boyfriend wasn't the most charismatic of people, but he was so sweet. Apollo dated Mia when we were seventeen. They were caught on North Beach, wrapped in a towel and nothing else. I couldn't speak to him for weeks, broke up with Brad during that time, and Apollo and Mia didn't last either.

"I mean, I'm happy for my sister and brother-in-law." Justin moves to sweep at my curls, but I evade his hand. He sighs. "But I wouldn't have let this one get away."

"That's going to get back to Mia." I lift my chin up to signal to the people making their way over as if one intrusion deserves five more.

"Psh. Everyone knows what a smitten kitten I am over you, and yet you just won't give." He snatches my hand and presses it to his chest.

"Ugh." I pull my fingers away and wipe them on my skirt. "Don't you have ten girlfriends you need to get back to?"

He bats his eyes at me. "Just biding my time until I can convince you to give me one night with those thighs around my—"

"Careful." Apollo squares his shoulders, and I settle in and take a bite of custard. Interesting. The protective streak makes my belly flutter.

"I was going to say *bike*." Justin waggles his eyebrows at me.

"Unsubscribe." I poke his shin. "I never signed up for this mailing list."

Maggie, the beach lifeguard, smacks Justin on the back of his head and introduces herself to Apollo, then sits next to me to talk about the Mossy. After Justin fixes his hair, he hits on me again.

Then Jennifer, the El Escape desk clerk, wanders to my other side to ask about the updates to the spa that we're doing over the break. She re-dyed her short teal hair, making her blue eyes even brighter.

Apollo eats custard while observing the four different conversations going on around him. Have I ever seen him so out of his element? He's an attention sponge. Soaks it up because it's how he was made. But this new Apollo, he's silent, seemingly content to listen.

Justin talks about taking his bike to the mainland.

Apollo's grin is mischievous. He glances at Justin, then back at me and rolls his eyes, making me laugh—apparently at the correct time, because Justin says, "Right?!" and laughs too.

I give a glare of chagrin back at Apollo as he takes a long lick of custard from his spoon that I feel all over me, and then neither of us are smiling. Thankfully, Jennifer tells me how much she loves the new welcoming spray I made. She wants some for her house and is curious about what the components will do for her mood. That gets me into an animated conversation with her and two others about what all went into it and how scent affects the nervous system. When her fiancé drives up, she hugs me, says goodbye to Apollo, and drags Justin away.

"You really found your calling, didn't you?" he asks, keeping his eyes on his bowl. "I'm not sure I've ever seen you so excited to talk about something. Maybe that day when the freezer broke and we had to eat all the sorbet before it melted."

I smile. Apollo didn't know me when I discovered aromatherapy, but he understands my heightened sense of smell. He called it my superpower once I'd finished chemo and after a year, everything returned to an oversensitive point.

"I really love my job."

"Everyone else does too. Your mom speaks highly of your skills and what you've brought to El Escape."

"She wasn't thrilled at first. She'd have liked me to stay and take over. There was a brief battle about it until she understood."

"That you weren't interested in running the hotel? I'm not sure anyone who knows you didn't see that coming."

I lift and drop a shoulder. "People still ask about it—why I didn't at least partner with my parents before..." He probably doesn't know Nico or that he bought El Escape after the hurricane wrecked it.

He stares off at the thicket of palms between us and the ocean. Fireflies twinkle in the darkness in rhythmic constellations, but watching Apollo's profile is more captivating than their light show. He wants to tell me something, but instead rips through the perfect line he made in his custard like a backhoe slamming through flat ground. He shovels the spoonful in his mouth and closes his eyes. The dip of his Adam's apple is followed by a lip lick and a long, tired exhale. "You wouldn't have been good at running the hotel." He gives me an apologetic squint. "Only because you have to love something to put your full attention on it, and you didn't love the paperwork or dealing with the staff management."

I open my mouth to protest, *I would have been great, thank you very much*, but he's right. If I'm not going to fall down an obsessive hole of perfection in something, I don't try at all. What's the point if I'll never reach a finish line, break a record, or have people look at me and know there's nothing better than what I just did. Even if it's brief.

Apollo touches my chin again, and I jerk back to attention. He balls his fingers on the table. "You okay? I'm sorry. That was—"

"You're right." I can't curb the irritation from my voice. He knows, because he *knows me*. Not the recent version, but the core me. I meet his concerned gaze and swallow hard. "So, you're working as a pilot in New York?"

Suddenly, I'm not the only one tongue-tied. He shovels another construction-grade custard collection past his pillowy lips. "I have been, yes."

"Is it busy?"

"I've been...busy." He clears his throat.

"That was a pause." And not a straight answer.

He grins. "Afraid I'm missing too much work by being here?"

"It is a long time." I squeeze my fists until my short nails bite my palms. "A jump-about timeframe." Every Simona Island kid leaves at some point to jump about the world. If it's not for college or a brand new life, homesickness drags them back about a month later.

He nods. "That's true. And kids from Simona either never leave or never return. And here I am."

"Until you set sail again." I grab my cup. I'm digging when I should retreat and change the subject. But there's a part of me that wants to interrogate him with a barrage of questions like I used to do when we were younger, before things changed between us. *Why the Mossy, why now, why not three years ago when you promised you would? Is this some weird revenge, or are you only occupying time during your vacation? Tell me everything.* But I keep my mouth shut. It's been too long. He may owe me an explanation, but I'm not innocent here. I ignored him first, but for good reason.

"Hey." His tone is serious. "I hate it when you're upset. You can always talk to me. You know that, right?"

That's the thing. I don't. Last time we had a too-honest conversation, we didn't see each other for seven years. We're not cut out for certain topics, but I'm afraid to even say that much.

I wave my hand in the air. "I'm fine. How do you like the States? It was an adjustment, wasn't it?"

He squints at me, eyes seeking...something I'm unsure of. "It was enlightening. How was your experience?"

"I learned a lot." How the best of friends click into place like an adjoining puzzle piece, and following what you love is the obvious path, and sex is fascinating. How aromatherapy and the psychology of it was ten thousand times better than hotel management, but telling that to Mama and Papa was ten thousand times harder.

"Care to share?" He settles his elbows on the table, now twirling his spoon in a drilling excavation.

I lift my chin. "I competed in a triathlon. Four of them, actually." I started training because he was leaving without me, planning ahead, and I couldn't imagine the island without him. Sure, I could have stayed, but I didn't have many options besides running a hotel I didn't want to run. I had an idea of what I wanted from my life, but I hadn't made that leap into action. But sharing that is too much. He doesn't deserve knowing his path led to mine. "That's why I left. It was great."

"Was it? And then you found massage and aromatherapy school?"

"Yes. I wanted to help with the hotel, but doing something that I actually liked."

"Of course, you did." He grins. "And you returned because your jump-about was over?"

"I'm here and can't imagine living anywhere else."

He smiles and finishes the last of his Island King with a groan. "Four triathlons by twenty-five is impressive."

"Is it?" I can't help that my chest fills with pride and that I'm addicted to the warmth that floats through me with praise. I want more.

"Absolutely." He sets his cup aside. "But jump-about's concluded. We're all grown up."

With him here, I'm not so sure of that. I'm feeling immature, unsteady, indecisive.

"Come on," he says, tipping his head toward the truck. "I'll take you home."

I sit frozen still. That's it? He doesn't want to discuss the Mossy or anything else?

"Or we can stay." He sets his hand on the table and leans close enough for me to see his eye color tinted by dim neon and solar light. "Start some rumors. Or *more* rumors, most likely."

The bench creaks when I struggle to detach myself from it. He keeps up with long strides, a smug smile on his face.

A spurt of farewell yells pop up behind us.

Justin calls my name.

Apollo loops his arm around me and tugs me close. I stumble but catch myself. Well, actually, he holds me up and continues toward the truck, opens the door for me, and shuffles me in.

We travel in silence that makes my heartbeat sound like "part-ner" instead of "lub-dub."

The island is talking about the new Mossy rule, so why aren't we? I twist my lips back and forth, chewing at them. I don't want to acknowledge this smack to tradition, but I'm forced to. We bounce over a bump in the pavement, and the old truck gives a creaking groan. I come close to responding to its vocalization to take care of this blasted quietude, so maybe it will be easier to ask a question or two out of a thousand. Who is he partnering with? Did he even consider asking me?

My brain is muddled enough without adding him as my main competitor to the mix. *Great.* And now I'm thinking of his potential to beat me. Can he even kayak? I glance at the round shoulder beside me. I don't know how he couldn't with that structure. It's time to focus on training more than ever.

Or maybe he's mustering the courage to ask me. Past him wouldn't wait, but this new version of Apollo seems more observant and thoughtful. That's it; he's giving me space to warm up to this idea, right? I wait, internally impatient, in the extended silence. While my heart races because I'm not sure what I'll say, it would be nice to know he thinks he could win with me as his partner.

"So..." His single, trailing-off word makes me exhale in relief. This is it. We're going to talk about it. It's not ideal, but I'm afraid it will be worse to choose anyone else, or no one at all. He taps a rhythm on the steering wheel. "When are we headed back to Uncle Artie's so you can make good on your loss?"

My jaw drops open as he pulls up to the curb. "But—"

He holds a finger up, leans over, and boops my nose. "Uncle Artie even said it. You owe me another. Next Friday, or should we do a mid-week nooner?"

A nooner? Really, Apollo? "I don't...I mean, but..." Partnering?

"It's okay, Xi. You can check your calendar." He steps from the truck, coming around to my side, but I jump out first and face off with him.

Maybe I should ask? He's fast and strong. We grew up pretending we were competing. It's likely we'd win together.

Except he's also Apollo—my kryptonite in human form. I'll find someone else. Someone who can keep up.

He steps close, tilting his head as he searches my face, then he brushes my curls behind my shoulder but doesn't drop his hand. He traces my neck and moves closer. Is he...thinking about kissing me? "Goodnight," he whispers.

I turn and leap for my porch, but I'm spun back into a cherry-scented hard chest. A wordless, jumbled mess of syllables in an octave I'm surprised I can hit stumbles from my mouth, but then Apollo's arms encircle me, and my entire body shorts out. If it were possible to get close enough to inhale a double rainbow, it would smell like this. There's a hint of amber and cinnamon on him too. I want to crawl up into him further to extinguish this tingling ache, but when I twitch to wrap myself around him and follow his collarbone with my nose, he gives me a squeeze, biceps hard against my shoulders, then he's gone, walking to the truck, shaking his head. "I really hate that she's right."

What? Tell me that wasn't a bet or something. With who? I glance down the street, but it's just us and the moonlight.

"Text me about another custard run." He slips into the driver's side without even looking at me and speeds off, his taillights disappearing around the turn until all that's left are the glow of porchlights and the silhouettes of rooftops against the dark sky.

8

WATERFALLING

I should take the few minutes available before I head to the waterfalls to work on a get-it-done blend that's giving me balancing trouble. Instead, I slump on my couch, hugging a decorative pillow.

My mother won't partner with me. Neither will my neighbor or Nico, and I'm so desperate that I nearly asked Camila, because my cousin is a runner, but she'd be too busy posing for photos and touching up her makeup before the finish line to win.

Mom tells me that numbers have grown because some chose their significant others as their partner, and there are nine other people who haven't picked. One of them is Apollo. At least as of ten minutes ago, he's still available. I'm just being obstinate about choosing, and it could cost me the Moss Boss trophy. Is that what I want? No, it's not.

I should call him, but I can't make myself do it. Not yet. I grab my phone and dial Roxanne.

"Guess who's just spent five hours in the car?" she says in lieu of hello.

"Day trip early on a Saturday?"

She snorts. "Potential client meeting. Five hours for a ten-minute conversation. I loathe them. But I've picked up Hadley and am now home, where the opening of the wine will commence in two-point-three hours."

"I want wine. I have a problem."

"Oh. Is it an Apollo problem?"

"How would you know that?"

"Oh, you're the sweetest." She gives a fake "Ha, ha, hahaha" laugh. "He's on Simona Island. That alone is a problem. I was just hoping your perfect little world wouldn't go all explody before I arrived for the Mossy."

"You're coming?" I'm on my feet in a flash. "Seriously?"

"Got my ticket. I can't be there until the day of the event, but Hadley is staying with her dad, so let the antics abound." When Roxanne has a moment to let her hair down, she doesn't waste it. She is exactly what I need to distract me from Apollo.

"That is the best news."

"Glad to know I hold a candle to the wonder that is your ex-soulmate. Explain."

In stuttery, broken words, I tell her everything from my military crawl out of the lobby to him hugging me. After a long pause that makes me look at the phone to make sure we still have a connection, Roxanne breaks out in raucous laughter. "You're so fu—" She clears her throat. "Fun. Yep. So fun."

"Tell Hadley Aunty Xia says hi. How is this *fun*?"

"Because you're going to ask him to be your partner."

I sputter like a yard sprinkler. "What? Why?"

"It's required for the Mossy, and you're asking me what you should do about a man who beat you in a race—"

"Because I fell."

"Pssh, details. He won, has massive shoulders for kayaking, and competes with you more often than he blinks. Please.

You've decided, you just need to do it. I give you permission. Go forth, young warrior woman."

I told her about his shoulders? I close my eyes and rub my forehead. "He does not make me feel like a warrior. I feel like I'm thirteen and have never spoken to a boy before."

"Which is why this is such a good idea. You'll settle down after working with him. Then when it's over, you will have proven to Simona that when it comes to Apollo, you can handle your shi—elf." She snorts. "That's right. Handle yourself, you little wackadoodle. I believe in you."

"I'm glad someone does. I don't think I can handle myself at all around him."

"You're going to win. Even if you have a partner who can't keep up with you, you'll find a way. This means too much to you. But also, let's talk about the important stuff." She lowers her voice. "What happened in that hug, Xia? Did you wrap your arms around him? Climb him like a tree? Give a little hump action? Tell me you at least performed the patented boob press?"

I cover my eyes. "No. None of those."

"Aw. You didn't reciprocate, did you? I bet you hurt his feelings. Now go make up or make out. Both, preferably. Either way, ask him or someone else. Sounds like Mama Nivar is serious about this partnership thing, and you know how she gets."

Ugh. I really do.

We say our goodbyes, and I stare at Apollo's face in my contacts, then open a message to him. There's nothing wrong with having a discussion. Could we make it work if we teamed up? This will be the first text I've ever sent to him. Feels more momentous than it should. After tapping and deleting twenty times, I push send. *Do you have time to meet up today?*

The writing bubbles start immediately, then his message pops up on the screen. *I'm busy at the moment. Let me see where the day goes.*

I drop my head against the couch and sigh. He's probably asking someone to be his partner, and then they'll be busy making training plans. I waited too long. Just like always.

The weather is turning summer-sticky. It doesn't last long, but this begins the time of year that locals thrive at night and stay in water during daylight when they're not working this little island. But the Mossy takes place in the afternoon, so a sweaty run it is. Diving into the waterfall will be amazing after three miles.

I get going, slow at first to find my pace. Heart pounds and blood pumps. I turn the music up since I no longer have earbuds and find the perfect rhythm, occasionally glancing back to see if Apollo is behind me. I don't want to be caught off guard again, but I expect it now that he's returned. As if he'd be where I am like in the past. But that was when we were kids.

His father probably loves that he followed in his footsteps and became a pilot. I bet Apollo does really well in New York too. That's clear from his social media photos. It didn't occur to me that some of those people hanging on his arm could be famous clients.

The sharp screech of a monkey has me stepping off the jungle's hiking trail and into a web of vines and roots. They grow thick along the ground in places. It makes the tourist-finding event even more treacherous when in a hurry. I slip my foot out from between two sprawling ankle-twisters and step back on the path.

The monkey either departed or is staying still and silent so it doesn't attract my attention. Little bastards are snide like that. Another quarter mile and I'm singing—more like panting—along with the pop blaring from my phone speaker while hitting my stride. I pass a group of tourists and Monique. She scrunches her nose and makes a hissing sound as she rakes her fingers through the air.

The rivalry is ratcheting up. I snap my teeth, fighting a grin. "See you at the starting line."

"You bet your speedy patooty, you will," she calls after me. "Hey!" Her yell turns me back around where I jog in place. "Who are you partnering with?"

I stop moving and put my hands on my hips. "Don't know yet."

Her eyes widen, and her mouth tightens into an O. She turns to her group but pitches over her shoulder, "You may want to get on that."

I fill my lungs to capacity and blow all the air out in a slow stressful stream.

The trek isn't as busy on the weekends with the typical honeymooners' departures and arrivals, but I hope the water-fall isn't crowded. I slow to a walk when I get to the bridge spanning the lake's main output river, stretching my arms above my head and breathing deep.

It's fairly quiet. A few couples swim in the crystalline water that winks like a polished gem when the sun peeks through the trees. Two men bask on the large, rounded stones surrounding the edge. A woman climbs the path to the upper overlook where you can jump beside the first cascade. They're not big waterfalls. One drops twenty-five feet from the pinnacle, the other spills a short thirteen, smashing over boulders to make a perfect roaring soundscape. It smells of moss and hibiscus. Clean water and mineral rock. I've tried to bottle it, but it's not possible. There are too many factors that alter the air from sunup to sundown through the year of tropical seasons. I'd have to harness millennia of life, and as much as I've studied, as skilled as I've become, I'm not that level. One day I'll get it right.

I pull the water-pouch backpack from my shoulders as I

walk toward the path that wraps up the curve of rock. After gathering a handful of assorted rings and my goggles, I strip to my sports bikini and shove everything in my bag. It fits with plenty of room in the natural cutout cubby between two car-sized rocks. There's someone's phone in there wrapped in an arm holster and a gray t-shirt beside that. Another local. Maybe a guide with tourists in the narrow indent behind the shorter falls. I climb, hearing cheers, then a scream and a splash from the brave woman who climbed up and jumped. I grin to myself and set my goggles over my eyes, looking forward to my own impending adrenaline rush, and crest the top of the hill, rumbling rapids loud in my ears. It's a drastic temperature change in the mist. The woman has cleared away from the jump path and is in a man's arms as they swim, talking close and bobbing in a circle.

The rings sparkle in the air when I scatter them to the water below. One long exhale and I follow with a swan dive. Other Simona kids could do a few flips and add a twist, but I usually land wrong. You only need to belly flop from twenty-five feet once to deter future experimentation.

Some days, when the tourist season wasn't in full swing, we'd stay here for hours, kids from seven to eighteen, trekking up the path, diving again and again. Older ones sneaking off behind the falls, youngers leaping from the stones at the sides while watching their idols twirl and cannonball from what seemed to be a hundred million terrifying feet. Apollo, Ziggy, and I acting as judges, calling numbers when we weren't jumping.

The water splashes more than I'd like, but the speed is fantastic. I don't need to kick to reach the bottom and spot my first glimmery circle. Scooping it up, I slip it on my finger before I come up for air, then dive again. How would part-nering work for this? It's meticulous. I can't be paying attention to someone else because I'll lose where I think the rings fell. And Apollo would pull all my attention. How is he at diving?

My task is a rhythm of breath holding, kicking, and seeking shiny metals among sandy silt, mossy rocks, and long threads of paper-thin green leaves of the underwater plants. Small, silver fish dart along the bottom away from me as I travel in a pattern on the hunt for rings. Except I can't find the last one. I have nine on my fingers, and I threw ten. Six more dives, and I pop up and pull my goggles off my head.

"You are focused," Apollo's voice says behind me.

I squeak and spin, treading water. He's lounging on a flat rock, basking in the sun in light blue swim trunks with a pattern of pink hibiscus. Droplets glitter against golden-brown skin, slide down mounded, tattooed pectorals in an alluring haphazard roadmap, then bump over gentle dips of abdominal muscles. *Jesus.* I dunk under the surface. It was an accident because my limbs forgot to function. I come up choking.

Apollo raises an eyebrow. "Do I need to come save you?"

"Please don't," I say, making honking seal sounds to dislodge the lake in my lungs. If he touched me, pulled me to him with those defined arms until I was against the tattoo on his chest, I'd drown us both.

"You sure?" His lips twitch, and he rolls the tenth ring between his thumb and forefinger.

"Hey. I was looking for that."

"I noticed. You missed it on the first pass. Didn't go far enough right in your pattern."

My mouth drops open in a huff. "Are you spying on my training?"

"Absolutely." His grin is too charming. I kick water at him. He turns his head as the splash hits, and when he glances back, there's warning fire in his eyes that makes my stomach do three flips from the cliff. "Was that a challenge?"

"No," I answer as he straightens, hands on the edge of the

rock, bent forward and ready to dive. Those shoulders are round pauldrons that probably feel like steel under skin. He's not huge, but he is firm and fitness-built. A body made for underwear modeling. I ball my fists to keep from making a "turn around" signal so I can see his back muscles and sink again in the water up to my lips. His grip tightens on the stone, but I shake my head. "Throw the ring. I won't look."

"Nope." He slides it on his pinky. It rests above his knuckle. "Toss the others. I want a go."

"But I should have gotten the tenth."

He flicks his eyebrows, tilting his head while he smiles in that way that requests me to play with him—his nonverbal request to chase him through the jungle or a challenge to jump from the cliffs. It's how he tells me I better try harder, because otherwise he's going to win. "Yep," he says. "But instead, I did."

This man's charm needs its own city to run. For a moment, I was worried he'd lost it. That muscles and diplomatic speech had replaced it along with a serious, curious stare that now overpowers his boyish grin. That's the give and take of adulthood; you make sacrifices for things deemed better. Homes replace toys, focus shifts to a specific interest instead of playing in many, and hours with friends fall away to hone personal career development. And sometimes the path warns us that some wants aren't worth the fall and inevitable end of precious things, which end anyway, because there's only so much a friendship can take. As everything beyond the vortex of Apollo is fuzzy white noise, I curse my stupid fluttering organs and the persistent thought that we could be friends again if he plays like this. Would it be so bad?

"Where do you go, Xia?" His lips twist, boyishness gone, curious adult gaze in full scrutiny. "When you look at me like that?"

Biting my lip, I pull the rings from my fingers. "Nowhere." I toss them behind me and drift forward the slightest bit, extending my hand for the tenth. "Gimme or throw it."

He rubs his thumb against the metal. "Nope. I could throw it and then tell you how to find it. That's a task in the race now."

It is. Has he already partnered with someone else because I was such a disaster last night? Is his comment a reminder that I'm partnerless? "Are you mad at me because of yesterday?"

He tilts his head. "Why would I be?"

"Because, um." I crinkle my nose. "You were...aggravated before you left."

He copies my wince. "I'm not mad." He seems sincere enough about it.

Dunking back under the water puts my hair in order. When I resurface, Apollo hasn't moved. The same penetrating stare bores through me, seeking my thoughts. It asks what I'm going to do.

"What do you want for it?"

He pulls his goggles over his eyes, purses his lips in thought, and slides into the lagoon with flawless ease. When he pops back up, he's close and drifting closer. He studies my face, and I predict his movements like the next series of mancala moves. He'll move in, I'll move away, he'll laugh and pout with disappointment. I'll splash him, he'll dunk me, and lord help me if I touch his chest.

We do the first and second move, but he doesn't laugh. "Do I scare you?"

"No." It's my feelings that scare me.

He changes course, turning to float on his back, face to the sky. "Good. Then how can I make you laugh with me like we used to? It's gotta still be in there."

Erase a confession, the most awkward night of my life, and years of ignoring each other. "You've been gone. It's..."

"Mmhmm. Different. I know. Remember Ziggy?"

He wants to change the subject to the son of Orchid River

Lodge's owner? I'm in. "Of course. You two were close until he moved away with his ma."

His eyes are closed, and he smiles. "We're still close. He's always had this method of getting to the bottom of things. A time-out from keeping everything inside that he calls a truth bomb."

"I remember that, though he used it mainly as an excuse to insult people."

Apollo turns in the water to tread in front of me. "You mean, when he would say, *Truth bomb, you're an asshole*? Oh, yes. But sometimes it helps because air needs to be cleared. And sometimes it goes awry because you can't undo some words."

His face says it all. He regrets telling me he wanted more all those years ago. Especially with what happened after that. We should bury those moments. It's what I want, except for the squirm inside and a voice yelling that it wants to be doused in dark, sparkling honey and tasted by pillow-soft lips over every inch forever. I tell that voice to shush.

"Are you with me?" he whispers.

I scan the area for people, but everyone here is unfamiliar and absorbed in each other. "Yeah."

"So..." He licks his bottom lip and drags it under his teeth as he watches me. "Truth bomb. I am painfully jealous of your silent speak with Jose. That was our thing. When you two were working through whatever it was you were mentally conversing about in the lobby, and then at Uncle Artie's, I thought my heart was caving in." He takes a deep breath, making a tiny wave of water lap over my shoulders.

I nod, chewing the inside of my cheek, because I don't have words for that. Good? That seems mean, even if it's true. There's relief that I'm not the only one with inner turmoil. I've always been jealous when he laughed with others without me. People joked about my role as the sassy girlfriend claiming my territory at ten years old. I just didn't understand what that meant back then. And by the time I did, I'd ruined the opportunity and he was gone. "I recall a silent conversation between us when Justin was talking."

He drifts closer, locks his fingers with mine, heating the contact to a boil, and tows me toward the rock.

He pulls himself up, then offers a hand. I take it, then I'm out of the water with a warm stone under my butt. I pull my legs up and hug them, and he gives another weary sigh.

"How's that truth bomb treating you?" he asks.

I give a silent laugh. "Okay." Is this my opening to ask? *Truth bomb. I want you as my partner.*

"Good, but one more. When we kissed—"

Oh no. I hold up a hand, batting his next words back down his throat where they belong. "Please don't."

"It's not that—"

"Please." I give him my most serious, threatening eyes. "Don't."

He wants to say it. His lips firm with it, probably aching to open and tell me that he didn't mean to promise to return for me. Or worse, that he did. I'm still not over the multiple doses of disappointment when it comes to Apollo.

I'm one small scoot from escaping into the water and swimming very quickly away. I cannot talk about this now or I'll break. The memories already bombard me, the dismay so thick I still haven't gotten over it. "Partner with me." My racing heart pounds in my ears. That escaped right out, didn't it? Can't take it back. "If you haven't yet. Have you? You're fast, as am I. I don't like this new rule, *at all*, but I think us partnering is needed. Don't you? Or do you?"

Apollo bites his lips together, then lets them pop out from between his teeth. "Really selling it."

"Sorry. I—"

"Okay."

"Okay like, it's fine, or like you want to partner? For an event that shouldn't have partners."

"And you just keep going." He laughs. "I will partner with you." His delight would be contagious if I wasn't playing through the risk this will entail: gossip, touching, sweating together...often. "We'll be great together."

9

TEETH

artners. Apollo stays beside me in patient silence as I take all that in. Giggling, a couple from the top of the rocks can't decide whether to jump. After minutes of squeals, laughter, and *you go, no you go,* they clasp hands and leap. Another day in paradise.

As soon as they're out of the water and walking the path, Apollo nudges my shoulder. "So that kiss between us..."

I knew he wouldn't be able to keep his mouth shut. He can't let things go.

I shake my head. "No."

"It was..." He scrunches his face. "Not so good."

A puff of a laugh bursts out of me. I didn't expect that, but still. "It was awful, and I don't want to talk about it."

"Worst first kiss you've ever had?"

"You aren't going to stop, are you?" I angle myself to stare at him, which is a mistake, because he's leaning slightly my way, peering at me past his round shoulder. I want to lean too. Lean and nibble that ball of muscle, trace the lines of his tattoo with my tongue. Then his lips. Apparently one worst-kiss-ever wasn't enough to teach me a lesson.

"Not my strong point. It was..." His eyes drop to my lips, and they tingle. "Wet."

I press my face into my hands and groan, then peek at him through spread fingers. "Yet dry. And the teeth."

"What was with the teeth?" He bares his and gnashes them at me a few times. "I think I got more incisor than tongue."

"I have never been so embarrassed." Or disappointed.

"It could have been worse."

"Worse how?"

He twists his lips and squints his eyes—his thinking face. "One of us could have burped. Or thrown up."

"Gross. Yeah, that would have done it."

"It could have been with someone else."

My lip may bleed with how tightly I have it trapped. What does he mean by that? Heat sears my cheeks.

"First kisses are always awkward." Apollo sits straighter, chin pointed toward the falls.

"First kisses are the best." I pointedly stare out at nothing. "But not ours."

"Definitely not ours. I mean, it's kinda funny." He pokes my side, and I flinch to jab him back and tackle him but shove my hands in my lap instead. Not my place. With a stretch of silence between us, his long exhale is part of the conversation. "It's in the past, Xia"

"Unless you keep talking about it, Apollo."

He nudges my shoulder, grinning wide and boyish and wistfully beautiful. It aches in my chest, the past him and this new grown version that's more...everything. "Now..." He stretches his arms up, showing off impressive obliques. He shows me the ring on his pinky. "I'll give it back if you collect more rings than I do."

I shove him off the rock, landing him sideways in the water, then stand and dive for the sparkles at the bottom.

I win by a lot. Far more than a simple head start advantage

would allow. While treading water, I hold up my ringed fingers. "You need to work on your breath control."

"Maybe you can direct me." Apollo drifts closer.

"Don't," I warn him, recognizing that mischief in his eyes.

He flicks water at me instead of shoving a wave at me with his palm. "Throw again. Tell me where to go."

I toss the rings and try to direct. "Left, sorry, my left—so right. I think. It's probably hiding in the rock bed. Or the patch of grass. No?" It's sad how bad I am at guiding him. After two failed attempts, I get impatient. "Can we just gather them right now? See how many we can each get?"

"That's not—" His forehead crinkles. "That won't help us figure out how to work together."

"Yeah, but we have time." Maybe I should just go. I nearly excuse myself from this lagoon of discomfort when he nods.

"Okay."

I win again. And again. He almost ties me the fifth time, and by then my muscles sting with fatigue. He's made me forget how intensive it is to dive for rings.

Fortunately, he doesn't ask me to throw them again. He grins and splashes me and makes the stakes of a race challenge; he'll get me a pearly phone case if I win, or I'll be forced to buy an orange one if he does. I flop over the stone nearest the second waterfall with a victorious smile.

"Don't gloat." Apollo lifts himself out of the water and crosses his arms.

"I'm not. I'm just happy to be on this rock, not swimming faster than you." The amber sunset looms behind the trees. "I should go."

"I'll take you home." Apollo's fingers paint an explosion of chills on my ankle right over the tiny sprig of lavender tattooed there, my only body art, but I can't make myself pull away from his touch. "I brought the truck."

"I'll run." I close my eyes as his thumb strokes the most delicious circle. Then he works down to the arch of my foot and squeezes. His hands are strong and confident with the ability to be so gentle, it makes my skin riot, and I want to sit up and straddle him, or better yet, drag him behind the waterfalls. That would be terrible. I stiffen to keep myself tightly glued to this rock where he will not see my nipples through this bathing suit. He massages a circular path against my tight sole, and I'm going to moan if he doesn't stop.

But he does stop. By slapping my calf. "No falling asleep. Let's go."

Then, he's back in the water and swimming toward the falls.

When I sit up, my shoulders are reaching for my ears again. I stretch my neck and arms, then follow. Those were Apollo's things in the rock cubby, and we gather our items in a silence that's thick enough to insulate all my thoughts and bounce them back at my face every two seconds. We're partners. *Partners.* As in, for the next month we're going to train together. Be standing next to each other. Oh my god, we'll be in the same kayak. They're tandem, so it's not like we'll be on top of one another, but still. Too close.

And everyone will see us together and think more of it than they should. What else was I supposed to do though? Lose? No thanks. Winning the Mossy is still my number one priority, and I just need to ignore what people may say and get used to being near this man. This gorgeous, good-smelling, makes-my-body-do-stupid-things man.

"Hey." Apollo's voice next to my ear makes me jump. He grips my shoulder and runs his thumb over my collarbone, and oh my god, I want his hands everywhere. "Just pulling you from la-la land. Would you like to head to the truck or keep staring at that rock?"

My laugh is faker than his vanilla air freshener, which I will have to endure again in a moment. "Sorry, I'm—" *Freaking out? Unable to stop thinking about your hands? Horny?* None of that will fly. "We're going to win. It's going to be great, right? Yeah. Truck's good."

I zoom the path and Apollo keeps up beside me, until I hear a loud voice and the thud of boots. I halt, but he continues a few steps before realizing I'm frozen like a rabbit trying to hide in plain sight. That's a Cliffs' tour guide, and Apollo works there, and I'm with him—in a bikini. He didn't bother to get dressed either. We're soaked, but because we were training, not doing any of the things couples do when they come here.

Apollo returns to me, and that's worse because the herd is coming, and now he's close enough to do those couple things and—

He settles a hand on the small of my back and guides me to walk. "Hey, Oslo."

The older tour guide stops his spiel about the waterfalls at sunset, and as soon as his eyes hit me, Apollo shoves me forward into the man's arms.

"Geez, Xia," Apollo says. "I know he's handsome, but you can't just go throwing yourself at him like that. I mean, the man is working. Hi, folks. Enjoying the tour?"

They laugh, I sputter, and Oslo gives a rusty snort and sets me on my feet.

Oh, Apollo is so going to get it.

I turn, and he's already running up the path. I leave the laughter behind me and give chase, but Apollo is so fast and clearly working with a hefty dose of stamina. He gets to the truck first and goes for the handle of the driver's side, but I'm close. I reach and he drops his stuff, darting away to the other side before I can jump on him and nip his neck. No wait. That's exactly what I can't do. Punch him? Seems maybe too much for our age.

He dashes toward the other door, but I'm there again, and he makes an amused "ack" and spins out of my grasp, sprinting around the front, turning back to watch me as I consider the best route to get to him and inflict some revenge.

"What are you going to do?" His grin is a challenge I'm all for conquering. "Hmm?"

I dip low so he can't see my path and duckwalk to the front, which he won't expect. Sure enough, I dart out, and he's right there. We crash together, and he ends up pressed against the truck, arms up in surrender, but there's a smile on his face. His chest rises and falls quickly under my palms, and my hips are touching his. I had a purpose, but I can't remember what it was. Now it's the muscles under my hands, the heat against my center, the panting puffs we share.

"You caught me." He wets his bottom lip, and a cloud of warm cotton engulfs me, so soft and insulating that our bodies seem to be the only thing in the haze. "Now what?"

I'm wondering that myself. What would it be like to kiss him again? Would he be all-in like he was before, even though that was part of what went so badly? I consider it. Especially when his warm fingers touch the bared skin above my hip.

He slides them on a path they've never traveled—at least, not this slow and meaningfully. "I want to—"

The crunch of shell gravel has me jerking my head to the side where a golf cart pulls into the lot. I move my hand two inches left, grip and twist Apollo's nipple. When he yells, his arms fall from around my hips and I leap from him, moving a full ten feet away so it's clear nothing was going on between us. Because there wasn't.

"Fucking ow." He rubs his chest and glares at me. "Get in the truck, vicious."

His demanding voice has me in the passenger seat before I remember that there is an onlooker. Camila steps out, staring our direction most likely. Her massive sparkly glasses are too dark to tell. She waves, as do we, and soon enough, it's just

Apollo and me and the hefty tension. I seriously twisted his nipple?

"First rule of partnering together. No nipple twisting." Then he has the audacity to glance at my chest, squinting like he's thinking about payback.

10

THE ROMANCE OF THE YEAR

I'm not sure anyone knows I have a partner yet. People are more enthusiastic about the Mossy, but I haven't exactly talked about it. I've said I was training, waved, and run off if anyone asked me how things are going. Should I make an announcement so it doesn't seem like I'm avoiding? Which I am.

I wave to the chefs and kitchen staff who mill around behind long tables covered in white cloth. Fruit, fish, and couscous salad from bright bowls sit between tiered, overflowing servers pressed close together. Fresh hibiscus and shells fill empty spaces. I take the table under the massive palm in the corner and eat while I check email and scan social media. After I find out my shipment will arrive tomorrow and see that Apollo hasn't added anything to his feed, I change my relationship status and put that Lavender is my new beau, then post that we're going on a date this week with an excited emoji. There. A little tongue-in-cheek notification in case people start to question my alliance with Apollo once the news spreads.

Well-wishes pop up one after another, with questions from those who don't catch my context. There are various forms of "you're dating someone?" Some of those are in all caps. I didn't realize how much I don't date until those comments. Roxanne texts me. *Lavender must be killer in bed to get a relationship status.*

Lavender is in my bed every night, I return. *And it's so good.*

Is there room in there for Apollo? I bet he could add a lot to the mix.

Olfactory imagination smacks into me, wrapped in lavender-scented sheets with a brilliant invasion of cherry. The heat from pillow-soft lips tingles my own enough that I have to brush at the phantom sensation with my fingertips. I glance around as if someone could see my thoughts. Couples lean toward each other in conversation, but a table of staffers are looking at me. Three of them jerk their attention to their plates, but the fourth, Jennifer's little brother, grins wide and waves. I return the gesture and shovel more fuel into my face.

There's no room for Apollo, because it would make partnering with him even more awkward than it already is, I write, peeking back up at the starers. They're huddled close and chatting. I bet there are under-the-table bets starting.

My phone buzzes again. *I'm proud of you. Have fun training with his sexy ass.*

Cozette pops into the dining hall, a sunbeam through clouds, and turns her toothy grin on me, beelining with a skip in her step. "Hey," she says, plopping into the chair across from mine. "How's training going?"

"Great so far. I did a lot of diving yesterday."

She sighs loud and slumps in the seat. "I love the waterfalls. And *behind* the waterfalls."

"Aw, did you join the behind-the-waterfall club?"

"If that means what I think it does, then yes. And if it doesn't...probably." She gives me a wicked little smirk. "Is that part of the Simona Island checklist? Rum punch, snorkeling, and waterfall fun times?"

"Definitely," I say, then finish my couscous. "And Uncle

Artie's, bog slogging, The Huts at midnight to see the fireflies, and a beach bonfire. Oh! And the cliffs at sunrise. Sitting near the edge feels like you're on a cloud with nothing underneath. God, I haven't done that in ages."

When I returned to Simona, it was one of the first things I did. But it was only me up there and two couples wrapped in each other's arms on the other side of the overlook. I hadn't watched it by myself until then, and it changed the meaning. Regular kids sneak out of the house while their parents are sleeping to get frisky, drunk, or pull pranks. Simona kids sit on the edge of their island and breathe the first rays of the sun with their friends. It's a shared moment of pure peach and fuchsia astonishment. Mind-altering, heart-swelling life at its most glorious. Unshared, it's still altering, but overwhelmingly so. I'd never felt so insignificant and exposed than I did sitting alone on the edge of my world and viewing a new day bursting open. I haven't been back since.

"Xia," Cozette says with a shiny glaze of pity in her brown eyes. "Are you okay?"

I swish my hand through the air. "Fine. Just in training mode. Thinking about the stakes of that win."

She raises an eyebrow. It's sculpted and sexy and damn Jose for making me into an eyebrow-judger. "And how is partnering with Apollo going?"

I pause mid-chew. Looks like the news has spread. The onlookers probably aren't taking bets; they're talking about my reunion with Apollo, and what do they think about that? Maybe Jose knows. Cozette hasn't been here long enough to have breached the full extent of the gossip circle of Simona, has she?

I wipe my mouth with the cloth napkin. "So you've heard?"

She props her chin in her hand. "The board of directors knows all the good stuff." She holds up a finger. "That I can't talk about. But anyway, how is it going?"

"We were at the waterfalls yesterday."

"Oh," Cozette says with the tone of "Xia and Apollo sitting in a tree, K-I-S-S"—nope.

"Not like that. He was already there, and I was diving for rings. We just happened to be in the same place at the same time."

"And became partners." Her shoulders lift and sink with her sigh. "I think you two will be amazing together."

I blink at her. "I hope so. I'm not thrilled with the rules."

"Your mom has told me. But she believes you will make the best of it."

I'm still not sure of that. It may have been a bad decision to team up with Apollo. Not because he can't be successful, but because I'm a wreck around him. Speaking of...I stand, probably too abruptly. "I have to go meet with your man for kayak training." And Apollo. He already knew somehow and asked if I needed a ride. Which I didn't because showing up together for a preplanned training session seemed too much.

She stands. "Can I come? I'm ahead of my to-do list with the break coming up and am itchy to learn everything about this Mosstastic tradition."

"Cozette," I say, grabbing my empty plate. "Tell me you're making up Moss Monster swears." It was difficult to stop cursing "holly bells" after the holidays.

"Muck yes, I am."

"I'll marry you, if he doesn't."

"Mossvelous, baby." She loops her arm in mine and sets her head on my shoulder. "Eh, I'll keep working on that one."

I drive the golf cart to the beach where we're meeting Nico. It's a short, rugged stretch that should be part of the course on Mossy day, though the location slightly changes every year to keep us on our toes. Cozette doesn't complain about my speed, and I ask her to be one of my transport guests on the day of the event, which she agrees to by clapping and bouncing the cart.

"Is it okay with Apollo?" she asks as I turn between palm trees and the waves crashing against the beach come into view.

I didn't think about it. At all. Would he be mad at me deciding who's in the cart? I can't exactly go back on asking Cozette now. "It's fine." It is. He won't care. I think.

The rickety little sports shack houses a tiny table, stool, and a variety of gear. Made of a hodgepodge of unleveled cinder block and wood, it's a funhouse building painted coral with a variety of patterned tin for the roof. Weather events have knocked it down four times, but we have pieced it back the same way.

"I'm in it to win it," Cozette yells at Nico as we slide into the space next to the rack of kayaks.

"Oh yeah?" He lifts an armful of paddles. His sun-bleached waves tousle further in the breeze. I don't think he's cut it since Cozette arrived five months ago, or worn a shirt for that matter. I see her in his clothing more often than him. I hop out of the cart and stretch my sore muscles.

"Do you kayak?" I ask Cozette before Nico gets to her and sexy-mauls her within an inch of her life.

She comes up for air. "Not really. I'm riding with Nico." Cozette tilts her head as he whispers something in her ear that makes her bite her lip. "Having a good day?"

"Better and better," he says.

Enough of that ooey gooey phooey. I'm happy for them, but a little jealous at how easily they fell together when they met. It reminds me of how easy it used to be with Apollo, until we hit a certain age and lust got involved. I pull my phone from my satchel to turn it off, but then check for messages first and find myself on social media.

Apollo commented on my date with Lavender: *Jealous.*

Is he now?

That has twenty-six likes and some comments. *You're ruining the romance of the year, @ApolloF,* from Demi no less. That makes me smile, until I read my cousin Camila's response: *I could keep you busy, but you're wrapped up a lot for a vacation.* She finishes with a heart emoji. My blood boils for no good reason whatsoever, but it helps that she has no replies and three paltry likes on that comment. They probably clicked by accident and didn't realize.

I shouldn't have posted. I didn't expect Apollo to respond. I scan the likes and cringe at the amount of Simona Island residents interacting with the post. I meant to draw attention away from Apollo and me, and instead I've added more things to talk about. Take me back to the days of gossip about a major spa in Aruba reaching out to woo me to work for them, or last year's Mossy win. If Apollo and my relationship was like the snapshots of loving vacationers, I'd be thrilled they were talking about us, but it's not. I'm the headline of the pitiful beached whale that needs help because it forgot it couldn't swim on land. Apollo is the beach my sad self flops around on, all stoic and perfect.

"Ready?" Nico asks, then looks past my shoulder.

I follow his gaze and another golf cart is roaring toward us, Apollo at the wheel. He may be better at the golf cart race than I am. Blowing out a long breath, I turn back to Nico.

He shrugs. "You knew he was coming, correct?"

"I didn't. You two know each other?"

"Yes." Nico pivots and ambles to Cozette, dragging her close as they make their way to a red kayak.

Just *Yes*?

"Good afternoon." Apollo slides in so fast, I expect the cart to fishtail. It doesn't, and he rolls out of the panting vehicle at a carefree walk. "Ocean." His voice is as velvet as if appreciating a feast of decadent dessert. "I can't wait to get in you," he whispers deep and with a hint of threat, staring out at the sea.

And there I go, flopping around. My stomach swoops, heat threading through me and pooling in places where it has no business going. Chills travel my arms and I pull off my tank and shorts to hide my trembles and throw them and my phone in the cart. This is ridiculous.

"Are you sore today?" Apollo asks, tugging off his shirt in that sexy one-handed way. His tattoos are still a fascination. Perfect black lines with random teal or purple triangles sprawl geometry over his chest. One is an intricate hexagon with an X marking the center like a labyrinth treasure map under the sprawl of chest hair. If I started at the edge, could I get to the middle? He rolls those pauldron shoulders, unseating my stare. "It's been a while since I swam that long."

I open my mouth, but only breath comes out and I shift on my feet, a nervous shuffle.

"Sand hot?"

Of course, it is—it's sand in the sun. "Yep."

His Adam's apple bobs, and he seems to be struggling with something but shakes whatever it is off. I read the intention on his face before he moves. When he jolts forward, my legs fail me and stay unmoving. I'm going to have to talk to them about their malfunction when it comes to him.

He wraps his arms around my thighs, then I'm hoisted over his shoulder, butt in the air and my hands on his warm, bare back. I yip and drop them, then swing in close enough to kiss the tattoo over his spine and plant them again to keep myself stable.

"You didn't tell me about training times today." His muscles are long and firm. I'm boiling and struggle to get down, but when he grips tighter, hand sliding up to almost cup my ass, I freeze and give up, flopping along for the ride.

"You knew though."

"Yes, I did." His grip tightens, and an odd thought that he may slap my ass runs through my head, making my breath quicken, or maybe that's just his super hard shoulder against my abdomen.

"Hey, um," I rasp, wobbly and small. "Watch my butt."

"Who says I'm not?"

I snort in disbelief, but he laughs, squeezing my uppermost thigh, and I fight squirming to get his hand two inches higher. "Just keeping you safe, partner. You know how it is."

I really, really don't.

11

WAVE BYE

*a*pollo sets me on the sand, and I dart to the shed on shaky legs to grab the blue kayak. "Let's start on our own for a couple rounds and see where it goes." I can't be in the same space as him and do well. He needs to see that I do well. The furrow is back between his eyes, but I turn and without a look, another touch, or a tackling kiss, I haul my kayak through the waves. It promptly crashes into my shin, and I bite my tongue to keep from cursing. "Ouch," I whimper through grit teeth.

The heat of his skin marks mine. I brush at the sensation, as if it will come off, so I can concentrate. When I'm at the edge of the surf zone, feet barely touching the sand, I jump into the front seat, paddling fast.

As I approach Nico and Cozette, there's a knock and my kayak makes a sharp left. I gasp, glancing back to see Apollo holding his paddle out, getting ready for another shove. I move quick to swing my stern away from him.

"Just testing your skills. Seeing what I'm working with." He grins, continuing on, but slaps his paddle against the water, spraying me with ocean.

I glare and put my goggles down. "You done?"

"Never."

Nico snickers, braiding Cozette's hair, then leans forward to kiss her neck. "Ready to be rescued?"

I want my neck kissed. Not by Nico, obviously, but it's been a long time since I've had that kind of affection. Chills climb my spine from the want of it. My eyes dart to see what Apollo's up to, but I force them to the horizon, the trees, Apollo's water shoe and strong calf—nope, back to Nico and Cozette.

"Shall we get started?" Apollo stares in my direction through mirrored goggles, chin propped on his hand. He's not paddling. His kayak appears to be anchored while mine is trying to return to the boathouse. I struggle to keep with the group and fidget with the Velcro on my paddle leash, tightening its already tight-enough grip, but mainly using it as an excellent reason to not look at Apollo.

Cozette stands on bent sea legs, then puts the back of her hand over her forehead. "Save me," she says in a southern damsel accent. She swoons over the edge, leaving Nico laughing in a tipping kayak. A second later, she surfaces. "Goggles. Need goggles. Bitey fish?"

Nico hands them over. "No, elskede. Besides, Xia is going to save you, if Apollo doesn't first."

My eyes flick to Apollo's, and in a flurry of paddles we begin. When I'm close enough, I slide into the pushing current and swim my way through blue-green water, holding onto the kayak's edge with one foot. The sandy sea floor is ten feet below her dangling legs and spattered with starfish, bumpy rocks, and a few patches of short grass. I pop up near Cozette. Apollo isn't on his kayak but next to it, giving up the game. He's smart, because I'm trying to save someone, and if he were to come in now with a two-person watercraft, it could endanger us all. That's been a problem in the past if the victims weren't spaced out well enough. Still, not a decent reason to force teams on us, because I've clearly got this. I loop an arm around Cozette and gently tug her toward the kayak, letting my hooked foot fall so I can maneuver her better.

"Yay," she says, adjusting her goggles. "My heroine."

"Don't 'yay' yet. Getting in the kayak is a bitch." I snag the handle again and jerk it closer.

"It will be easier with a partner," Nico says. "Don't help, Cozi. Make her work for it."

Apollo's beside Nico's kayak, talking with him—unfortunately, too quietly to be heard over the ocean and sea birds.

"Ugh." Cozette relaxes, making it more difficult to line her up for entry while keeping her head above water. "Actually, this is kinda nice."

"To you," I say, struggling with the drag of waves and my disobedient kayak that's intent on running away.

I finally get the thing in place and help Cozette onto the deck right behind the front seat, dunking under to push her out of it. Apollo and Nico cheer as I move to the bow, grip the opposite side, and with two long breaths of preparation, kick myself out of the water and across the deck. A simple twist and my ass lands in the seat. If this were Mossy day, we'd be ready to head back to shore.

Cozette hugs me from behind. "Mossnificent!"

"Indeed. I hate it when I can't get in the kayak."

"Here's your reward." She lifts her mask and plants a sloppy kiss on my cheek.

I laugh as I catch my breath.

Apollo makes it onto the deck of his kayak with four tries, and I try to tame my pride. Once he's settled, he smirks at me as if he can read my mind, then rolls his eyes, confirming my suspicions. With Nico's prompting, Cozette swoons her way back into the gentle waves after resetting her mask and checking the water for fish.

Apollo is fast, and after "saving" her, he receives a kiss as well. Then, while Cozette and I practice again, the guys dive in and talk in murmurs that have me wishing the sea was silent and I was closer.

"So, Cozette..." I grin and flutter my eyelashes at her as I paddle her toward the guys. "Is this where the kayak portion will be?"

"Mm-mm, nope." She slides from the deck and swims toward Nico. "Secret courses are secret."

As Cozette backs away, it reminds me that Mama has been avoiding me this week. Maybe she's afraid I'll press like I always do—but it's only in jest. I never expect her to give me hints. As head of the Mossy board of directors, she gets a lot of questions like mine, but the stakes are higher with me headed toward the Moss Boss title. I'm sure people gossip about possible nepotism, though the notion is ridiculous. Maybe that's why they decided a partnership was better this year. I'll have to ask Mama about that.

I flutter my eyelashes at Cozette again. "Not even a little hint?"

Nico snorts as he pulls himself back onto his kayak. "You're in trouble now, elskede."

"Yeah," Apollo says. "That's always made me give her whatever she wants." He sighs long, but I refuse to look at him.

"That cuteness is a weapon." Cozette reaches for Nico and whisper-yells, "Save me."

He grins and lifts her in with his hands on her ass. "I've got you."

"But..." I blink puppy eyes and pout my lip, drifting closer to them, playing up this tease. "Just maybe, a tiny, itty-bitty—"

"Bye, friends," Apollo says, handing his paddle to Cozette while smiling at me. "Xi and I have some partner practice to tackle."

"Catch up soon then, yeah?" Nico says, digging his paddle

through surf, dragging Apollo's kayak behind them as they escape, abandoning me.

With scrunched eyebrows, I watch our chaperones take a wave to shore.

Nico yells over his shoulder, "Are we doing this again on Wednesday?"

"Working all day Wednesday," I yell over the cacophony of waves, paddles, and the roar of my racing heart.

"Thursday," Nico yells, glancing at Apollo, who pauses his breaststroke and nods.

Then Apollo sets his eyes on me. "You have good balance alone. Little shaky with another in the boat though."

"Am not." Fine. So, it's difficult to steer when someone else leans to look around me or shifts to get comfortable in the bare kayak seat. The weight they add changes the angle and effort of paddling.

He raises an eyebrow and approaches. "Ready?"

I tilt my head. "For what?"

"Coming up," he says, reaching long, veined arms across the deck to grip the handle opposite him. I want to lick the valley between his deltoid and biceps.

He pulls to get in, and I try to counterbalance, but it's too late and I hit the water, capsizing us in an epic entrance fail. Glad I didn't take my goggles off.

When I pop through the ocean's surface, Apollo is righting the kayak. He turns toward me, raising that eyebrow.

"I wasn't ready."

"Mm-hm. Let's try again."

"Can we just *not* maybe? For today?" I can't focus on anything but my mouth on his body and how odd that would be.

He tows the kayak closer. "Did you ever play a team sport while in the States? Kickball, softball, volleyball?"

"A couple of times." I couldn't bat to save my life, which was so embarrassing, and volleyball was too chaotic. How are you supposed to get the ball when other teammates are going for it as well? Makes no sense.

"Okay, so we're a team, right? This is now a team sport."

"But it's not because..." I crinkle my nose, then blow out a long breath. The rules have changed. Just because they're wrong doesn't mean they aren't the rules. I'm not ready for this or Apollo. This was a mistake, but I'm locked in now. "What do you have in mind?"

He moves closer. Too close. "We practice getting in and out of the kayak at the same time to see how we can keep balanced so we don't capsize." He pats the deck, then dunks underwater and pops up on the other side. It's a bit easier to function with space between us. "Ready to try?"

I bite my bottom lip and reach to grip the handle across from me.

Apollo counts down. When he hits "one" we throw ourselves over the deck. With our weight difference, the edge catches me in the gut and flings me forward, face-first back into the sea. When I surface, Apollo's there, arm looping around my waist, the contrast of cool water and warm skin sending more heat into my cheeks.

I try to turn and shoo him away. "I'm fine."

"So that's something to work on."

I glare. "I just wasn't ready."

"Let's talk about being ready then." He hoists me over the edge of the kayak.

I flop in with the grace of a tuna, legs sprawled until my body catches on that Apollo is no longer touching me, and I rotate to get into the seat. That doesn't stop my skin from prickling, butterflies in my stomach more like hummingbirds, when he pulls himself over the nose and straddles it facing me, nearly knocking me back into the water.

He looks over me, searching, and pauses on my leg before

reaching down to gently touch my shin. The pain makes me hiss and flinch.

"This from running into the waves?"

My face heats even more. Can he please stop seeing me fail so much? I have to pull it together and get better at this fast. "It's no big deal."

"You need ice on that." He glares at the raised bruise.

I readjust my goggles. "Ready to try again?"

"Let's talk about it first."

"No, I can do it."

"You mean *we*."

I stumble over some syllables and slip back into the water to try again.

"Shift your balance to follow me." He hesitates, allowing me to pull myself over the deck, but the second he leaps, I'm off-kilter and barely able to stay on the boat, having to cling to the handle.

When we're holding on the edge and bobbing on the waves, he pulls his goggles to the top of his head. "Have you kayaked with anyone else before?"

"Have you?"

"Yes, but I asked you."

My jaw aches with how tightly my teeth are clenched as I get ready again. "It's different when they're already in the kayak. Why are we trying to enter at the same time?"

"And if I'm the one retrieving and you're attempting to stay on the deck? That's going to go great if you keep fighting the shift."

I do not like his sarcastic tone. "What? How am I fighting the shift?" Whatever that means.

"You're trying not to rock the kayak as if someone is already in, but I'm not."

"Well, maybe you should be."

"And what happens if I'm faster in the water?"

My jaw drops before I can help it. "You want to find out?"

He rolls his eyes. "That wasn't a challenge. I'm not playing right now, Xia. I'm thinking of the reasons I may be better in the water and you better on the kayak, except you can't stay on deck when someone else boards. But hey, we'll get it."

I have no idea how to do this. This event was designed for one. It was just fine before this bullshit rule. "There's no rule about using two kayaks. We can work on increasing our times individually, then both help the 'victim' into your kayak, since you have so much experience with it."

His expression goes from frustration to deadpan annoyance. "Let me get this straight. Your suggestion for working together is not working together?"

"That's not what I said."

"Actually, it is." His jaw twitches, and he looks out to sea as if it may hold the answers to our partnership. "How about tomorrow we run and talk about a game plan, then work on this some more?" The gentle way he says this tells me he's worried about how much I suck and that his plan is better.

My shoulders prickle with irritation, tightening my muscles. "Or we can just get it down tonight."

"You are..." He trails off, his lips twisting to the side.

Awful at this. Just terrible because I don't play team sports or have other people in my kayak like he does. My defensive shield cracks, and I slump. My streak is over. We're going to lose because of this stupid—

Apollo grips my shoulder. "Hey. We'll get it. This is our first day working together. Things like this take time."

They don't with me. I'm good or I'm not. And he certainly sounds experienced. How many partners has he had before? My throat tightens, and even if I knew what to say, I don't think I could without sounding like I was talking out of the stretched neck of a balloon. I'm not doing this in front of him. I'm embarrassed and disappointed by my inability to be a good partner, but it's even worse that I can't be a good partner to Apollo. *My Apollo*. Not mine, but just...

I shake my head and focus on making words that won't give away my distress. "I think we can keep the tasks the way they were and do them side by side."

"If we do that, we're going to lose. It's partnered. You're going to have to learn how to work with me."

I push away from the kayak. "Well, ditto." I turn and swim for shore. Fortunately, the waves aren't mean to me this time, and I stay on my feet out of the water.

This isn't going to work.

"Hey, wait." Apollo hops out of the beached kayak and jogs toward me.

"It's fine."

He snatches my hand and drags me toward him, cupping my neck and making my knees Jell-O when they should kick sand on him and continue stomping off. He ducks his head to put his eyes on my level. "Sorry. That wasn't handled well. I know this is hard for you."

"How would you even know that, Apollo? You haven't been here. You have no idea who I am now."

That muscle in his jaw tics. "Then let me learn. We're going to have bumps along this road, but you can't just retreat. That won't help anything."

I breathe in the scent of cherry and ocean and island. I can't be angry with that mix. "Fine."

"Stop saying *fine*."

I sneer. "Fine."

12

JUST INHALE

I'm sorting the fresh lavender into bunches and placing it in the fridge's storage drawer when Jose walks in with a big canvas tote. He sets the bag on the couch, then spreads his arms wide. "Hug. Me."

"Did you have a bad day too, or is this a pity hug after my 'Apollo's a butt for not listening to me' text?"

"Today was rough."

I kick the fridge closed and wrap myself around him. We stand there for a good two minutes in a fuzzy, huggy cloud, transferring positive energy through our tight squeeze.

"So many tourists," he mumbles into my hair. "And they all want to tango immediately. As if I will bestow upon them flawless moves in one thirty-minute session. I am not a genie in a bottle, Xia. They cannot rub me the right way." He pulls back and arches an eyebrow. "I mean, maybe—"

I smack his chest. "Let's have a drink. One. Not that it matters because I'm probably partnerless after today and someone else will be on the path to Moss Boss."

"Don't be dramatic, Xia. You know that's my job." He takes a deep breath. "Though there is something you need to see."

"What?"

"We require drinks for this."

I hoist up his tote, making my way to the kitchen with him on my heels. "What do you have in this thing?" I set down the heavy bag and peek in.

He pulls out a full corked jug of mojitos, a big container of cut limes, and sprigs of mint.

I glance over his shoulder and all around until he does the same.

"What?" He plucks and shreds a mint leaf.

"I was looking for the other people who are going to drink all this alcohol." I signal to the half gallon jug on the counter.

"Well, I wanted to invite your new partner, but I thought you may faint if I did."

"Nope. I'd have pinched you." I pass him, making pecking motions with my fingers as Jose squeaks and bats at me, sending fresh mint scent into the air. Snagging the rollerball vial of Great Day in the Morning from the fridge, I move the charcuterie board on the counter to the round kitchen table. My El Escape catering friends put together the snack for me, since my version of cooking is putting leftovers in a box and bringing it home. I made fun requests, and as usual, my coworkers went above and beyond. They arranged a cat face from remnant fruit bits, with random cheese and vegetable pieces assembled into a mouse. That's as healthy as it gets. The rest are tostones, a few with sculpted smiley faces in them, deep fried frituras, and a sea of M&Ms that I added because... mancala and mojito night needs all M&M things. I'm only having one each of the naughty stuff.

Jose shakes his hips when he spots the food and indulges me by plopping in a kitchen chair and displaying his wrists. I press the rollerball to his pressure points and rub until marjoram and sweet orange hit the air, highlighting the soft notes of mint and lime.

Pulling two mango stick whiskers off the cat, I raise them to my cheeks and wiggle them. "So. How's life?"

"Oh, don't you dare spout a mundane question, directed at me no less, when it's your dumpster fire we need to extinguish." Jose stands up to pull glasses from the doorless cabinet.

I wince. My home is minimalist and clean all the time because people walk in frequently, but I have no idea how to fix the cabinet without replacing all of them for consistency's sake, and I can't afford that yet. So it's there, blatant as a missing front tooth. "I should just move," I grumble.

Jose chuckles, assembling drinks. "Tell me everything about this new *partnership*. You two were looking coquettish for custard." He turns back and whispers with his hand cupped against his mouth, "And each other."

I roll my eyes and bite into a tostone. The fried plantain disk is deliciously savory, but not quite as crisp as it should be since it's no longer warm. Still good, and those who live on leftovers may not complain. "We were not. And even if we were, today sucked and he's probably jumping the partner ship." I snort. "Ha. Partner ship."

Jose raises an eyebrow. "Oh, darling, you're the most precious little thing with blinders on I've ever seen. Let's talk custard first and then you can tell me about the suckage, which I'm sure isn't as bad as you think."

"It's so bad."

"Pssh. Now...custard shop." He pitches his voice to mimic my tone and accent. "You two were all whispers and touches and sexy."

"We were not. Now let's talk about you." I grin wide and bat my eyes at him until I remember Cozette and Apollo's comments. Weapon of cuteness? He'd give me anything? Right.

"I'm ready for a break, Walt is the best, but my work wife is a mess. There. We've talked about me." He hands over a mojito filled to the top of the glass and dances his other hand above it like he's blessing it with magic sparkle dust.

"I'm only allowed to have one of these. Don't let me forget."

He retrieves his and sips long as he makes his way over, shaking his hips. "You and Apollo were *close*. Holding onto each other as if the only thing you needed was to crawl into each other's skin, but like cute, not creepy."

I laugh. "How could you have even seen that?" Thinking back on that moment raises the temperature. "You tossed me into him, and he made sure I didn't fall. And you were next to Uncle Artie two seconds later. That was it."

He gives me a guilty puppy face and takes a long drag from his glass.

"There's something wrong. What's wrong?"

He hangs his head and sighs. "Okay, look." He holds up a finger like he does when he needs me to pay attention during a difficult salsa routine because I could get hurt if I don't focus. "If I show you something, you can't..." He waves his hand through the air, then pulls out his phone. "You can't, like, swim to Panama or anything. Not allowed. Got it?"

Oh my god, what did he do? "Okay?"

"Swear. On your distillation set."

He really means business. "I, uh, swear. What is going on?"

"This isn't a bad thing. It's sweet, actually, but will be a bit of a shock too, and I don't want you upset."

I nod as he swipes at his phone, then turns it toward me and does a full-on, grit-face wince. I look at the screen and die.

There's a picture of Apollo and me from Uncle Artie's. Apollo is bent over me whispering in my ear, hand gripping my hip. My expression is how I imagine I looked when I received my first box of lavender from France—eyes half-lidded, lips parted, face flushed with awe. On top of that, his head is turned to show the slightest grin and his intense focus. Like I'm his world. It's sweet and terrifying. Simona Island has the wrong idea, but damn, if we don't look beautiful together. Oh, that's not good.

Jose waves a hand in front of my face. "What were those whispers about?"

I think back to that brief conversation, though in the moment, it was hard to compute with the scent of Apollo all over me. "He said I'd changed, that I was more confident."

"That's interesting. Not as sexy as I'd like, but interesting. Then you got all sassy with him."

"When did you see that?"

"When I turned around and you were sassafrassing all over him. I'd wondered what I'd missed. Then Kingston posted the picture. What raised your hackles?"

I close my eyes for a split second before looking at the photo again. "Apollo said that people couldn't *not* watch me. So there. It's out of the bag. I am clumsy around him, but to point out that I'm a spectacle is just rude."

Jose puts his hand on my arm and rests his forehead on his thumb and middle finger with the other. "Oh, honey."

"Why are you 'oh honeying' me?"

He taps the screen. "*Xia.*" And now I get stern voice?

I stare at the photo and take in Apollo's expression—the mirth, his eyes on me, the pouty-lipped whisper. He looks... "No."

Jose cackles and slaps his knee. "Yes! You were hot as hell and obviously he likes watching you, so he'd think others do too. One and one, baby." He thrusts his pointer fingers in the air and moves them together, entwining them and making kissy noises.

No. He's wrong. I touch the photo, and it shifts down to show comments from the residents of Simona Island. I catch a couple words like "cute" and "aww," but what most grabs my attention is the video of me falling. Except it wasn't actually of that moment but the one after, when Apollo was leaning and cupping my face with his thumb on my cheekbone like his only purpose in life was to comfort me. The comments below all fall along the lines of more "aww" and "so glad to see them back together."

This is so bad, I'm shifting the line of how bad I thought it was, because we've gone beyond. Far beyond. Like everyone is mooning over us beyond. They have no idea.

And why shouldn't they? Freaking look at us. "Oh, honey," I murmur and down half my mojito.

A notification dings on Jose's phone, and I hand it over. He tilts his head and taps buttons. There's splashing noises and cheering. "It's Indigo and Bodhi."

"They're partners for the Mossy." I stand and look at the screen.

They're diving for rings at the waterfalls, Indigo on the rocks pointing this way and that, screaming directions. "Left, farther down." And Bodhi pops up holding a ring. Indigo screams, and the screen turns around to Kingston's grinning face. "Under two minutes. The Mossy just got real interesting."

"Oh my god," I say while hyperventilating.

I wake with a headache even lavender dabbed on my temples can't curb. Jose failed to remind me of my one-drink rule because he was a mojito ahead of me during a panic mode freakout over what I need to do to win the Mossy. Remnants of an intense M&M night scatter the kitchen. A wooden board with only crumbs remaining. During our win-the-Mossy game plan session, we ate the mouse, cat, and all their friends, then Jose insisted on mancala to lighten the high-strung air.

A half-finished game still sits on the table. When Jose realized there was no hope for a win, he became more interested in giving me the fifty-question examination of my Apollo feelings.

He aimed the hanging pendant light in my face and played bad cop, to which I rolled my eyes and downed the rest of mojito two. Fortunately, Jose was three-mojitos-distracted, and before I could really dive into my increasing confusion, he forgot he was interrogating me, moving along to wax poetic about Walt's hands.

I get coffee brewing and check my social media with a nerve-ball in my belly in case I did something either very smart or very dumb. An unsettled relief takes over when I discover that I didn't join the Simona Island residents' group. It would be odd because I'd be front seat for Apollo and Xia rumors, even if I really want to see that picture and video again, but I'm still tempted to join so I can keep an eye on more competition updates. The embarrassment of what people think has wilted overnight, overshadowed by scarier problems. I've replayed from memory the way he was looking at me in that video, and it was more than checking on a competitor, even more than the friendship we'd once had. It was the same starry-eyed adoration he wore right before his lips touched mine.

How could he look at me like that the second after I failed at simply staying on my feet? Has the universe not given him enough examples of how wrong we are for each other? Anger threads through me, fresh and hot, amplified by the fact that he didn't return and he's only here to visit. There's no future for us, so why is he torturing me with touches that no one else has ever come close to replicating? It's only making me have to smash down more stupid hope I have no business feeling. He is infuriating. I have to be remembering the photo and video incorrectly. My three sips of mojito really skewed my perception.

I have to get over that, ignore what I thought I saw, because he's my Moss Monster partner, and if we can't put aside our personal problems, we're going to lose. *Under two minutes.* And that's in one of the two water events. If they're just as good at kayaks and I'm flailing about like I did yesterday, there's no point in showing up on Mossy Day.

As I pull a flowery mug from the cupboard, there's a knock on the door. No one knocks except—

I fumble my empty mug to the counter with a clunk. Why is he here so early? I squint at the clock, then realize he's not early at all and attempt to sprint to my room so I can not look like I do, but my pinky toe catches the kitchen chair and shoots pain up my leg. I curse and hiss, hopping toward the bedroom when the doorknob turns. Apollo steps in, glancing around my place, which isn't put together like it should be because of M&M night. He tilts his head as he takes me in, eyes trailing my half-hearted side bun, then my face, which I'm sure is nothing but dark circles and morning breath, my shoulder where the strap of my tank top refuses to stay, and my braless tits shouting, "Welcome," with how they tingle. I'm afraid to look down, to move at all, so I stand frozen on one leg, holding my aching toes and blending in chameleon-style with the kitchen.

His lips purse. "That is not running attire." He approaches with the sleek grace of being up for hours, then pauses and glances toward the hallway. "Are you dating someone?"

The coffeepot beeps and I limp away to shakily pour a cup and take a long swig of caffeine, scrunching my face at the bitterness. I forgot cream and sugar, but gulp anyway, holding a finger up while my cloudy-cotton thoughts shift and sharpen through the ache throbbing against my skull. "No."

He pulls his eyes from the hallway with a look of relief. "How's the leg? Is your shin worse?"

I wave him off before he can get closer and probably be all sweet and touchy. "No. I just stubbed my toe. It's fine. I'm fine."

He saunters forward, making my breath stall in my lungs, and takes a mug from the toothless cabinet to pour coffee for himself, then turns to the fridge, opens it, and stares long at the bottles of essential oil and bins full of lavender. Pulling the glass bottle of cream, he checks the expiration date, shrugs at my glare, and tips a little in his cup, then returns to me, pausing over my mug with raised eyebrows. I nod, and he drops in a nice amount. "You look like someone rocked your world, then you stole their drawers."

That makes me give a raspy morning laugh. "They did."

The frown he gives me isn't friendly. "Um—"

"Rum," I murmur against the edge of my mug. "I should know better than to tangle with that troublemaker."

His shoulders lower, and he grips the silk, tugging it down an inch. "And these?"

My skin bursts into tingles. I grab the sugar jar, spin the top, and dump an even spoonful into my cup before nudging it toward Apollo, failing to ignore that he's still pinching fabric hard enough to drag it down and off and this can't happen. Nope. No. I'm angry. And I suck at being a partner. He's only visiting.

I shrug a shoulder and tug my tank strap up where it doesn't want to stay, grip my waistband, and step back from him. "I'm going to get dressed."

I retreat, shutting my door and sitting on my bed to try to collect my thoughts. He's checking on my dating status and touched my boxers. Why would that matter to him if he's leaving? He wouldn't be thinking about a hook-up, would he? That's what Simona Island seems to assume. That may be a worse idea than partnering, even if the thought of having him in my bed makes me squeeze my thighs together to disrupt the ache.

I have it all wrong. I'm misinterpreting his signals. I need to get dressed, go run, and train, unless he's here to dump me. I don't think he'd do that though. He's stubborn. I can be stubborn too, and maybe we can figure out a way to do the tasks close together but separately. That may be the ticket. It's too late to prevent gossip from spreading, but if we figure this training thing out, get better quick, and win the Mossy, no one can say anything bad. It will all be worth it.

When I come out of the room, Apollo's leaning against the counter holding a box. "You're sending a package to Athena? What is it?" He lifts it to his ear and gives it a little shake, then turns his head and sniffs it, making me have to cover my lips with my fingers.

"Something for nausea. I'm mailing it today. Need to send her anything?"

"Not at the moment. You've been talking to my sister?"

"I wanted to congratulate her."

The angle of his eyebrows pushes a rush of endorphins through my bloodstream that my best oil concoction would have trouble keeping up with. Is it possible to bottle a sweet expression like that? It's marshmallow whipped cream, the purest chamomile, and a rainy day snuggle-fest, but on a face.

He clears his throat. "Do you need to postpone running? I can grab something for breakfast." He jerks a thumb at the fridge. "Unless you eat essential oils and flowers?"

I shake my head and wobble on weak knees to my coffee cup and drain half the glass now that it's cooling, inhaling the soothing and rousing scent. A last sip and I'm ready enough. "We have a problem. Well, problems. Multiple."

"Yeah. About yesterday. We're going to get it down."

"We have to. One of the teams did a ring retrieval in under two minutes."

He hisses through his teeth. "And we're at what? Six?"

"Much less if we go individually." *Hint, hint.*

"But we're not on our own, Xia. So they're good at diving." He shrugs. "Fast on foot?"

"Indigo's not."

"Then we've got them there, and it's a lot of running. We're fast. You said multiple problems. What else?"

I chew on my lip and stare into my mug at the light brown

yumminess. "People are talking. About us. There's a photo from Artie's and a video on the Simona Island residents' page. Have you seen it?"

His grin drifts away. "No. What's the video of?"

Where's a hole to fall in when I need one? "It's when we were racing and I went down."

"What? Who would do that?" There's that protectiveness I shouldn't like so much.

"It's, um—not right when I fell, but it looks..." I swish my hand through the air. "Like something's going on between us, which it's not, but people are talking about it, and this is the Mossy, so, um, rumors are amplified."

"Interesting." He taps a finger against his mug. "Who posted it?"

"Kingston."

He sighs and shakes his head. "That makes sense."

I blink at him. "How?"

He drains the coffee in his mug. "Kingston, like others on the island, is a hopeless romantic." Heading over to my sink, Apollo holds the scrub brush up to sniff the soap and nods like it was expected that I added ginger and cardamom to it. "Does it bother you?"

"That people think we're a thing when we're not? Yes. I don't like it when they assume and build these elaborate, completely false accusations."

Apollo turns back around and takes my dish towel, drying his hands. His lips are set in a tight line. He knocks a knuckle next to the cabinet with no door. "Is this a style choice or do you need this repaired?"

My cheeks burn hot. "It's hard to match. It doesn't bother you?"

"It does. I think I need to fix it."

I glare at him. "The rumors."

His lips quirk as he pokes at the bare hinges. "Not in the

least. It's Simona Island gossip. They're looking to 'ship everyone because there's a lot of love here. It's a real fairytale."

"I'm not Cinderella."

"I don't know, Xi." He stands up straight and steps closer to tap my nose. "Can I see the video?"

I shake my head and flinch to touch my warm cheeks. "I'm not part of the group it's posted in."

"Then how'd you see it?"

"Jose."

He glances around the kitchen like all his theories assembled into one fact, calming the electricity in the air. "Are we running today?" He checks a watch on his wrist. "I have an hour and a half, then I have something to do, but we should talk about working together and how to tackle training."

He's been busy to be on vacation, and after Camila's comment, I'm not the only one noticing. Maybe he has brunch scheduled with his mom and sister. "O-kay." I put too much question in my voice, and his eyes lift to mine, and yeah, there's guilt there in that micro-wince. He waits as if wanting me to ask, but partners or not, it's none of my business. I stretch my still-sore toes and head toward my running shoes.

13

PEOPLE ARE LOOKING

"*L*ike that," Apollo says, breathless. "Right there."

I tighten my grip. "Like how? There?"

"Close. So close. Keep going. Faster, Xi. Eyes on me."

Electricity zings through me like it does every time he looks at me as if I could do anything and do it really well.

"Ready?" he asks. "Move. We're coming. You good, Cozette?"

Cozette stays relaxed except for a nod. "Moss definitely."

I drop my legs over the sides of the kayak and tuck the bar of the double paddle under my arms as Apollo makes quick work of the last few feet of water and hoists Cozette onto the deck. I tense my thighs and steady her as Apollo moves to the front seat, grips it, and pulls himself in while I lean to counterbalance his weight like we've practiced over and over. One shot. We win. *Finally*.

"You rock!" Cozette yells, pumping her fist in the air.

"Thirty-six seconds from dive to entrance." Nico claps from the other kayak. "It will probably take you an additional forty to get to shore, but if you stick to this and train more with running into the water, you'll be under three minutes, which is exceptional."

Exceptional. I'm glad Apollo convinced me that we couldn't do the event separately and needed more practice. Nothing can stop my grin. Not rain or no-show clients or a hefty whiff of body odor. Not even stupid Kingston with his stupid phone as he watches us from the shore with Vic and Camila. He's not getting another compromising video of me for the Simona group, that's for sure. We nailed this practice so hard.

Apollo grins wide and holds a fist out for me to bump. "Good work."

My insides salsa.

Cozette sits up and stretches. "Well, I have a client teleconference and work whatnot. You two are doing amazing. How are the other events coming along?"

I fail to hide my grimace. They aren't. We're good at running beside one another, but I suck at directing for the Ring Retrieval and suck at being directed, and we haven't even discussed the Beach Tray Dash or Lost Tourist events, because not being able to stay in the kayak seemed to be the biggest, most dangerous issue. I can't imagine we'll have trouble carting "tourists" with Apollo at the wheel and my superior tour guide spiel, and we're getting the Wave Rescue down. Two out of five isn't bad, right? That won't win the Mossy though.

Apollo clears his throat. "We're improving and have time to perfect all the events. We've got this."

We do? His grin says he thinks so, and I breathe a little easier.

We make our way to shore, keeping Cozette with us so we can practice paddling with a third person in the kayak. When we get there, Camila saunters up to hug Apollo, who keeps the contact brief and steps back.

"Looks like you two are working well together," Vic says, distracting me from whatever Camila is whispering to Apollo.

"Yes, I think. Some. We're, uh—"

Camila's giggling a lot. Kingston strolls up, nudges her into a conversation, and now I don't have to rip all my—or more likely Camila's—hair out. Not that their chat should bother me. My chest squeezes tight.

Then I remember I'm supposed to be talking to Vic. She's biting her lips together like Apollo does when he's trying to not laugh or say something he really wants to. What in the world were we discussing? My face burns.

Vic rubs my shoulder. "You're doing great. I'm proud. It was nice to finally see the action." When my eyebrows furrow, Vic continues. "I keep trying to track you two down when Apollo tells me you're practicing, but I just miss you each time. So sneaky." She grins like that's a thing she approves of, and I tilt my head.

Apollo steps beside me. "Ma. Enjoying spying?"

"Oh yes." They stare at each other in some silent conversation before she pats his chest, pivots, and heads toward the parked carts. "Off to work then. You two have fun."

"What did Ma have to say?" Apollo eyes me intently.

I cross my arms and turn to him, wanting to ask what Camila said, but instead I tell him, "She was glad to get to watch and that we're doing great."

He purses his lips and nods, then grabs the kayak and drags it toward the shack. Why do I feel like there was more to that conversation?

"Are you dating Apollo?" Camila's voice rings like a church bell from inside the belfry.

I spin so fast the centrifugal force sends a tomato over the edge of my plate. I snatch it from the air and put it back, my eyes flitting from face to face. Unfortunately, we were over-heard. There are plenty of side glances and whispers from coworkers and guests alike.

"No. Tambien cállate." As if she could shut up.

Her dusty rose lips curve, and today she's pulled her sleek, chamomile-colored hair into a high ponytail, so tight it changes the shape of her arched eyebrows. "No?"

"No. Seriously, keep your voice down. People are looking."

"I enjoy when they look." She studies her rhinestone mani-cure. It's gorgeous like a bridal gown—a once in a lifetime, sparkle-encrusted fashion statement—except she's always styled to this level. "You two spend a lot of time together. Simona is talking."

"You were at our practice last week and saw that we're part-ners. Obviously, we're spending time together." Apollo and I run neighborhoods while waving at residents, jungle paths while discussing island businesses, and the beach while confessing how hard it was to find peace with the lack of ocean sounds in the vastness of the United States. But besides our training schedule, Simona has nothing juicy to talk about. There've been no more house walk-ins, no talk of mistake-kisses or bets, but I fulfilled my obligation and paid for a late-night Island King custard. While we were there, Apollo gave me a pearly teal phone case; he smiles every time he sees it. We are on even ground.

I sigh long and obvious, turning back to the lunch buffet to gather black rice and curry. "People always talk on Simona."

"Well, Nena, you should listen."

"I'm not a baby girl any longer, cousin. And what should I be listening for? There's no gossip-worthy situation between us. We're boring. Move along."

She puts her hands up. "Okay, I won't bother you about him. Just..." She trails off, peering over my shoulder. "Never mind. Adios." She pivots and walks off, leaving a trail of expensive but mediocre perfume in her wake. It's painfully floral but with coffee, I assume to mellow the five to six varieties of power-scented flowers. There's also vanilla and a touch of amber, which would be lovely without the garden attached. I should make her something to fit her chemistry.

"Enjoy the day, Camila."

"You too, Nena." She blows a kiss at my scowl and sashays her tight shorts toward a table with a man sitting by himself.

I head back to the chaos of the spa. And it is chaos. There are massages to give, questions to answer about my products, and a team meeting about how we're going to move furniture around for the painters in a few days when the clients' leave. Yet I'm preoccupied, wondering why Camila thinks I should listen to gossip. I have a good idea about the subject of rumors surrounding Apollo and me. We need to ignore them and keep training. I'll continue pulling myself together like I'm not a disaster zone around him, as if everything's fine. Over the past few weeks, we've given them nothing negative to talk about, and yet Camila's words have crawled under my skin. I'm half-paying attention the entire day because my mind is on Apollo. What is he doing when he's not with me? Watching television? Catching up with friends? Laying on the beach all hot and sweaty? Should I know more? I shake that thought right off. That's a slippery slope I will not enter.

Yet my curiosity refuses to be tamed. I pull out my phone to text him. *What are you up to today? Are you helping out at the Cliffs?*

We text now. Daily. It's little things about training—except he doesn't respond to my message now. Not at all. It lingers there on my phone, which I keep checking in an unprofessional manner. My muscles lock up in my shoulders, and I have to stretch my jaw because it's so tight. Is he mad at me? Maybe he's regretting partnering because the Mossy is closing in and we've trained for one event; and that was intense and annoying, and I'm still not sure I'm consistently good enough. At least we shined in front of an audience. When the last client leaves, I sweep, getting lost in the back-and-forth brush of bristles.

When I'm done there and my phone continues its silence, I head in to see what Jose is doing and get tackled in a hug as soon as I step into the club.

"Dance night on Friday," he sings, shimmying his shoulders, then bumps my hip until I dance to no music with him. It does make me feel better, but he notices my frown. "What's wrong?" He pokes at me, repeating "What's wrong, huh?" until I bat at his hand.

"I sent a text wondering what Apollo was up to today and he didn't respond, so I'm pretty sure he's fled from the island on a plane he's probably flying, and I should be happy, but I'm not and—" My phone buzzes.

Sorry. I was talking with someone. Headed to dinner. Want to go?

Yeah, I do. But where? In public? Like on a date? No. I send, *Sure, partner,* and immediately cringe. That's accurate though, right?

Jose slaps a palm against his forehead. "Put the phone down, darling. You're no longer trusted to use it properly—you know, for things like sexting and midday trysts. The important communications."

I drop my chin to my chest, and Jose squeezes my shoulder. "Come dance Friday with us. It will be fun and crowded. Very chill because you need to chill."

I really do. That will be the final day before the guests leave. Locals itch for the last party that sends off tourists on Saturday, starting our Mossy season for real and bringing in friends and family over the next week. The spa runs at half the workload for most days, but we're closing for painting and deep cleaning this year, leaving room for me to catch up on oil-making, maybe enjoying beach time, and getting into a solid training schedule.

I twirl to the door. "See you then."

14

WET RAT DREAMS

The rest of the week speeds by on oil sales, aromatherapy sessions, and so many massages, it replaces the exercise I would have gotten had I been able to escape for an hour from sunup to sundown. Meals are eaten while refilling supplies, and social media checks are so impossible, I'm positive Lavender is ready for a breakup since I missed our date. Bedtime comes whenever I trudge home, kick off my pants, and fall facefirst into bed.

It's odd not seeing Apollo. I grin wide when I get a message from him mid-afternoon. *Kayak at four? Two runs. Half hour tops.*

The last time we met up, we had dinner and talked about how we would tackle the rest of training once the tourists left. I was quiet, keeping an eye on everyone blatantly keeping an eye on us. Apollo asked for to-go boxes and got me out of the only pizza joint on Simona so quickly I could have kissed him. But I didn't.

Since we didn't get far into the conversation, we didn't plan for the other events. *No waterfalls?* I text back. We've been focusing on the kayak so much I'm nervous. It would be tragic to lose because of the Beach Tray Dash.

Not enough time. Thought we could do something quick and fun. When the tourists leave, we'll buckle down.

That makes sense. *Let me check with Stella to see what else needs to be done*, I type.

Is that a yes?

I scan the schedule on the computer, exhaling at the blocks of empty appointment slots. We're getting so close. When Stella returns from the back hall, I'm stretching my hands. "Would you mind if I left a bit before four?"

She locks our fingers, then squints at the screen while she rolls my wrist around, rubbing her thumbs over my palm to stretch the overworked muscles. I groan and let the counter keep me upright.

"The schedule says we're all done here." Stella finishes my impromptu massage with a squeeze. "Go. Enjoy the day. Tomorrow we move out the inventory for the painters, and I'm sure you want to box the aromatherapy products."

She is correct.

When I arrive at the shack, Apollo is leaning against his golf cart and thumbing through his phone. He's wearing a tank and yellow trunks. His ankles are crossed, his bare feet buried in soft, white sand. His grin makes my stomach somersault.

If I've missed him this much over a few days, what am I going to do when he leaves? I straighten my spine. I'll keep living my life and he'll keep living his. We'll see each other on holidays, and I won't fall all over myself because I've reacclimated to him now. That's easy enough.

"I think my sister may name her baby after you," he says. "She got your package. The shells and rocks were a nice touch."

Everyone needs a dose of home every once in a while. "I'm glad." I consider telling him about the mixes I've been making with him in mind, but my tongue won't work again. Too soon. It's weird to tell a man that you've been trying to make a mix to complement his natural scent, right? It is. Especially when his smell is ingrained so deep in my brain, I can build an olfactory picture with what would match.

"Hi," he says, eyeing me with warmth that rivals the hot springs. He squeezes my fingers and stays quiet and close. Do I have something on my face from lunch—a grain of rice crammed in the corner of my mouth? His attention is around that area, but I already checked myself in the mirror before coming here. Don't lick to check. Do not. I do. Just a quick sweep. Nope. No rice or crumbs of any kind. Then why—

Apollo keeps my fingers in his and leans until his lips are mere inches from mine. While I don't run or liquify into the sand—yay me—I suck in a breath so deeply, the world blanks out for a second and I'm left with my rapid pulse.

He moves closer, to the side, cheek grazing mine. "You have a really strong grip," he whispers, giving my ear drum a heat stroke.

"Sorry!" I let go of his hand with cramping fingers. "Massage. Today. Lots of, um, them and kayak." Now I can run. I move forward, trip, and bounce myself into a jog, then spin and walk backward to show how wonderfully agile I am.

Apollo follows. Or prowls. Hot and sexy and swoony. I turn to watch for those sneaky divots, and when he catches up to my stride, his arm brushes against mine as we stroll to the kayaks. "Guests clearing out yet?"

"No more appointments, but I'll have to go back if we get too many walk-ins. Are you helping your mom out?"

"Everyone has been a blur for five days. Whoever made the break rule was a genius."

"I'll let Mama know, if I ever see her again."

Giving me a confused glance, he helps me pull the red kayak from the rack. "Everything okay?"

"She's been busy. Too much to say hello or check in with her daughter. I get glimpses of her in my peripheral vision sometimes, but that's it."

"Mm-hmm." His jaw flexes as he grabs two buoys.

"What?"

"Are you headed to the El Escape club tonight?"

"You know about that?" I snatch one of the white oval floats from him by its frayed yellow rope, but he doesn't let go and instead drags me closer—close enough to kiss again, but on my lips.

He releases the buoy, and I flail backward. "I was invited."

Once I regain my balance, I kick sand over his triathlon sneaker until it's buried. "Were you?" It would be like Jose to sneakily invite him without telling me.

"Just said I was." He grins wide while digging a starting line, then pulls his sand-filled shoe off to dump it out and brush off his foot.

I fumble with the kayak. "And..." I gulp. "Are you going?"

He straightens, eyes wide. "Are you asking me to go out with you, Xi?"

My jaw drops. Isn't he in a mood. "Uh, I—"

He pushes me toward the line he made in the sand, fingers sparking electricity against my back. He swings a buoy, launching it out past the waves, then tosses the other one a good distance from the other. "Of course, I'll go with you."

"You're such a brat," I mumble.

"You love it. New game. We start together, park between the buoys, and each go for one. Whoever gets back into the kayak first wins. If that's me, you owe me a dance tonight."

How can I be both giddy and so nervous, nausea tightens my stomach? Can I just have one emotion at a time? "What if I don't go to the club?"

"Then I won't either and we can talk more about training. Maybe watch a movie." When I only blink, he shrugs. "I hate going places and having no one to dance with. It's embarrassing."

I scoff and roll my eyes. "You've never been out in Simona and not had a full card."

"But *you* would never dance with me."

"We did."

"To radio songs, bouncing on your couch. At the beach as we tried to figure out moves the adults were able to do. Not publicly. Not now."

And that thought makes my insides itch. He's seen me do a couple moves with Jose. I've inadvertently stoked his curiosity, and if he wins, I will pay for that in rumors. "Fine. If I win, you..." I purse my lips and watch the two bobbing white buoys as I think. There are many things I'd like Apollo to do with me. Making a bet about any of those is asking for more than I can handle. "Let me try a few new essential oils on you for a men's line I'm working on." There. If I win, I can get what I want without being weird.

He holds out a hand. "Deal."

We shake on it, and he leaps into a sprint, dragging the kayak along.

"How do you think that's going to make you win?" I yell-laugh. "We're both starting in the kayak."

He only cackles and attacks the waves like Poseidon. Why didn't they name him after the god of the sea? Seems obvious for a beach baby deity.

We get through the surf and into the tandem kayak, him from the left, me from the right. The buoys aren't far out, but navigating to an even point is difficult.

"Ready?" Apollo places his paddle across the deck.

I do the same and stand. "On the count of three?"

He faces me in a crouch, staying balanced on the rocking waves. "On the count of three and a hand slap." That would prevent anyone from leaning to off-balance the other or getting a millisecond head start.

"Fine."

We count together, eyes locked. "One. Two. Three." We slap hands and launch into the water. I peek back to make sure Apollo didn't forget to dive shallow, because we're closer to shore than usual, but he's glancing back at me. We exchange a quick smile and turn. The water is choppy and difficult with stronger than usual currents, but I reach my buoy in what I feel is an appropriate time. Until I turn around and Apollo is about to pull himself in.

Looks like I'm dancing with Apollo tonight. I slowly breast-stroke to him and drag myself in while he's performing a victory dance—a shimmy with his shoulders up to his ears and his knees twisting to the sides. I give the kayak a jerk, but he's expecting it and crouches, holding onto the seat. His grin is smug.

"That is not good for your joints." I fling my buoy between my feet while I wrestle my hair into a bun.

He pauses. "That's too bad. We'll be doing this move tonight."

I fight a laugh. "One more time?"

"You're really stacking up the debt. What's your bet?" His eyebrows raise as he snatches and hurls my victim out farther than where his floats.

I narrow my eyes. "Same thing. Scent experimentation on you for a new men's line I'm working on."

He nods. "An aromatherapy consultation."

That drops my glare. I'd do that anytime. "For where?"

"Undecided."

What, is he planning on tricking me into going to New York with him? Wait—what if he is? I can't live there, I live here.

Whoa. I need to slow down. That was an epic leap of over-dramatic proportions. He probably wants the consultation for the truck or his mom's house or maybe to make fun of Demi by calling her apartment stinky, which I doubt it is.

"Did I make you short out?" Apollo's watching me from his seat, chin propped in his palm.

"No, I'm...just..." I thrust my hand out.

He grips it, giving a solid pump. "First one who enters the kayak takes it back to shore as fast as possible as additional punishment to the loser. Plus, we're past our half-hour allocation, and I need to go." His thumb stokes my knuckles, stirring up chills. "Unfortunately."

My brain is all fuzzy from his touch, and I bite my smiling lip like I'm flirting with him, then snap out of it, pulling my hand away with a jerk that makes him raise his eyebrows.

I stand so quickly we tilt, and I tap dance on the deck before tripping on the edge of my seat and crashing into the water. When I come up, Apollo is staring down at me, still on the kayak.

"So, on three?" I ask. "Yep. One..."

He snorts and gets to his feet. "Two."

Together we say "three" and he dives while I launch into a strong stroke. I'm not letting up this time, and the current seems to be in my favor. I snag the buoy's rope and launch back to the kayak as he's approaching. That shock of adrenaline, knowing I'm on the edge of a win, helps me burst out of the water, twist to get my seat, and then I'm paddling to the beach on a wave, leaving Apollo swimming hard to catch up.

"Ha!" I yell, leaping from the kayak and doing my own victory dance.

Apollo glares as he swims in, stumbling out of the surf, but his lips are twisted to the side, like he's putting up a good fight to not show amusement. "Practicing for tonight, cowgirl? Got your invisible lasso?" He shakes his head, sending a spray of water sparkling into the late-day amber light like a slow-motion movie scene with the hottest-man-of-the-year cover model.

I throw my imaginary rope toward him. He jerks his hips,

an expression of shock in his eyes, then dances a step toward me with every pulling motion I make.

"You got me." He blocks the sun, casting me in his wide-shouldered shadow.

My mind visualizes snagging the drawstrings on his swimsuit and dragging him against me when a whir of an electric engine sounds behind me. I turn to see a golf cart driving in. Camila stops feet away, and I step back from Apollo. What is she doing here?

"There you are," she says, sliding from the vehicle.

Was I missing? I open my mouth to ask if something happened at El Escape when she makes her way to Apollo and splays her nails on his bare, wet chest. "Where'd you go last night? You escaped."

Nausea hits me like a sledgehammer to the gut. My brain blinks white-light rage, or maybe that's just the stupid, sunshiny hope of what can never be draining out of my body. *Again*. What is it about this man and me?

Apollo doesn't move. Not toward her, but not away either. "I went home." He clears his throat, and when his eyes lift from hers to mine, I bolt. I don't want to see whatever truth or apology or nonchalance is in his gaze.

I trip over the kayak and yip, but haul it by the handle so it appears like I meant to run directly into it, as if a kick would have moved it all the way to the shack since practice is over. It's so over. I fling it in the rack and smack the buoy on the hook. It falls—of course it does—and I try again with shaking fingers.

"Xia?" Apollo asks.

I throw on a smile that I hope doesn't look as if I'm about to hurl and stare over his shoulder at the ocean instead of into dark honey. This was what Camila was hinting at, and I'm a fool for staying out of the loop, blind to seeing it and deaf to hearing about it. They're fucking. I shouldn't care one iota, but I really and truly do, and I need to get away and deal with this, because it's too much. I'm acting like my weird self, I can't stop it, and nobody needs to witness the catastrophe that is me.

"You okay, Nena?" Camila loops her arm in his, pressing her tits against his biceps and pouts her lip. I have the urge to throw her into the waves and see how the wet rat look works on her, instead of her perfectly put-together beach-model allure.

Apollo takes a step to the side.

"You look a little..." She wiggles her sparkle nails at me. "Yucky."

"I'm fine," I croak. "I forgot about a walk-in this afternoon, and it's been over a half-hour and sales. You know?" Wow. None of that made sense. I bite my tongue and stare at my scurrying feet, which thankfully don't stumble. "Work. Things." Shut up, shut up.

Apollo calls for me again, and when I ignore him, he says he'll see me tonight. Sure, if he's not too busy banging Camila. I throw a hand in the air that hopefully resembles a wave, slide into my golf cart, and rip-roar out of there with a final glance of him peering down at her with crossed arms and Camila up on her tiptoes—

A dip in the sand makes me squeak and focus on the path I'm traveling. Looks like I'm not the only one seeing more of him. I rub at the tight, searing heat in my heaving chest. Guess that's what's keeping him busy. My teeth clamp together. I will not shed a tear over this thing that is none of my business. It's not. He's not mine, and soon he returns to New York. Done. I turn onto the path through ferns and palm trees and stop the cart, dropping my head back to blink at the beige, plastic ceiling that wobbles like I'm under the waves, looking up at the sky. I should have seen this coming, should have paid better attention. Long vacation in a paradise full of people holding hands and making out all over the place? Why wouldn't he be enjoying hooking up, no-strings-attached style?

A cruel little demon says that could have been me, but it's

wrong. As much as I'd like to say I could handle it—a night or ten exploring things about each other we never did—I can't even handle a conversation. And I thought I was doing better around him.

I don't go back to the spa, nor do I go home. I head to the silent rocky southern beach no one goes to unless they're hiding because the terrain is either rock or sludge, and it smells like seaweed on the verge of rotting—salt and old eggs. At the shoreline, I pace quick strides, rock to rock. I've gone from klutz to jealous girlfriend. Well, that's not exactly true. If it were, Camila would have taken a dip in the waves.

She was probably the one to invite him tonight, and I have to dance with him because of a bet. *Wonderful.* Maybe I can call in sick or make an emergency trip to the Aruba spa until tomorrow. I halt and growl. No. I will not stop my life because of my feelings toward Apollo, however confusing they are.

Whatever makes me a fool around him has to go. If Simona Island watches me stumble and flinch and fumble my every word at the club, I may as well hide my head in the sand for the next year. I need a better plan. Warrior woman 2.0.

I text Roxanne. *Attention: Opinions on club clothes needed.*

15

TEAL TRIMMINGS

*R*oxanne is brilliant, and I feel a thousand times better after talking with her. Until I walk into the club of lights, fake fog, and a sea of gyrating bodies.

I'm Florida-club Xia tonight. My hair is in wild spirals, my eyes smoked with plum and charcoal, making my muddy green clearer. Roxanne convinced me that Simona Island was ready for the bright teal clubbing dress that I've only worn on uninhibited evenings with her. Now I'm not so sure. My usual dance night attire is loose, knit harem pants with a tight, cropped top or even a floral, swirly skirt that has a nice swish. This stretchy scrap isn't in the same orbit. It coats my curves like paint, and its frilly hem ends at my upper thigh. The back is so open, the only way it stays on me while dancing is because a silver chain holds the fabric and kisses my shoulder blades so I can shimmy without ending up naked.

Heads turn as I saunter in, and I fight to keep going forward instead of backing my heels out of this room. I didn't want to be the topic of gossip...except I already am. I tighten my posture, put on a sexy smirk, and sway my hips to the booming bass. I look good. They'll have nothing to say tomorrow but "whoa."

The impressed whoa, not the I-can't-believe-she-did-that whoa I've been stuck in since Apollo's arrival.

People mingle and twirl, both resort employees gearing up for some calm time and honeymoon lovers clasped together in their own sexy world. Walt's tortoiseshell glasses and highlighter-orange shirt glow beneath the flickering club lights. He flips bottles, his brow glistening with the effort of satiating this final-crowd-before-break. Six others are corralled with him behind the circular bar, including Jennifer, just as focused on slinging drinks. She fills a pitcher of frozen pina colada from the half-full machine and circles the crowd, pouring the concoction for whoever raises their glass to her.

"This is chaos," I yell to Walt.

Walt squeals when he sees me and crawls across the bar to kiss my forehead, giving me a whiff of sweat and rum. "You are drinkable. Why have I never seen that dress?"

I wince and shrug a bare shoulder. "Because I've never worn it here. You okay? Need help?"

"It's starting to slow down. All the Cliffs folks are here too. They shuttled over." He thumbs behind him and yells, "Kingston and Margie didn't know they'd be working tonight."

"Yes, we did," Margie laughs. "We bring a crowd, we work it." Two full tip jars sit on the bar, which is not the norm for our all-inclusive resort.

Kingston gives me a heart-eyes grin and looks around the room. He's going to be either disappointed at the Apollo-Camila development since he's such a *hopeless romantic* or thrilled for new gossip fodder. If he's posted a video of her and Apollo—my stomach drops again on this rough rollercoaster I'd love to get off.

"What are you drinking?" Walt yells, coming close to stare in my eyes with a bit of worry in his.

"Something highly alcoholic."

"You got it, beautiful." Walt peeks at me while he mixes. "What's wrong? Want me to get Jose?"

I need to pull myself together. While he probably wasn't heard over the pounding beat by anyone else, I can't look concerned about whatever is making Walt frown at me. Boobs out, hip cocked, confidence face on. "No. I'm fine. Just need to warm up. It's been a while since I've had a club night." I toss my hair and shimmy my shoulders. "Think I'm ready?"

He passes me a drink that's one hue off from my dress. "You mean, is the club ready for you? Doubt it. Go, enjoy, and dance with my man."

"On it." I navigate toward the rows of half-moon booths that face the small stage, trying to keep the contents inside the martini glass while being bumped by guests bounding toward the dance floor.

Giniki sings "Lambada" over the speaker, and I peer up at the window outlined in rainbow rope lights on the second-floor overlook. Our DJ has on neon glow bracelets, necklaces, and beads in her short braids. Her lipstick glows blue in the black-light-lit booth.

"Xia!" Cozette shouts from a table with Nico. "Get over here." She signals wildly.

Nico snags her drink to prevent her from knocking it over and laughs.

I hug them both over the table, settle on the cushy blue velvet next to Cozette, and try to avoid talking about my partner by asking her about upcoming events. She gets as excited about that as I do aromachology, so she's not difficult to distract.

"You're not checking your phone," Apollo says in my ear. I squeak and jerk, turning to come face to face with him as he leans close, elbows on the back of the booth. He waves at the others.

I pinch his arm and he hisses, then mouths, *Ow*.

"Don't sneak up on me."

He smirks. "I texted you."

I'm well aware but refused to read them because he'd see that I'd looked. I wasn't ready to respond. Trailing my hands over my dress, I shrug. "No pockets." I take my drink and sip like I do not care.

"I can see that." He plucks my dress's chain, and it's like he's toying with my detonation button. All hot, tight anticipation. I should not want him to push it, but I do. I really, really do.

"Beer?" Nico asks, climbing from the booth.

"Yes, please," Apollo says.

"I'll join you." I go to follow, but Apollo slips onto the edge of the seat.

"Nope." He props his arm on the ledge behind me.

I eye the other side to freedom, but Cozette is perched on the edge, smiling like everything is just dandy. I sip my pretty teal drink.

"You abandoned me today," he says. "What's that about?"

I blink at him. "You seemed in capable hands." I put way more spit into that than I'd intended. I turn to focus on Cozette or the crowd or the air to my left.

The heat of his body soaks into my side, and the cherry is joined by a faint soap scent that includes fig and cedar. It's not perfect, but it's good enough to make my mouth water. "I'm in no one's hands, Xiamara." My full name, in the timbre of his voice, may as well be his finger trailing up my bare spine.

"None of my business." I wave him off, but he drops his arm from behind me and catches my fingers, locking them with his. I stare at our entanglement resting on the thigh of his coral-colored chinos.

"It is. You ran out of there after manhandling a kayak. It cried for an hour. You need to apologize."

Cozette snorts, pressing her fingers to her lips as she watches the dancers.

My jaw tightens. If I would have just seen that they had

something going on, I wouldn't have acted like such an ass in front of him. "I was—"

"You don't have to explain. I know you were all offended because we're dating and Camila showed up, doing her Camila thing. It looked bad."

My mouth pops open. Apollo lets loose a glorious laugh as his grip tightens and he reels me closer. "Shh." He cups my cheek with his other hand to keep my attention on him, and my body shivers to its quietest state. "You're so cute when you think I don't know you. You've never liked being left out, and Camila is a frenemy for so many on the island. You especially." After a sweep of his knuckles against my jaw, he drops his hand. "I can explain."

My brain catches up to his words when he squeezes my fingers, and I blurt out, "Not necessary."

He raises an eyebrow. "We bumped into each other at the airport."

"Seriously. It's fine." If there is a punchline about cockpits in this story, I'm going to scream.

"She was picking up a parcel for Angel and I was talking with Alvaro, and when I was done doing that, I went home and was asleep three minutes later. By myself."

He was talking to the owner of the airport? I open my mouth to ask why when a clink on the table brings my attention to Nico as he sets down a frothy mug and another drink that matches my dress, this one in a rocks glass with ice. "From Walt." Then he's gone, stealing Cozette for the salsa beat playing through the overhead speakers.

"So..." Apollo says, dragging both drinks toward us. "When she showed up after I so elegantly escaped last night, I was going to use you as a shield, but you dodged. Next time, you stay and protect me from your cousin. Partners do that, you know."

I smile over my glass. "Think throwing her in the ocean would be considered protection?"

"Maybe too far. A smidge." He strokes his thumb across the back of my hand, and I realize we've moved closer, arm to arm. "You still mad?"

"I wasn't mad at you." Confused, territorial, hurt in the pettiest way, but I was angrier at my reaction than anything else. Apollo doesn't seem to mind though. I take another sip. "It's none of my business anyway."

"No?" He presses his leg against mine and leaves it there.

What does he want me to say? That I wish it were my business, more businesslike than we've ever been? The long-haul, lifelong-career kind of business? Not possible. My resume doesn't match. I'm not willing to relocate—probably—and I'm not even sure what this company is looking for in a candidate. I glance out at the crowd and am pleased to find that we are apparently invisible on this excitement-fueled evening.

"Hey." He pulls at my hand again, tone serious. "Talk to me."

How can I? I love seeing him. And while I'm not coming close to beating any of my personal records or training like I would were I doing this alone, running and practice are new joys with him beside me. Losing that—losing him—seems impossibly painful.

Apollo's grip loosens on my fingers just before readjusting and pulling my hand to his chest, which expands under my touch as if maybe I help slow the speed of his axis too. He blows out his breath, releases me, and leans to take a long swig of beer. "You owe me a dance."

"Um."

"You're not getting out of it."

I glare at him. "When have I ever not repaid a bet?"

He purses his lips in thought, then slides out of the booth. "Good point. Let's go."

I'm not ready to be in his arms. Will my legs even work? There are so many people here. And then, the best sight pokes his perfect hair through the crowd.

"Jose," I yell so loud half the room pauses and glances our way.

He squeals—bless him—and rushes forward. "I didn't know if you'd come. Hi, Apollo." He flicks his fingers between him and me. "Are you—"

"I need to warm up." I bounce out of the booth to leap on Jose, not even able to look at Apollo. "Dance with me." I drag him until I'm at the crowd, and Giniki announces a samba.

"Oh," Jose says. "Are you sure because—" He points over my shoulder toward the table, but I do not take the bait of glancing back.

"So sure." I grab his hand and get in the starting position he taught me years ago. "Please."

"Perfecto. You remember this?" He notices the dress for the first time. "Holy shit, Xia." He spins me, and the frill flips high. He drags me close. "Um, is that only for Apollo because—" He looks left, right, then back at me. "Darling, the room has noticed."

"Roxanne convinced me. Is it bad?" I follow his steps and peek at the others. Nico talks with Apollo, and Cozette perches on Nico's knee facing us. She points at me, then fans her face.

"Oh baby, it is bad in the best way Simona has seen in a long time. I wish I had your thighs, and he wishes he had your thighs around his—"

I put my hand over his mouth. "No, he doesn't. We're just partners."

Apollo's eyes lift to mine as if he heard my whispers, and his scowling lips soften, then quirk up.

I sidestep the wrong way, and Jose whips me and my attention back to him. "Uh huh, I see." He spins me three times, walking me backward, then dips me low and waggles his eyebrows. "You need a positive spotlight to step in. I have the best idea, gorgeous."

"I don't need a spot—"

He jerks me up and whisks me into rotational spin toward the bar. People move out of the way, clapping as we pass, and I'm only saved from flying out of orbit like a poorly hit ping-pong ball by my trust in Jose. He pushes me, but never more than I can take, which would get me hurt. When Jose came to Simona, that was a trait that reminded me of Apollo. We slam to a halt, and I gasp for air and laugh as the dizziness drifts away. Jose kisses my cheek and waves his arm dramatic-presenter style to the bar. "Let's dance."

I shake my head. "I'm not bar dancing—" And then I'm grasped and on the bar. "Jose," I whisper-yell through a gritted-tooth smile because people are definitely looking.

He pops up like his natural dance floor is this narrow lit-glass runway and cups his hands around his mouth. "Salsa!"

Shimmying up next to me, he cups my hip and waves like a parade king as Giniki repeats, "Salsa! It looks like we're getting a show tonight from our fabulous dance director Jose Cortez and the lovely Xiamara Nivar."

The surrounding crowd puts their attention on us as Jose takes my hand and twists me around to show me off to the onlookers. Warrior woman 2.0 dances on bars in front of all of Simona Island—and Apollo, apparently. I can do this. Probably. When he pulls me into a starting stance, his brows furrow. "You're wearing panties, right?"

"Oh no," I gasp, giving a fake wince, then cackle at his expression.

With his hand over his heart, he huffs out a breath. "You are behaving so badly tonight." He jerks me against him as the song starts. "I love it." He gives me instructions before each move. "Counterclockwise twice, reverse, come close." I take half a minute to settle into the fact that I am on a bar and center-stage. Apollo has never seen this side of me. He missed this part because it's something I grew into without him. When I peek down to see how close we are to the edge of the bar, I make a tiny stumble and Jose tugs me against him. "Stop thinking, Xia."

Like that's possible. "Si, Jose," I coo, straightening my spine and getting my mind on the game.

Our legs stay against each other as if I'm standing on his feet as we move backward.

"There now. Better." The twitch of his thumb guides me along with his words. "Clockwise." Three steps. "Again." We are the breeze over water. Muscles ease and tug with fluid grace as he dips me, fingers trailing my neck and chest, then I'm whipped up against him and slide down, acting as if his leg is a firehouse pole as he circles his hips. With a jerk, I'm up and we're smiling, hands locked, stepping in time. "Full rotation to the ground. You ready?"

"Uh, bar," I say.

"Si. You can do it." Holding me, my back against his front, he forces my rhythm to keep up. "And three, two, one." He whips me out and I tighten my balance, letting him spin me like a top as I crouch lower and lower until my legs burn. Twisting to settle on my hip, I safely land on the glass surface, and the crowd is a chaotic rally of cheers. Jose pulls me up to take bows, which I cackle during because I'm dizzy and elated. Before I'm able to slide away, he lifts me in his arms in a cradle, making me yip with shock and then full-out screech when he tosses me off the bar.

16

LA BACHATA

I land in Apollo's arms with a grunt and cling to his shoulders before turning to scowl at Jose. But he already has Walt on the bar, and they're mesmerizing in their movements in sync with each other and the pounding bass and bright spinning lights.

"That scared me," I say, forcing my head away from Apollo so I don't jam my nose against his neck to get a better inhale of him.

"I've always got you."

I guess partners do that. I pat his chest that is too hard and close, then ball my fingers and keep my hands to myself.

He lowers me until the toes of my shoes bump the floor but keeping one arm looped around me. "It's my turn."

"But—"

"It's *my* turn. Don't make me steal your invisible lasso and rope you in. I want you."

I wait for him to finish his sentence with the obvious "to dance with me," but it must have been implied because he links our fingers, right hand to right hand, and puts his left on the small of my back. Now he's not only tugging me into the dancing crowd but pushing me too. I'm caught. And it's hot in here. Like maybe too toasty for danc—

Apollo halts, wrapping me close as the song falls into a foggy silence, then bumps out a slow, familiar drumbeat that pulses through my bones.

"La Bachata," Giniki sings.

My eyes widen, and I glance around for the others to save me, but pairs form with no concern to my reckless heart rate. *Not the Bachata.* It's sex on a dance floor, and Kingston is here with his phone. I go to signal to Giniki, thinking maybe she will change it to a line dance if I appear desperate enough, but she's not in the booth.

Apollo's hand fits my hip as if it lives there. He leans to talk over the humming crowd and music. "You are incredible. You've always been athletic but—"

"Wait." I must not have heard that correctly over the quick, rolling vocals. "I'm sorry, I've always been what?"

His brows furrow. "Athletic. Fast. Strong."

"I was a klutz. Still am around—um...sometimes. I have off-days." The ones when Apollo is close by, and why am I bringing his attention to my flaws? We should talk about our running times.

"You were not a klutz, but I'm not going to argue with you because we're dancing now." He presses closer to me.

I'm breathless and not from exertion. "Uh. But this is the..."

His fingers touch between my shoulder blades, right over the chain. He strums it, and my eyes half-close as the fabric tightens and shifts over places already on high alert from his proximity. "Bachata." His voice is a growly hum in my ear. "You ready to pay up?"

"Yes?" I bite my lip. *NO.* I swallow hard and glance up at Apollo.

He steps and I back up, too far because his fingers splay and he tugs me closer. I step on his foot.

He chuckles and grabs both of my hands, jiggling them. "Get it all out. We've never danced together over the age of twelve, so we may need a few tries."

I take over shaking, then shimmy, adjust my heels, and toss my hair that's probably getting frizzy with the increasing sweat and humidity. I can do this. Or it will be another kayak disaster. Fabulous.

He crosses his arms. "Now we definitely get another dance. Who knew you could move so slow?"

I hold my hand out. "Oh shush."

He grins and spins me into him, then out, then back. It's jerky and jostling in a way that's intentionally playful.

"You're going to make me hurl," I say, smiling.

"Can't have that." He pulls me against his chest, thigh between my legs, palm on my lower back to keep my hips to his as he rolls them in time to the music. Though I'm a massage therapist, I've never truly considered how many nerves are in the hand until his fingers weave into mine and our palms kiss. My inhale is sharp as my skin simmers and melts at every point of connection. I follow his every motion—slow, rhythmic, swaying steps, then arching quick with determination to the driving beat. If Jose and I move like wind over water, Apollo and I move like fire. Simmering, cracking heat. The way he leads isn't joyous or playful; it's licking, white-hot flames. I swear steam moves from our glistening bodies, but it's probably the fog machines.

The crowd falls away to hazy lights that make his gaze impossible to stray from until he spins me out and back, bringing me close enough to count each eyelash. His heartbeat thumps under my palm, adding a perfect harmony to the thrum of guitars and slap of bongos. I run my nails across his tense muscles until honey sparks with smoldering embers. Fingertips blaze down my spine, and when they burn a path up again, I lean against them, eyes closed, and give over to this dance I'm not even sure is the Bachata anymore.

The rhythm changes, and our hips slide apart, then back for more in our own dance where graceful spins feel like rolling in sheets, and every shift together is impossibly right yet still too distant. His fiery touch weaves up my arms to my neck, stoking the flame before simmering to the sweetest warmth as he sets his forehead to mine.

We stay that way, glued to each other as we find that rhythm is one more thing we have in common. He spins me out, and when I whirl back, my knee clutches his hip, and his fingers slide up my sweat-slick thigh. I clutch fabric, then slip under the sleeve of his shirt to trace the dents of muscle leading to his shoulder. I was correct. Steel under warm skin.

His breath steals mine as honey glints under pops of colored light so close that I get the most mouthwatering inhale of deep cherry, stronger with warmth and sweat. I want to bottle it. I have to taste him. Heat ripples from his lips as we make a slow turn—

Someone gasps while another shushes them. A sung "Oh" draws out and makes my hair stand up, not with sexy energy, but like my skin is cringing.

It abruptly jerks me from the throbbing, intense connection to Apollo, and I trip over his leg, but he's still wrapped so tightly around me that it probably wasn't even noticeable to anyone watching. Camila stares with wide, amused eyes through the fog, next to Mama who's practically bouncing, until she realizes she's been spotted and then she does a quick turn toward Camila to act like she wasn't just homed in on Apollo and me.

"Xi," Apollo whispers against my ear, but all I can focus on is the crowd watching us. Like, just us. The spinning lights of the club pierce my eyes, and I wave, stepping back from Apollo.

"And that's how you Bachata, am I right?" My laugh is tight

and pitchy, but the surrounding people clap and go back to dancing, since Apollo and I have stopped fornicating for their entertainment. I sneak a peek at him. He looks concerned, but I can't deal with that right now because I can't breathe. "Thanks for the, uh, dance—or bet," I manage to squeak before I stride through the crowd away from him, away from Mama, away from all of this. If I don't fall before the exit door, no one will have much to talk about except for believing the rumors about Apollo and I are true, which they're not.

The worst part of it all is I want them to be true. Kissing him again feels like the best bad decision I could ever make, but it would ruin the progress we've made as partners and as…friends. Reconnected *friends*.

On shaking legs, I move fast, slipping through gyrating couples. I veer a hard left, dodging, weaving, ducking, and spinning my way to the exit, nearly running by the time I dart into the dark outside, make a U-turn to slip into shadows, lean against the building, and inhale cool ocean air. "Oh my god," I pant. "Oh *my* god."

I pull off my heels. Every inch of me aches and throbs, even though the bass is now muffled through a wall. I'm so turned on, the swell and heat between my legs make each step a reminder of his hands on me. It's difficult to walk, but walk I do.

With sneaking steps, I get to the side parking lot and drive myself home. I leave the lights off and rush to my bedroom, lean against the wall, and run a hand up my stomach, noticing how my skin seems to tighten with desperation. This is a brand-new level of turned on, and it's so chaotic and intense, I'm a little frightened of it. This built-up tension is too much, and when I cup my sensitive breast and squeeze, I whimper in the quiet.

I have the most crystalline picture of what could be between us, but it's a ridiculous fantasy, so I need to cut the bullshit hopeful voice loudly asking, *What if?*

No. We tried and we failed. We didn't talk for ages.

But did you really try?

I shake my head as if the movement could dislodge the thoughts. We don't work together physically, even if we can dance. That proves nothing except that we both have rhythm that kind of matches and an attraction that will torture me until he leaves.

Since that's the truth and my body is hyperfocused on the fantasy world, I flop back on the bed and arch as I thumb my rigid nipple while replaying his scent, his breath against my lips, and the tingle of his fingers tracing my skin. The pressure of his hard thigh almost had me to this point on the dance floor. When I raise the hem of my dress and envision Apollo's finger teasing over the hot silk instead of my own, I have a difficult time imagining what he'd say to find me this soaked. I've never known him sexually. Well, there may have been fantasies, but they were mainly kiss-related and happened before the horniness-destroying moment when we actually kissed. So I hold onto the way he says—or rather, exhales—my name. "Xiamara." I've felt his hardness against me, and I let it roll out in my mind. He'd rub against me, tug my panties to the side as I arched just like this...

A knock on the door has me sitting up so fast, tiny silver stars blink against the darkness.

No.

Oh shit no. Why now? No, no, no.

17

NOPE. NO MORE

*A*fter tugging down my skirt and attempting to shake the desperation off my face, I take a deep breath, turn on the living room light, and open the door.

Apollo's facing the end of my walkway where his truck is parked, but he turns and takes me in from head to toe, not helping the ache that must be extinguished.

"Hi," I say. "What do you need?"

His chest rises and falls, and his eyes narrow.

I smile wider, trying to calm my deep breaths. *Everything is fine, Apollo, see? Now go away so I can get back to thinking about you while I take care of the raging fire you started in my loins.*

He tilts his head. "Can I come in?"

But we would be alone inside. I step out on the porch, crossing my arms. *Mistake.* Sensitive nipples. Oh god. All that smiling and focus on easy breaths goes right out the window, and I bite my lip, full-body blush activated.

The corner of his lips twitch. "We need to talk. Inside." After a moment of standoff, he adds, "Please, Xiamara."

Oh hell. I move aside, squirm, and when he slowly passes me, I follow, closing us into this room of energized lust. I may be a tightened rubber band. Or a thread pulled so tight, I'm fraying, but I can be cool about this. My every thought has a side question of "why aren't we having sex yet," but that doesn't have to affect a simple conversation. He looks good in dim, warm light and in colorful club spotlights, and I've made a mistake looking him over because I now know how his chest feels and how his biceps and shoulder and thigh feel between my—

I reverse that train of thought right out of my skull. "Need something to drink? Uh, I have water, tea, lemonade, coffee, tea —I already said that, didn't I? Or maybe—"

"I'm good. So that dance was...intense."

I cross my arms. "Why did it have to be La Bachata?"

He shrugs. "That's what came on. And..." I can see him fighting with his words. Chewing them into order. "I liked dancing with you. A lot. Did you enjoy dancing with me?"

That stumps me. Of course. Best dance ever. It got me so worked up my nether regions have called in a state of emergency, but I can't tell him that. And why does he look so tortured? This was just a fulfilled bet, and I don't know how to react. Do I apologize for getting handsy? Laugh it off with a joke about humping his leg? Because, damn, was I grinding that muscle-clad thigh. Great, now my body is firing off another round of the lust hormone blend.

He takes a step closer, dropping his head to stare me down in a challenge for my words. I'm expecting him to make a bet any second, and with my track record, I'll lose and then where will we be?

"I can't, um." I drop my eyes to the floor. "Everyone was watching. There will probably be another picture on social media any minute. Or a video."

"Is that what's bothering you?" He slowly reaches out to take my fingers in his, but the contact sends a jolt through me, and I jerk away. I rub my forehead, put my hands on my waist, then cross them over my chest, which puts pressure on my aching nipples. So I drop them, because no place seems right for my hands right now except on him.

When he gives me a hurt expression that cracks my soul, I put my issues aside and slide my fingers into his. "Sorry, it was just a lot. Out there. Dancing."

He grazes my knuckles with his thumb, making me clench my thighs. "We were good together. We'd probably be good at other things too." His attention drops to my lips. "Or better."

"Like we were at kissing?" I shouldn't have said that out loud.

"Well, since that seems to be on your mind..." He full-out grins, and I think my panties are incinerating. I can't look. It would be really—I do. I'm not on fire. He tugs me closer. "I'd like to try it again."

"But the first time was—"

"I know. But that was then and this is now."

He pauses when I give another little "But." *Kiss me?* What would it be like? We shouldn't. It's a terrible idea, but if this will prove our bad chemistry so we can get back to training, then I guess...I wet my lip and nod.

His pillowy lips quirk. "I'm moving slow, so you can run. Watch out for walls and doors."

I glare, and some nervous tightness inside me unfurls. His lips touch mine, and I gasp at the shock of the softness. Heat washes through me, making my eyelids flutter closed on a moan. There's no way this could be happening, right? Maybe I orgasmed myself to sleep and this is a dream. He moves so slowly into a full press that I push forward out of impatience. I can feel his grin. It's not bad. It's not desperate or dry, wet or toothy. It's not awkward. Not at all. His scent so close is better than lavender. Better than anything I've ever made.

"This okay?" he whispers, the vibration of his words tickling my lips and making my brain go haywire.

I answer by sliding my teeth over his bottom lip, whether from teasing about the past or testing if it's terrible, I don't know. He hums and lifts my chin with a finger, then gives me a timid flick of his tongue. I tilt my head and melt closer, wrapping my arms around his neck.

This kiss sears. It's the type that will replay every minute for the next few days, and even if I want to wish it away, scrape at it, or cover it with an assortment of others, it will hold fast in my memories as a reminder that two people can make the Earth move and stop time.

Apollo Fischer kisses me down to my soul.

When he parts from me, setting his forehead against mine, we're both panting.

"That was an improvement," he says with a grin.

I launch myself at him. Just crash mouth-first on tiptoes, sending us into an off-balance dance. Apollo catches on quick, kissing back hard with a grumble I feel in my clit, and then backs up, dropping away from me as he sits on the couch. He wraps his arms around my middle and looks up at me, lips wet and flushed, a question in his gaze.

Straddling his lap, I wiggle to get my dress to ride up so I can get closer. Apollo grumbles a "fuck," sliding his hands up my thighs, under fabric to grip my hips, dragging me forward until the ache between my legs makes contact with the bulge in his pants.

I whimper into his mouth because the pressure is just everything I need. And the warmth of his body, and his eyes on me, and his trailing hands that make my skin hum.

He crushes me flush against him, fingers in my hair, tilting my head so he can sip kisses from my lips. I roll myself against him, and he exhales a long sigh, eyes fluttering closed. This is out of the realm of reality, but we're here—him and me.

His touch lands back on my thighs and slowly slides up to palm my ass. His jaw tightens, and he thrusts up into me. My gasp gives him access to twist our tongues, which I like very, very much. The reverberation of his groan makes me tremble more.

He skims up to thumb the bottom side of my breast, and when I arch, he whispers, "Yes," tickling my lips with his soft voice, and fully cups me, squeezing. That fantasy version Apollo who didn't quite know what he was doing was a faded shadow of this man with his sure touch and determined stare. "Ride me."

My hips automatically get to work, and with him holding me tight against him, sharing panting breaths between tasting his perfect lips, it's impossible to keep from grinding harder against his stiff length, putting the best ever pressure right where I need it. Have always needed it.

"Like that," he groans.

I clench. Hard. It's as if my clit tightens with a huge inhale, then screams out waves of intense bliss.

When I return to the world, I tremble, setting my forehead against Apollo's shoulder. He kisses my neck and follows the swoop until his teeth gently surround my trapezius, making me groan and my hips to give one more slight thrust and clench and pulse.

"You always smell so good," he says in a rumbly whisper. "Like walking through a field of flowers. Sunshine." He kisses where he nipped, and the contrast is the first sunbeam after a hurricane—all warm, sweet hope. His hands come up around me, and he makes a slow circle on my back. "You good, vixen?"

I give a hum, grinning against his neck, because I don't have words right now. Apollo is good at this. We're good at this together. His erection is an impressive thing still firmly pressed between my weak thighs. We should fix that.

"Bed," I say in a husky whisper.

He nudges my cheek with his until he can brush our lips together. "I'd like to talk about some things first."

I'm too relaxed to sit up, so I stay put. "Like what?"

"Tomorrow." The slow sweep of his hand up and down my spine pauses. I wasn't thinking about tomorrow. Just now. Tonight. Not what this will mean when we have to train together and face the people who saw us dance—

"You tensed." Tilting me, he settles me on my back on the couch, then lies between my legs, but lower so his chest is over my stomach. He thumbs my shoulders. "When we go to bed together, you won't regret it."

"I—" Don't know what to say.

"No regretting this." He kisses me again, a brief brush that has me relaxing. "I'm going to go." His movements are slow like he's studying the exact texture of my lips, just like I'm doing with his. So soft. Just...so soft, it makes my chest ache with longing because we have to quit. "But we're training tomorrow, after you move furniture. And after that, we're doing more of this." He sweeps his tongue against mine.

Unable to stop myself, I moan and open to him, running my fingers over the back of his neck.

He grins against my lips. "I like the sounds you make. Especially when you come." With that, he pushes himself up, stare trailing over me, my legs spread, skirt hiked up past my hips. "Mercy, Xi. Just...mercy." He blows out a breath and I sit up, noticing the wet spot on the bulging front of his chinos.

I cover my eyes with my hands. "I ruined your pants."

He tugs my fingers from my face and pulls me into his arms. "You ruined me long ago. Haven't been the same since."

Something inside me shatters apart. What am I going to do?

18

A-W-K-W-A-R-D IS HOW YOU SPELL XIAMARA

I barely slept, rethinking everything since Apollo had arrived and upturned my world. Keeping up my protein and hydration is key for prepping for the Mossy, but I grab the sugariest pastry at breakfast and cram it down my gullet while sneaking to the spa.

I'm avoiding eyes, but I still get stopped by a few coworkers to talk about my debut on the bar. Only one mentions me dancing with Apollo and how I better save a salsa for them next club night. It's almost as if our dance wasn't that big of a deal, at least to others. It was huge for me as was what happened after. I pull my phone out and read Apollo's previous texts for the tenth time. After my escape from watching Camila perform a patented boob-press all over my man—I mean partner—his first message was a joke about him needing to up his game for the golf cart transport part of the Mossy. The second wanted to make sure I was okay, and the third asked if he could pick me up and take me to the lounge.

I chew my cheek and type out, *Hi.* That's dumb. *How are you today?* Also dumb. *Sorry for dry humping you on the dance floor, and then on the couch until I came and probably left you in a really uncomfortable state.* I don't dare write more than a few words of that one. Delete so much. *Are we meeting in the jungle today?* I push send and promptly have a mini panic attack. Maybe I should have waited for him to reach out. Is he thinking about me as much as I am him? Because my mind has been homing in on every sound, hoping yet nervous that it's his footsteps, his honey gaze, his lips.

Stella comes out of the hall with her arms full of empty boxes. "Hey, are you ready to shine up this place?" She drops her armload and turns to me. "You look tired." Her eyebrow raises. "Did you have a good evening?"

"Yes. But I left early and went to bed. At home. My home." I inhale deep and wait for her reaction to last night, because she was there along with most of Simona Island, but she only gives a closed-mouthed grin and starts toward the shelves with a box. How much did she see? Are Apollo and I doomed to be Moss Monster gossip fodder for the rest of the year?

She approaches to take my face between her palms and presses her thumbs between my eyebrows. It would be weird if it weren't Stella and her vast knowledge of the Yintang point. We stand still another minute to activate the calming effect, then Stella drops her hands and I grab a box, making my way over to the shelves to unload inventory. My phone doesn't buzz. Maybe he's sleeping late. At ten in the morning.

Stella shoos me after forty-five minutes, and I'm going to climb the walls if I don't have something to do for the next three hours, so I pull the lavender from the fridge and get lost in the distillation process. The pattern of condensation is equivalent to watching a favorite show but smells better. The sharp tings of boiling bubbles against thin glass create the most meditative melody. I sway to the rambunctious rhythm. By the time I stand upright from pipetting the remaining grams of oil into vials, I'm starving.

I lift my phone and snap a selfie of me kissing the last vial.

Before opening social media, I groan at Roxanne's newest message: *How did it go?*

Well, I type, *I danced with Apollo and then dry humped him on my couch.* I push send and smile, imagining her drop-mouthed expression when she reads that.

Chomping on a granola bar and still smiling from the thick scent of lavender in my house, I post my photo with the caption, *Finally got around to that date.*

My phone buzzes in my palm. It's Apollo. *Yes! Below the rope bridge! Ready now? Want me to pick you up? I can.*

He seems excited. Has he ever used an exclamation point with me? We shouldn't be in the truck together though. It's too close, and then there's dinner to think of, and it's a lot.

I chew my lip and type a response. *Meet you there. Leaving in five.*

Okay, he texts back. *Have I told you that your lips are very distracting?*

I grin. *You haven't. Should I write something else?* I mean, he's just one big ol' distraction with all his parts. What would I even focus on?

Well, they are. See you in seven. I'm timing you.

I dash through the house to get ready because I need to see him more than I need to hide. It's going to be weird between us probably. Where would things have led if the first time we'd kissed it had been anything in the realm of yesterday? I pull on my shoes and shake my hands out. I can't consider that; that was the past, and I can only control the here and now.

How am I going to handle the here and now? I jog out the door and wave at my neighbor Edison, who's lounging like the biggest cat in the jungle on his front porch couch. Then I'm off and speeding toward the hill that Apollo says looks like a narwhal. Granted, it used to have a huge half-fallen tree sticking out the side—its hornlike tooth—but that's gone now. Still, I'm caught in a happy reminiscence as I park on the road next to the path. There are a couple other vehicles here besides the truck, and I wrinkle my nose. If it's weird between us, we may have an audience.

The humidity clings to my skin and makes breathing thick as I jog. It's going to rain soon.

As I turn the corner, I trip. Apollo looks up from his phone, smiling wide.

He pushes off the rocks and prowls toward me. My heart thumps as if trying to escape to get closer to him, and I glance around for others, because that look—oh, that look. He halts so close I can feel the warmth blazing off his skin. "Good afternoon. How are you feeling?"

I don't realize I wet my lips until his focus drops there and sticks. "Good. Um...you?"

His grin grows impossibly wide. "Even better now that you're here."

"Good day?" Must have been, because he's vibrating with energy.

"Great day."

Guess his vacation is going well. That thought chills my libido, until he runs his knuckles down my arm, making me inhale hard and louder than I'd like, but when he dips, I dart to look past him and through the thick trees. His exasperated sigh tickles my cheek, and he takes my hand, dragging me off the path and into a short, leafy copse.

He spins me toward him, and I dance backward until I bump into a tree trunk. Apollo kisses my gasp, and his needy groan gets my body fully onboard with this tryst. With the slide of his tongue against mine, the sounds of the jungle quiet, the humidity falls away, and it's just gasping breaths and cherries and honey eyes I want to be stuck in for good. I touch his sides and slip my hands under his shirt to map his defined obliques. He cups my face, studying me. I may just die of warm, gooey overload right here, right now.

He stays still as if asking a thousand questions I don't have answers to, and my heart pangs, my eyes burn, and I spiral into a serious emotional overload.

"Don't stop kissing me." My voice is a thready, weak wisp. I need him—need this—so much. What happened last night ripped down a wall inside me, and all of me is clambering to catch up on this exploration.

Apollo slowly leans in and presses a heartmelting kiss against my lips. It speaks, whispers "forever." But it's misleading, and that hurts more than it should.

And what about Simona's gossip mill? They probably already think we're doing this and more, and if we're caught...I jerk my head to the side and put my hand on his chest. "No, wait. People."

He thumbs my lip. "Are great, but I'm most interested in you."

"But training. Others."

He slides his palm over my ass, sending me arching toward him. "Training others? I don't know, vixen. I think we should just focus on us until the Mossy." Then his lips are grinning and on mine again, and it scrambles my brain.

I love how he relaxes when I trail my fingers down the indent of his spine. And how he seems to be mapping my hips as if he knows one day he'll need to find them in the dark. He parts from me and slides his nose over my jaw and under my ear, and my lids drift closed when he inhales.

The sharp *tap tap tap* of rustling palm leaves makes my eyes pop open as Apollo kisses my tingling skin.

I jolt back from him. "So how would you go about finding a tourist, Apollo?" I ask loudly, darting out from under his arm, tugging at my disheveled shirt and shorts. They're too tight and itchy, and I'd like to be naked.

Apollo stares at me, lips parted and eyebrows up. I crinkle

my nose, give him an apologetic shrug, and redo my falling bun.

He drops his head back and growls at the sun before looking at me again. "Okay. Lost tour guide training. How do you navigate the forest when you've done this in the past? I've heard while you're the best in everything, this is one of your strongest events."

That makes me puff with pride. "Have you?"

"Mm-hmm. How'd you do it?"

I peek around the trees. It sounds so silly to announce out loud, and what if he tells someone? I'm being stingy, since he is my partner, but it's an award-winning secret and what would people think? I tear through this event like I have a map of the jungle in my head, but there's more to it.

"You don't want to tell me?" he asks, brow furrowed with hurt.

"It's not that. It's just silly." Right now, my skills seem magical, and when the curtain is lifted, things aren't so sparkly. The frayed ropes, the shoved aside failures, the broken pieces are revealed. Then what?

"How silly can it be if it helps us win?"

I step out of the hidey hole of trees and back onto the path.

"Any day now," he whispers behind me. "We're losing sun. How embarrassing would it be for the future Moss Boss to get lost in the jungle?"

"Future Moss Boss? You think we'll win?"

"Of course." He sneaks a kiss on my neck, making me jump. "If you ever get around to telling me your navigation secrets. I use a compass, but I've heard you don't."

"Takes too long." I clear my throat. Here goes nothing. "Listen. What do you hear?" The forest is busy with sound.

He puts on his concentration face and closes his eyes. "Ah, bugs...buzzes and chirps, birds, a particularly squawky one, and the monkeys, of course."

The primates shuffle around and yell like brazen pirates. I point in their direction. "The bulk of the primate population stays exactly southwest, and they're not quiet. They howl and screech, especially when people are close to their territory. If I listen, I can tell where I am even if I can't see the tip of the southern mountain with the rope bridge, or if I'm far from the river that flows south from the waterfall. I have a map in my head of where everything is on the island, and the monkeys are my compass."

It's easy to get turned around during this event while searching for people—which is why the Mossy board members tape the area off—but I can navigate with my eyes closed, though I shouldn't because of those shoe-grabbing roots.

Apollo tilts his head, studying the canopy. Realization spreads over his face, and I hold my breath. "That's brilliant, Xi. Okay, so where should we head?"

He used one of my favorite words. Brilliant. Right up there with exceptional and perfect. The only thing that keeps me from doing a victory dance is how it would look and that he's not going to like my idea.

"I think we should meet at the K-tree." Does he remember how to get to the landmark whose sprawling, thick limbs make a K?

He grins and tilts his head like he's listening. "So..." He points south. "That way?"

"You remember. Yes, but we should take different paths." I hold up a finger before he can complain about it being a team event and all that. "We're going to have to find someone, and in real situation search-and-rescue, people spread out. It's a waste of time to stay side by side, especially if we have a plan for how to get back to each other."

He stumbles to a stop and looks at me until I get that uncomfortable itch, wondering if something is stuck to my face. Sucking his lips into his mouth, he nods and lets them pop out again. "Yeah," he says almost with relief. "Let's try it. What's your plan?"

"I'll take west until I hit Orchid River, then I'll go south while you just try to find the tree. It's on the coast over the two streams coming off the river. If you make it to a third, you've gone too far."

He lifts a foot to readjust his slip-on sneaker. "And how do we find each other if we get separated for too long?"

"Listen to the monkeys and make your way to Orchid River, following it up. Wait at Alligator Head Rock."

"You remember my landmarks?"

I glance up from setting my stopwatch. "Of course, I do." He's always made me look at things differently. "But the clues will hint to more commonly known locations and direction. Meeting streams, the azalea forest, the rope bridge, and so on."

"I remember all of those." He leans toward me. "Kiss for good luck?"

I haven't heard anymore unruly palm fronds, but it would be just like Kingston to stumble on us and snap a picture. "Later," I say and point at my watch. "I'm timing us. Go."

With a quick pivot and dash into the woods, I navigate the forest floor for rocks and ankle-twisting vines. It's relatively clear if I keep from clumps of trees. When I step on the bank of Orchid River, I check my watch. Almost four minutes. This event could take up to a half hour if we're not careful.

I keep to the river, monkeys to my right, then veer left, aiming for moss or rock to prevent disturbing the temperamental primates more than we already have. Hushed voices make me slow, and I pause for a moment, tilting my head. It's either teenagers or Apollo has run across some tour guides. As I edge closer, his timbre confirms he's the one ahead. "A few more days and it will be official."

"Eh. It makes sense to me," a female voice says.

"Nope." And that's Demi. "She's going to kick your ass seven ways to Sunday, brother. And Ma and Ilaria will too."

Did I hear that right? Who is she talking about?

"D," Apollo says. "How can this be bad when I'm—"

A twig snaps under my shoe, and the chatter ceases. I'm not one for listening in on conversations, but for once I kind of want to. Too late now, so I speed up my pace and pop out of a thick patch of hibiscus. Apollo stands with Demi and Monique, and all three look as if I interrupted something that wasn't meant for my ears.

"Hi," I say and wave, because what else am I supposed to do?

There's an uncomfortable moment of silence before Monique smacks her hands on her hips. "What's your time? I need to know how long I can nap before you catch up to me."

That makes me snort. "Um..." I keep my eyes on my watch. Less than seven. "Looks like...I'm never going to tell you that because you are the enemy, woman." I glance up and plaster on a grin at her beaming face.

"Fair enough."

Demi smacks Apollo's shoulder harder than expected by the sound of the clap and his wince. "Catch up later, yeah?" She nods at me. "Good luck with the rest of training, Xia."

Monique takes her hand as they shuffle off, Monique glancing back to give me a tight smile, then sending another one toward Apollo.

I'm fairly certain they were discussing the Mossy and probably me, but I don't like how he looks kicked. What else were they talking about?

"Does your sister hate me?" I whisper, moving closer.

He blinks out of whatever sullen trance he's in, eyes going soft and apologetic. "No. Quite the opposite. You found me." He signals behind with a thumb. "K-tree is still here."

"It is. Where's Farid?"

"Not sure."

I pluck a leaf from a nearby shrub and rip it into strips, letting them float to the jungle floor. I want him to tell me about their conversation, but I'll look like a gossip if I confess I was listening in. "So, how are he and Monique doing as partners? That's what you all were talking about, right?"

"They're doing good, but she won't share times. We should probably get back to work on this, because they're going to give us a run for it."

"Are they?" It hasn't escaped my notice that he didn't answer one of my questions.

"Yes. So how would splitting up help us here?"

We already discussed that. "Cover more ground." I cross my arm, feeling chillier by the minute.

That chill grows colder when Apollo scratches the back of his neck and nods. "Makes sense. Okay. Want to review landmarks?"

No, I want him to tell me what he was talking about instead of agreeing with separating for this event. I pull my phone from my pocket and text him the picture of the map I made two years ago. "There, landmarks. Check your texts."

He pulls his phone and taps at the screen. It buzzes so many times, I'm afraid it's not going to stop. When it finally goes silent, he looks up at me, his expression pure guilt, but he remains quiet.

I ask an obviously prying question. "Everything okay?"

He nods. "Yes." With a glance to the screen, he crinkles his nose. "I just need to take this. I'll be right back."

Now who's running? He sets off toward the tree line while I stand perfectly still and watch his retreat, my head tilted, my chest tight. I feel too much for him, and he has a life back in New York. Is that a girlfriend he's going official with? That would indeed make me and both our moms kick his ass. He wouldn't do that though, right? No. He hasn't changed that much. Whatever it is, it's none of my business. My life is here, his is not. All I want is to win the Mossy.

When Apollo returns at a jog, he's grinning wide. Must have been a good phone call. He steps close, but I move back.

"What's wrong?" he asks, glancing at his phone.

"Nothing. Ready to get to work?"

His demeanor sinks. "We can do that."

That's all we're going to be doing from now on. Train, eat well, train some more. No kisses, no touching, no being a klutz. "Let's go."

19

THE LONG FALL

"*W*hat in the hell is going on with you?" Apollo looks like he's ready to throw the tray of cups and stomp off into the sunset. "Talk to me."

"About what?" Should we discuss his nonstop phone calls, the odd times he's unavailable, or how much I hate that this event is partnered? Who passes trays off to each other in resorts? Not many.

"How about why you're so pissed at me?" He plops the tray down on Blob Rock, and one cup tips into another, spilling seawater yet again.

"I'm not pissed." I'm just not kissing, touching, or coming near him. It's better this way.

"Ever since the jungle, you will barely acknowledge my presence. The progress we made as teammates took not one but nine steps back, and now you want to do everything separately."

"Well, I don't want to add to all the drama in your life." Whoops. That slipped right out.

"What?"

I step away and chew my lip. "Look, you're busy, I get it, but winning the Mossy is everything to me. I'm content with my life. Obviously, yours has plenty of excitement to keep you busy, and I won't interrupt that. Once I—we—win the Mossy, we'll go back to normal."

His brow furrows, and he's back to searching the ocean for answers. His lips move like he's testing out a conversation without making it live. "Okay, I can't figure it out. What are you talking about?"

"The whispers. The phone calls. You being so busy on vacation. You avoid talking about your life in New York and—" I shake my head. "Never mind. It's none of my business, but I'm not interested in being your island fling." My words catch up to my brain, and I wave my hands between us. "Not that I expect to you to marry me or anything." Wow, do I want to run.

Why is he grinning? It's not funny. "Xi." He steps closer, capturing me around the waist. "This isn't a fling."

I roll my eyes at him but can't find it in myself to struggle out of his perfectly solid hold.

He raises an eyebrow. "You don't believe me?"

"It was only a few kisses." And one intense couch dry-hump orgasm, but hey, who's counting?

He brings his other arm around me and tugs me closer. "You should have brought this up sooner if it was bothering you. We could have been doing way more than kissing all this time." He leans like going in for a potentially public smooch is the most natural thing, but I turn my head to check for others. "You done scouting yet?" he whispers in my ear, then nips it, sending my body into a full lust-clench.

I glare up at him. "They're so bad about gossip. We may as well have a Simona Island *Times Daily* front page spread featuring something someone wanted to keep private."

"I'd be happy to be on the front page with you."

"Gah," I say, but then giggle because he's too charming, the brat. "We need to—"

"Kiss again, I know." He leans close. "It's been so long, Xiamara. Torturously long."

"We can't," I practically whine, pushing away from him. "We shouldn't have in the first place."

"Yes, we should have. I couldn't have gone on like that."

"Why not?"

"You seriously haven't figured that out yet?" He's staring at me, blinking, and when I'm about to yell that I clearly don't, he takes a huge breath, laces his hands behind his neck, and grins —not a happy one though. An I-can't-believe-this-is-happening one. "Do you have any idea what it was like to watch you date other guys, to be so close to you, I could have kissed you a million times? I couldn't continue, but I had no clue how you felt because it's you." He signals at me in a way of frustration that would make me laugh if his words weren't punching me in the face right now. "But then...then I thought I understood because of what happened with Brad." He drawls my first boyfriend's name in a sneer. "It wasn't me who changed the game, it was you."

"What happened with Brad?"

"You didn't talk to me for two damn weeks after the thing with Mia, and then you broke up with Brad. I asked him why. He said it was because you were always so hung up on me."

I open my mouth, then shut it as I consider the memories. "You were my friend. I wanted the best for you. That wasn't Mia." I rub at the knot in my chest, but it only sends my skin into a fresh tailspin.

He presses his lips tighter together. "Think a little harder over that one."

Fine, I was horribly jealous. A fresh surge of irritation rises. "But you left and that...-hurt." I don't even know why I said that. Him leaving wasn't the part that hurt so much. It was what he'd told me. A promise he didn't keep.

He takes a step closer, ducking his head so that I get his full, intense focus. "I *left*? I had to go to college, Xia. I needed to—" The muscles in his jaw tick, and he growls. "I reached out. *I* tried."

I swallow hard. "You told me you'd come back, but you didn't." I don't like the tightness in my throat, but it can't be helped.

The anger slides off his face, sending his eyebrows to another, softer angle. "I didn't think you cared. We'd been friends forever, and just when I think we have a shot, you shut down. I thought you'd process it and then we'd talk. We didn't. You gave up on me."

I wrinkle my nose. "I'm sorry," I whisper, balling my shirt in my fist. A tremble starts in my hands, my shoulders, my teeth. Too much adrenaline mixing with all the emotions from earlier. Too much truth.

Apollo runs his knuckles down my arm. "What happened in that moment, Xi? What was so bad that you let us stay apart?"

I shrug. "There was an expectation. It should have been perfect because it was us and I lo—" Oh good god, I nearly told him I loved him. It's true, but still.

He slowly rolls a finger in an air-circle. "Go on."

"We knew everything about each other. Almost. We should have known each other that way too. And here, Simona, is...we see fairytales come alive daily."

"And we weren't. In that moment."

"Yeah. Back then, I should have just talked to you about how it wasn't going to work out instead of avoiding you."

"Why wouldn't it have worked out?"

"We're not compatible."

"Not—" He makes a sharp huff that's almost like a laugh. "Xi, I hang on your every word—*when you speak*—and at the club, uh, after the club..." He pinches between his eyes before looking back up at me. "I want to kiss you today and again tomorrow. And the day after that. And the day after that. What do you want?"

I want that too and beyond. I want every day, but like it always is with us, that's not in the cards. "I want to win the Mossy."

His shoulders sink like his balloon heart popped, and I'm compelled to give him more even though it will only prolong the inevitable. "And I want to kiss you too."

He steps forward with a quickness, lips pressing to mine, hands sliding around me to pull me closer. Every reason we shouldn't do this flutters out to sea because it's just so good. Nothing should be this altering when it's not permanent. The sting will be hard when he leaves, but I want to see how he moves inside me and what time will do if his kiss already stops it.

"Come to my house tonight." I nip his lip.

He groans, fights back with a harder press, then gives me this fierce stare that makes my heart flutter and my core tighten. "Am I invited to your bed, Xi?"

I reverse gasp. It's like my libido just kicked all logic out of my body and dragged my breath along. "Yes."

His tongue peeks out to wet his bottom lip. "I can't wait to see your room. Touch your sheets." He trails his fingers down my arms, and I grip his shirt. "I especially want to touch you. And know how you taste." He leans back, smiling nonchalantly like he didn't just destroy my panties.

"Ippa," I say, unsure what I was going to say instead of some random, non-existent word.

"Oh yeah?" he asks. "You're right. I think it's a great idea to go out tonight."

"Huh, wha?"

His amusement fades to a sweltering glance at my mouth. "Tonight. Let's go out for pizza—" He tilts his head, taking in my expression of what must be terror. Not ready. Too soon. So many eyes. He thumbs my bottom lip. "Or make a trip to the grocery store, and I'll cook."

"You cook?"

"My mother is Haitian and my father Italian-German. Of course, I do." His gaze only leaves my lips when I frown.

"You didn't before," I say.

"Like you, I didn't have to. But Nonna told me I needed to learn for my woman."

I straight up glare. "What woman?"

He arches an eyebrow. "My future woman."

I want to ask. I do. *And what about now? Is there someone in mind?* But his eyes are mancala winning all over my face, and I bite my tongue.

"Tonight." His kiss is an undammed waterfall, pouring out impatience for this new path. "Now that we've kissed and made up, think we can get in some more practice?"

At five, Apollo shows up at my house smelling like soap and him. His shirt doesn't hide the memory of what's underneath now that I've seen him, and my hands trail his muscles when he wordlessly steps into me, lifting my chin to sip a kiss from my lips. My body hums, then I do.

He grins, and his mouth touches down harder before he pulls away and incinerates me with boiling honey eyes. "Do you have leftovers in your fridge?" His voice is a low octave that resonates between my legs.

I blink up at him. "Fruit and a lentil dish."

He tips his head back and forth, then sighs. "Let's go to the store."

He tugs me outside, down the path, into the truck, and I'm fine, elated in his presence even, until we pull into the parking lot. It's a bland rectangular building named Groceries because it's Simona's only one-stop shop for most things you need to live in a house on the island. It never needed a fancy, distinguishing name. Down the street are farm stands, custard, and the resort restaurants, but this is where *everyone* shops. And here we are. In the parking lot. Together.

If that doesn't say something important and isn't noticed— well, there's no way this won't spread around Simona with a speed that rivals Jose's patented hip swivel. Just being in Vic's borrowed vehicle with her son has probably graced the social media group. I should have changed maybe. Checked my hair and put on some killer red lipstick. I hope I don't trip, and I can speak, and I don't panic and run for it. That wouldn't look good.

"You are freaking out," Apollo says, drumming his fingers on the steering wheel.

"I am..." *Not* won't pass my lips. I go to shake my head but nod instead. "Okay, yes. I am." I blow a long breath as if coming to a stop after a five-mile run.

Apollo un-clicks his seatbelt and shifts to face me. "Why are you freaking out?"

I chew my lip, but he tugs it from the vise of my teeth.

"Work it out with me," he says.

The single pull door with the handwritten sign that says, "No seriously, PULL," stays closed for now, but how many are inside? Who?

Apollo dips his head so we're eye to eye and tucks a curl behind my ear.

I fidget with my pinky nail. "When my chemo sessions ended and my hair started growing back, we went shopping as a family and were bombarded. It took us an hour and four thousand questions until we could return home. This kind of news—" I signal between him and I. "No matter what it is, it's big. Everyone will know."

Jennifer's mother comes out with two canvas totes, and I slide down the seat.

"I'm okay with that." His lips brush against my temple, and blossoms of heat in my stomach unfurl like he's the sun. "But you are not?"

"I am, but just, the thing is—it's like, so much. And then the Mossy and then you're—"

Leaving. Going. Gone.

Then I'm left with the questions to navigate on my own. And there will be questions. Instead of a cancer quiz with pity eyes, it will be one about Apollo with even more pity eyes. Poor-Xia-can't-seem-to-catch-a-break-unless-she's-winning-the-Mossy eyes. And what if we lose?

He snatches me, tickling my waist for a second, but only to get me to relax enough to pull me against him. "Xia," he whispers against my lips. "Are you ashamed to be seen with me?"

"No," I coo, turning to straddle him and cupping his cheeks without thought. A tremble starts in my chest and expands until I drop my hands to his chest to keep from jiggling his face.

Chewing my lip, I rest my head in the crook of his shoulder, taking a long inhale of him. I don't want whatever we have to fizzle because I'm weird about this gossipy fishbowl we live in. There's zero reason to be ashamed of walking into a store with Apollo unless I stumble while doing so, but it's just...this is *that* moment. The one between not together and together. This is temporary, but how temporary? Maybe we're only exploring this path on our way back to friendship.

Apollo aims the keys toward the ignition. "Hop off me. We'll scrounge."

I push his hand aside and reach to open the door. "It's not you—it's completely me. But I'm not ashamed in any way to be seen with you. Okay?" I stare at him with serious intent.

He takes my fingers and threads them with his, settling them against his chest. "The look on your face right now...I missed that. The protective streak that runs so deep in you. I thought I broke it when I kissed you and you wouldn't talk to me." I nuzzle his nose with mine, shaking my head. "I really am sorry I didn't answer your calls. Before. When you were gone."

"That was hard. I missed you so much. And I'm sorry I didn't come back when you expected me to."

That only slightly soothes the sting, because he's still not back. What does this mean for us? I want to ask, but it's all...a lot and I'm afraid maybe this is just closure for us. I'm not ready to hear that. Not after learning we're not bad at kissing like I thought. Now we know. Is that all?

"Do you want to go home?" he asks, lips downturned.

"Let's go," I say. "It'll be fine." After a thousand rumors, a million side-eyes, a triathlon of gossip that I'll solely bear, and I will, because it's Apollo.

We unfold from the truck, his fingers latched tight with mine. Then we're walking through the parking lot, feet in a synchronous rhythm that is far slower than my pounding heart. This is it. The moment we are going to be outed and judged and watched even closer. Apollo pretends to push the door, grunting with fake effort, until I smack his shoulder and pull, and we step inside like we've walked onstage. I'd prefer to hide behind the curtain for this particular show, but Apollo leads and I follow, giving a wave to the three patrons and two cashiers, who are staring. One holds a box of cereal, paused over the checkout machine.

I stumble, and Apollo kisses my knuckles. "It will be okay," he whispers. "You like pasta, right?"

Doing a bobblehead nod, I squeeze his fingers. "What person who runs six days a week doesn't like pasta?"

"None." He grins wide and grabs a basket.

We make our way through the store, Apollo grabbing ingredients, me following and ducking behind him whenever I see someone. He clucks his tongue and drags me close after my third attempted escape. "Too late, vixen. News of our engagement has probably already reached our mothers."

"You think?" Hell, he's right. "Maybe that will make my mother talk to me."

"She's giving you the silent treatment?" He's gone still and at full attention, which sounds a warning bell that tingles my ears even though it's imaginary.

"She gets busy sometimes and gets lost in work. But it's been different. It seriously seems like she's avoiding me."

His stare as he watches my face makes me wonder what my expression is doing. Am I bristling? A little.

He moves closer. "Red sauce or white?"

20

CAN'T FIGHT ALFREDO

"*C*all him," Apollo says, cutting broccoli. "You know you want to."

I do, but my confidence has wavered, and I'm scared to ask Jose to scour the Simona group for our grocery excursion. I push my phone farther away on the counter and focus on this beautiful man cooking, something I had no clue he could do. My kitchen smells like El Escape on pasta night. Though I've used the stove only once or twice, I have basic cookware because that's what normal people have in their homes.

Apollo steps between my legs and holds a spoon toward me. "Taste."

I raise an eyebrow, and his hand settles on my thigh, then slides to my hip. I sip and moan at the creamy, cheesy sauce. "Alfredo?"

"Yes. Good?" He's watching my tongue travel my lips.

"So good." I then taste again before he pulls it away and licks the spoon, keeping his eyes on me and, my god, when did he get so sexy? I want to be alfredo sauce. Something I never thought I'd consider. Alien, sure. I love sci-fi. Shifter? Who wouldn't rejoice at having the ability to fly or run through a forest at midnight and still see? But alfredo sauce?

"Your lips do this thing when you're thinking." He sets a palm on the counter beside my hip and leans. "They twitch like they want to release those words, and I wish they would."

"I have ridiculous thoughts sometimes."

His exhale travels from my chin to my ear, where he plants a kiss that makes me woozy. "I love ridiculousness. We used to talk about the most bizarre things."

"We did," I say, heart settling into a triathlon beat. We speculated what the people on other planets were like and acted out the behaviors of odd, fake animals that we insisted went extinct. We were going to revive them one day. Make them anew Jurassic Park style, because their DNA had to be somewhere and cloning was a thing.

"So, do it now. What were you thinking?"

I hesitate, then explain. Maybe it's to relive the comfort of telling him anything when we were young or perhaps to test him, seeing if he will run out the door or make a you're-wacky face. He fails miserably by appearing proud-slash-elated and stirring the alfredo with fresh vigor, bringing it to his lips and tasting.

Each teasing lick makes me antsier. Before I have a chance to leap on him, he assembles everything on two plates and sets them on my little table, now adorned with the fuzzy-leafed plant in a bright teal pot Apollo snagged at the store because all homes need a houseplant. "Come. Sit."

We discuss our families, talk American sports, and speculate about the other Mossy teams while we eat. The vegetables are crisp and match so well with the alfredo that I wish I could cook so I could make this. I'm going to need it again, and soon. While I'm cleaning dishes, he pulls out a cupcake that he'd pretended to sneak into the basket as if I wasn't right beside him every step at the store.

I finish up and approach, grabbing my glass of wine and taking a swig, while Apollo grasps my hips and pulls me close. I end up on his lap, straddling him, and he holds the cake out to me for a bite. Every lick, swallow, and moan are studied by the other. His lips dance up my neck, and I tip my head back and exhale tension as if he's giving me a full-body massage. He wraps me up in his arms, and I don't believe I've ever felt anything so right.

His kiss tastes of wine and Apollo. My fingers drift into his hair. Muffled taps start slow against the windows, then move into a quick, hard downpour.

"I've missed that sound," he says, dragging my hips against his.

"Yeah," I murmur, following the tendon in his neck with flicks of my tongue. "Soundtrack of home."

"So true." He slides his hand under my shirt to travel up and thumb the clasp of my bra before retreating. "And other sounds." He inhales against my jaw, sending chills over my skin, then grazes my ear with his teeth. "The waterfalls."

I arch into him. "Monkeys."

"Your laugh," he rasps.

Does he mean that? I pull back and study his eyes. "Your accent, especially when you say my name."

"Xiamara," he says, sexier than ever. "And as if you weren't irresistible enough, I'm adding your moan to this list. If I hear another, it's going to be tough to keep from laying you across this table and touching you until you give me a thousand more. What do you want?"

The clench between my legs about doubles me over. I want to respond, to say so many things I've never said to him before to watch his reaction, but I'm reluctant, worried I'll ruin it because what wants to escape is, "Please stay and never leave. Pack me in your suitcase. Give me chills and make me tongue-tied forever." That would be too much. Unneeded and hurtful because we both know better.

"Say it, Xia." He inches forward, running a knuckle over my shoulder. "Tell me what you just thought."

I can't. I get a night or two, a partner for the race, then disappointment and closure. My cheeks heat. "I want you in my bed. Between my legs."

There's a sensory delay in the room. No movement, no breath, nothing except the ping of increasingly heavy raindrops against the windows.

Apollo exhales, slipping fingers behind my neck and pressing his forehead to mine. He touches my lips before pushing his thumb between them. Did I say his eyes were honey shimmering in a sunbeam? Now, they're at a rolling boil, dancing with steam and disappearing into the blackness of his pupils. They move from my sucking mouth to laser in on my gaze. "You want me?"

With everything I am. I lick his digit, then nip it until his jaw clenches. "You know I do." I reach between us and brush my fingers over his straining erection, making him bare his teeth and inhale a hiss. "No more waiting." Touching him more is on my to-do list. Exploring where I haven't explored before.

He cups my hips in both hands and pulls me against him so I can feel what I'm doing to him against what he's doing to me. "Bedroom?"

"It's a small place. You don't know where it is?"

"I do, but I'm being polite and letting you lead." He pinches my ass hard enough to make me jump, then kisses my growl. "Show me."

I unwind from him, take his hand, and walk down the hall, leaving the light off as I kick off my sandals and crawl onto my bed. My bedroom's infuser glows pink against the stark corner of my room where it sits on the nightstand, kicking out a stream of lavender mist.

Apollo follows, grabbing my foot and kissing my ankle, fingers so gentle against my calves, it's ticklish. His lips find a spot above my knee that makes me fall back and close my eyes at the nerves he's dancing with. I didn't know that felt so good. The button on my shorts pops open under his thumb, and the skin under that is kissed too. A tug. I clutch his shoulders. The inhale of his breath against my panties. My hips lift for him without thought, and one layer goes.

He avoids my sex even though I'm arching, twisting, needing him there. Instead, he keeps slow movements of fingertips along muscled curves, lips following. "We're doing this then?"

I spread for him, eyes closed while the zing of sensation travels everywhere he touches. "Are we?"

"Yes." His voice doesn't waver. There's no question to it or reluctance.

"Good. I need you." I clutch his hair and lead his face between my legs.

He lights up my skin as he works his way down, thumb traveling the silk over my slit before he drops a hot kiss exactly where I want him, except covered.

"More."

"Keep talking." He kisses higher, leaving his fingers teasing over the thin barricade.

I tug at his shirt, and he drags it over his head in a quick movement, but then slowly edges mine up. I'm going to explode. Not with an orgasm, but from the frustration of wanting his hands all over me, inside me, and—

"Out loud, woman." He bites my nipple through my bra, and I squeal at the sharp shock of pleasure.

"I want you." Even to me, my voice is sex-infused desperate. "Everywhere. All at once, *now*, Apollo." I widen my legs, reach for his pants, and push at them, fumbling with the button. "Now."

He lies beside me, arms behind his head, freeing me to fight with his clothing while palming what's underneath. "I like seeing you falling apart because of me."

I fell long ago. I can't say that, even though the words try to spring out. Instead, I occupy my tongue with that sexy vein and drag his chinos and boxer briefs down his strong legs. Goodness. He's big and hard and a little voice says he's mine, but he's not. I'm not sure what's between us, but for tonight, I won't fight wanting him.

Wrapping my fingers around his length, I look up at his face. He's breathing fast, watching me with an unfamiliar expression that fills me with lava-level heat that simmers in my bones. I run my tongue over smooth skin and take him between my lips.

"That's hot as hell, Xia." His voice is thick. "Yes, like that." I work him until his muscles tighten, and he groans. "Moan for me, then stop or this is going to go faster than I want." I grin around him and do what he says. He gives a long, drawn out "fuck" before tugging me up against him and turning until I'm underneath again. "Do you have any idea how much I need you?" His expression tells me this isn't a hypothetical question.

"A little." Time for honesty. "You're so playful that I thought I misinterpreted how you look at me." He has that expression now—heat, sweetness, and maybe a touch of concern or reluctance.

"I think we were playing a different version of hide-and-seek." He moves to his knees, towering and bare. Faint light follows the planes and dips of his structure. I lose my air. He drags my disheveled shirt off, blows out a breath, and watches his hand as he slides it over my skin, making chill bumps rise.

His gaze is addictive. I want him to see all of me. I tug the straps of my lacy bra over my shoulders and arch to unfasten the clasp. He runs a finger from the hollow of my throat, down my sternum, until he takes the lace with him, humming an appreciative note, then falls over me and kisses one nipple, then the other, playing as he figures out what makes me put his curls in disarray.

"I'm going to come if you keep doing that." I grit my teeth and try to pull him closer with my legs, but he has me pinned and is frustratingly calm.

"Really?" he asks, grinning up at me. "Let me know when you get close." He slips a finger under my panties and circles.

I gasp at how sensitive everything is and rock against him. When I'm on the edge, I lift my hips. "Don't stop. There. Th—"

He gives me a wicked smile, and his hand leaves. He kisses my whimper and stays too still for me to do anything for relief. When my breathing slows again, sensation mellowing, he tugs down my panties and pays attention to my clit and the lips of my sex. I'm panting like I've run six miles, and he's as calm as if he's walking into a warm-up.

"Yes. There, there, there." I grip his hair and the sheet as my hips move faster, grinding against his perfect tongue. He moves away. "No, no, no," I say, right on the edge, with fire flowing through my veins.

"Are you ready for me now?" he asks, giving hard kisses over my stomach and sternum, settling back in for round two with my breasts.

"God, yes." Maybe he wants me to hold out for him. That makes sense, I suppose, though an early orgasm beats none at all should things not go as well as we'd like.

He roots around in his tossed-aside pants and comes back with a condom, sheaths it on, then puts my leg over his shoulder and fingers me fast and hard. I move with him. Quick grinds, so close to that delicious sensation that is revving up to be grand. My back bows in preparation for this ride.

He leaves me again. I bite back a curse, and if this ends up a failure like our first kiss, I'm not sure what I'm going to do. I ache from my bellybutton to my knees. I'm trembling, and I glance at the clock, but Apollo is grinning. Mancala-win grinning. What's he up to? Can he let it go until I come?

His mischievousness shifts to something sweeter, and he kisses my shoulder, my neck, my chin and ends up at my lips, staring down at me. "You ready?"

I nod.

"Out loud," he whispers.

I run my hands over his back and lower to grip his very toned ass. "I want you."

"Where?"

We kiss for a long moment, inhaling the scent of each other, my body humming for him and mellowing from the irritating ache of near orgasms. "Inside me." And because I win a smile for that, I keep going. "Deep. I need it."

His lips part in a hot exhale as he inches in, filling me. And he does fill me, completely, stretching me while his eyes stay on mine in a connection that is soul-touched and open. It's a lot. I could tell myself this is a moving on thing, or that he's just another man in another moment, but I'd be lying. This is Apollo Fischer, and nothing about him during our entire lives has been *just another*.

He slides his arm under my knee and brings it up high. I moan at the tightness and arch into him as he gives slow rolls to his hips. He feels amazing, and when he steps up his pace, I do too until we're racing and I'm—I'm—"I'm going to come."

Three more thrusts, and my body is so close to singing, I can feel it in my teeth. And he pulls away. My hips pump in the air, and I curse loud. "Oh my god, why? Why when I'm so very there and ugh! Need it. Want. Please." I reach to finish off the ache, but he grasps my wrists and pins me.

"Xia," he coos, and I gnash my teeth at him, but that only makes his grin wider. "There you are. Hello, Xi, vixen, my Xiamara." Ignoring my gentle chomps on his lips, he kisses me until my muscles go slack. "You think I'm going to go fast? I'm not crossing the damn finish line in record time when I've waited so long. No, no, no. We should play."

My mouth drops open. "But I need you." I squirm against his hips, now pressing to mine. "We can do it again in a bit."

"You have me. We'll do it again. If we can move afterward." He grinds slow against me, but not inside where he should be. "Then again and again." He kisses my neck to my ear. "Again and again."

My eyes roll back. "I can't, I—"

He catches my cheek with his palm and strokes. "Do you hate this?"

"Yes." I crinkle my nose. "No. But I'm there. On the edge. All over."

He tugs at my lip with his teeth. "Up to your eyeballs?"

"Almost."

"Perfect. Let me know when." He pulls me with him as he kneels and has me straddle his lap, sliding back together, sending fresh chills over my bare skin.

In two thrusts, I moan "when."

"Liar." He grips my ass, thrusting hard, and I cry out, gripping his shoulders. He uses his outstanding muscles to wake up every atom in my body with jarring pleasure before he growls, pulling out and sitting back to grip the sheets. "Fuck, this is torture." He prowls forward, caging me in beneath him, then circles his thumb against me until I'm close yet again.

"Then why are you doing it?" I ask, squirming away because I'm shaking with almost-thereness, and for some reason, I love it. Maybe because it's a new type of exploration. Or maybe because it's him.

He fists his cock. "Because it's also really, really fun. You trust me?"

"Yes." The word is a moan, and the truth.

"You want to play with me?"

"Always." Dammit, that was too much of the truth.

He grins wide and crawls over me. "Let's play."

As the rain provides background music, we work our bodies together, a triathlon of learning each other. When we're communicating openly about what feels best, too much, or not enough, he drags me on top of him, eyes grazing every inch of me. Sometimes we pause to touch with lips or hands, or just to stare at each other, and it's overwhelming. Just when I think my soul will explode into a thousand specks of glitter, he slides back in and takes me hard, driving that expanding ache into my bones.

We get so close to that ending moment of pleasure, a remnant of the precipice settles in until I'm in a constant state of riding the orgasm line. No—coasting on the high of it. I'm flying with Apollo, lost in the clouds, in a new atmosphere I wasn't even aware existed.

I suck his finger, and he has to retreat for a minute. He bites my shoulder, and I have to push him away and breathe through a clench that is so deep I think all my organs are in on the action. Against his ear, while he's thrusting a hard rhythm, I ask if he's enjoying fucking me and he goes harder, until we both need another break.

My words affect him. He stares at me with intensity, stroking my lips as if they're goddesses divvying out divine gifts. I want to give him everything. His eyes are my anchor, his skin a blazing territory I've never mapped before this moment. The newness of his weight over me is pure, delightful revelry.

When we're slick with sweat, raspy-voiced and trembling with the overload of endorphins mixed with adrenaline, Apollo kisses the back of my neck. I reach back to grip his hair, arching, wanting to absorb into him. I'm wound so tight, I'm spinning.

"Apollo," I whimper. "I'm going to break into a thousand pieces. Don't let go. Please. I need you."

He tightens his grip around me, pulling me tighter against

his chest. "I'll never let you break, Xiamara. I've always got you. Ready to come?"

"So much." I put my hand over the one he has on my breast. Everything is too much, yet I never want it to end. "Yes. Please."

He slaps his hips against my ass, pressing me forward over a pillow, and shifts his hand, finding my swollen ball of flesh with a rapidly circling finger.

I drop from the skies and crash hard into the molten lava center of the mother planet of all orgasms. Full-body pulses ratchet through me, ungodly cries of pleasure bursting from me in a way that's impossible to hold back. Apollo joins in a moment later with a hoarse, grunted curse before curling over me, body twitching along with mine in surprising synchronicity.

Time isn't a thing anymore. It's the puffs of breath against my ear, the radiant heat surrounding me as we collapse in a heap on my bed. It's my eyes fluttering closed. The furrow of my brow when his weight leaves me for too long. The hum of thanks when he returns to run a cool washcloth over me, then drags me into the most perfect hug I could ever imagine.

It's my mind too exhausted and pleased to be afraid. It's being cocooned in a love so deep, my soul sighs in contentment.

21

FROM NOW ON

*A*pollo lies beside me on his stomach, hugging a pillow. His lips are slightly parted. So this is how he sleeps. There's a thrill to seeing this part of him—the new-to-me bits that make him the Apollo he is today. Sure, we've napped together before, watching a movie or during a bonfire when the adults wouldn't stop talking, and we'd give up whining, curl up on a blanket, and hold hands until the murmurs lulled us into dreamland. But he's an adult now, naked, with a tiny furrow in his brow as if sleep takes great concentration. I kinda love this new page in our...whatever this is.

He snorts and burrows deeper into the pillow. I bite back a laugh and moon all over his peaceful, sleeping face, high-lighted perfectly by the fuzzy morning light. But nature calls, as does getting these last days of practice started no matter how sore I already am. I slip from the bed, or try to. My thigh spasms, and I bite my lip to keep from hissing at the pull of furious muscle. Oh my god, what did I do? Could have been sometime in the sex marathon. Or when I came out of the after-glow trance and crawled on top of him. It did feel a bit tight, but all my muscles feel tight in this final training push. I rub my palm against the knotted muscle, and it is a solid, heated knot. That is not good. At all.

I whimper when I stand, throw on a shirt, and hobble to the kitchen for ice. I couldn't have strained it, right? That would take me out of the Mossy. Pure panic spikes my adrenaline. Pulling a muscle during sex four days before the event of the year, my one shot for Moss Boss? What is wrong with me?

Hobbling back into the bedroom, I whisper-curse as I put on pants and grab my phone. And now I know Apollo is a heavy sleeper. I lean against the dresser, babying my leg, and text Roxanne: *I spent the night with Apollo and strained my thigh muscle. What should I do?*

My phone buzzes two seconds later. *Holy Hades on fire, are you two banging and you didn't tell me? #insulted*

Focus, best friend who went to school for nursing, I write back. *What do I do besides ice and rest? I have to run the Mossy.*

Give me five. Dropping Hadley at school.

I sulk and try to stretch, moving to the kitchen so I can whisper-scream in peace. The muscle loosens a bit, and I think maybe it's fine, but when I move it back to resting, it bunches back up again. My phone buzzes and I jolt.

"Good morning," I whisper, heading to the front door.

"Deets," she says, then yawns. "First, how was the sex? It was sexy, wasn't it?"

I sigh as I step outside, then sit in my single plastic chair next to the door with a whiny, "Ow, ow, ow, motherfricking ow."

"Is that a best ever ow? Or like—"

"Rox, I pulled a muscle. This is serious."

"Fine," she says with a huff. "Sex talk later though. That's what the doctor said? It's a pull?"

"I haven't been. I don't like going. The receptionist is nosy and always asks me how I'm feeling as if I've caught cancer again like a virus."

"You're going to need to go. Did you hear it pop while you were doing the thing we're not talking about?"

"No. But it's knotted up tight."

"Swollen? Forming a bruise?"

I run my fingers over the skin of my thigh. "No. But it really hurts. I can barely walk much less think about running."

"Huh."

"What kind of huh are we talking about here? I can't see your face."

"That's the you-need-to-see-a-professional huh. Seriously, get to the doctor and quickly, because if it's only a slight pull, you may be able to wrap it, and with anti-inflammatories you can still run. Though it could be something else, worse or better. Go see them. And then call me."

"I will as soon as I have an answer."

"Well, yeah, but also about the sex stuff."

"I think that was a mistake."

"Ooh, was it bad?" I can imagine her scrunched freckle nose, her lifted sneering lip.

"No. It was..." I squint one eye and look to the sky for words to explain the overabundance of emotions.

"What? Too fast, awkward but decent, amazing but he ran out two seconds after busting a nut and you're insulted? Which is it?"

"It was perfect." My whispering voice catches. "Fairytale, fall in love, want to do it forever because the world falls away perfect. And that's the problem."

"My lord, woman, how is that a problem?"

I rub the knot with the heel of my palm. I feel off beyond the pain. Drained and shaky. "He's leaving, and I've lost sight of my goal. I can't win with a pulled muscle, and what am I going to tell people?"

"That you got a sex injury you didn't notice because orgasms fix everything. Oh! That's what you need."

"Rox, not now. I love you, but no. This is bad. I've ruined everything."

"Woman, go to the doctor. Let me know what they say."

We hang up, and I hobble back inside.

"Xi?" Apollo calls from the bedroom, then steps out, fully dressed New York chic style, hair wet. He strides across the room and pulls me to him, making me hop and wince before he can kiss me. "What happened?"

"Uh, I might have a pulled muscle."

"What? Where?" He steps back and looks me over, and I miss the touch and how good he smells, like my soap.

"Thigh. I need to go to the doctor. Are you leaving?"

A flash of panic widens his eye. "Pulled?" He drops to a knee and gently touches exactly where my injury is. "Here?" When I gulp and nod, he stands back up and checks his phone. "Okay, so, doctor. Now. Let me—" He swoops me up in his arms and takes me to the bedroom, rushing to get me dressed.

I fasten my bra under the shirt, pull my arms in, and loop the straps. Apollo tosses pants at me. This is a new level of weird-next-day. I wasn't mistaken about last night's very intense sexy times, right? That felt...right. I'm paying for that today, I guess.

"Ready?" Apollo barely looks at me as he lifts me and heads to the door.

I have him put me down and do a hobble of shame down the path. Simona Island will already have questions from last night's grocery store outing, which will be exacerbated by having the truck in front of my house all night; no need to add why he's carrying me everywhere. God, this is embarrassing and at the same time heartbreaking. If it's a sprain I can't manage well enough to compete, what will happen besides losing the Moss Boss title? Will Apollo run it on his own? What made-up rule did the Moss Monster board create for this, or have they not discussed this kind of thing yet?

Apollo helps me into the truck and runs to the other side, jumping in and taking off, even more quickly than usual.

"You have to be somewhere?"

His Adam's apple bobs, and he nods. "Yeah. Um, I'm going to drop you off." Jaw working, he smacks his palm against the steering wheel three times. "Then I'll be back."

I know he can feel my gaze on the side of his face. How could he not when I'm staring through his skull seeking answers?

He turns on the main road. "Does it hurt?"

"Yeah." Along with other things. He's distancing himself already. Maybe out of preparation in case I can't run the Mossy, or maybe because we had sex and that was closure for him. We did all the things, and now we know what that would be like. Now an injury? Wrong turn. Again.

He stops the truck out front of the big white building with solar panels lining the roof. All of the island's medical businesses are in this clinic: physical therapy, dental, chiropractic, and oncology, though that's more like a satellite station go-between from larger inland hospitals.

"Xia," Apollo says, turning toward me. He's saying goodbye. The first one. He leans, and I fight not to fall out of the truck and hop inside. "Stop overthinking, please. I have a really big morning, and then I'm all yours. We need to talk about some important things. I'll bring over dinner? Can we do that?"

Important things like great sex, we should keep in touch. Maybe hook up when he's on the island. How the Mossy is going to work with my injury that shouldn't have happened. "Sure." I open the truck door.

"Wait, I've got you." Before I can protest, Apollo is out of the truck and jogging around. "Let me carry you."

I shake my head. "It's fine."

"Xia—"

"Seriously. Just go do whatever it is you need to do." I step out, wince, and hop toward the door.

Apollo growls and scoops me up, ignoring my protests but pausing at the door, where he stares at me. "This isn't how I expected the morning to go, and I don't like it."

"Sorry to put a damper on the day."

"It's not that. I'm worried about you, and I have to go do this thing, but I need to be here too. I *want* to be here. I'll be as fast as I can. I lo—"

I gasp and kiss him. He couldn't have been about to say "love," but what would that substitute be? Loathe leaving you? No matter what, I can't hear that right now because I'll cry, and it will make even more questions for both me and any sneaky onlookers. "Put me down. I can do it. Go, and I'll see you later."

He walks inside with me, marching in front of three wide-eyed people sitting in the lobby.

"Xia?" Phyllis comes around the desk to check my pulse. "What's going on?"

"Possible muscle pull, right thigh," Apollo says. "Need anything else?"

"No other complaints?"

The muscles in my face ache along with my leg. "My Mossy partner won't put me down."

"I see that." Her concern for my potential emergency shifts into such wide-eyed glee, there's no doubt that I'm utterly screwed. This is going on social media the second I'm in an exam room. "Well then, I've got everything I need." I'm sure she does.

I groan and attempt to separate my body from Apollo's as much as possible with him holding me.

He settles me into a chair, moves another one around in front so I can put my foot up, then leans and kisses me, hard, setting his forehead to mine and making my stupid body all

shimmers and goo. "I'm sorry I can't stay. I'll see you in a few."
With that, he jogs out and I'm left biting my kissed lips.

I clear my throat and give a wave to my audience. I'd tell
them it's nothing, or say something like "Partners, am I right?"
but it's a little late for playing things off.

Phyllis taps her pen against the desk like a gavel against a
lectern, grinning at me. "We're all so excited to see what
happens at the Mossy. It's going to be very interesting this year."

The others in the lobby nod and give affirming mumbles.

Mr. Walsh leans forward and scratches his white beard.
"Just make sure you pay attention during the tourist hunt.
Those jungle vines take someone out every year and you've
really been..." He laughs and squeezes his beard like he's
wringing a washcloth. "Well, they don't say 'he knocks me off
my feet' for nothing."

Oh no. "That's—there's, I mean—"

Phyllis's chuckle is sandpaper against a burn. "You two are
so dang adorable, I can't stand it. You're always so..." She signals
to me with wiggling fingers. "Put together. Not around that man
though."

"Nope," Mr. Walsh says, leaning back in his seat.

"Stop, you two," Duchess Borno says, bless her ancient soul.
"Look how red she is. You're embarrassing the girl."

Kill me now. Me and this body I have no control over when
it comes to Apollo.

"Xia?" Dr. Smith calls.

I jump up and promptly hit the floor, stars dotting my
vision and pain ricocheting through my thigh.

22

DON'T MESS WITH THE SACRED MOSSY

"*D*ehydration?" I ask Dr. Smith. "That's it?"

She nods. "Yes. You haven't been taking care of yourself in this heat, Xia. More fluids, more electrolytes, vitamins. That is a beastly cramp. You're lucky it didn't happen running while your endorphins were high."

Well, actually, my endorphins were in the stratosphere. I've lost sight of my goals, only taking care of my libido while everything else took a back seat. Still, this is the best-case scenario; so good it slightly takes the sting from my shame that everyone is aware I'm a walking disaster zone...that can't properly walk. "No tears, sprains, or strains?"

"No, but I am concerned you've overworked yourself and will be sore for a couple of days. You need rest, ice, massage. Only walking until the event."

I blink at her. "But—"

"No." She waggles her finger at me. "Rest. From what I've heard, you and Apollo are doing just fine."

When I can stay on my feet. But seriously, fine isn't good enough, especially with this setback.

She pulls a bag of fluids and some tubing from the drawer,

laying them on the counter next to a glass jar of cotton balls. "Are you as annoyed at the new rules as a few of the other contestants?"

"It's been okay." At first, but now I can't imagine running without Apollo beside me. Or kayaking without him flicking water at me with his paddle until I tackle him and we both fall in. I still suck at the waterfall event, but getting into the rhythm of passing trays back and forth was like learning to dance again. "The others are annoyed?"

"A few. Some are happy, the real team player types." She flicks her arched eyebrows and grins. "The Moss Monster Meet hasn't changed this much since they added the waterfall event, what...fifteen years ago? And that was discussed for a year. This new rule was so sudden. But your mother always knows what she's doing with things like that." She grins wide at me, and I plaster on a smile.

Mama really does. Though she thinks over things for a while before she moves on it, considering every angle for risk. That's why she's so good at managing El Escape. Why was this rule so sudden? Especially if people are complaining. She doesn't make decisions that get complaints because she's open about almost everything. Unless it comes to me, because I don't like being discussed. I scratch at a tiny hole in the thin, blue sheet on the medical table.

Dr. Smith pulls on gloves, letting them snap. "Let's get you hydrated and back home, though you should consider PT and massages until the race. I'll call Jamie over, yes?"

I nod, thoughts numb, as I hold out my arm.

"Still nervous about needles. It's fine. This is nothing. No big deal."

Why does this feel like a monstrously big deal?

A half hour later, when most of a bag of fluids has been dumped into my system, there's a knock on the door and Apollo walks in, approaching the bed to take my hand. "Phyllis told me what's going on. That's great. I'm mean, not great, but no damage." Of course, she did, because patient confidentiality doesn't exist on Simona Island. Apollo's phone buzzes, and he glances at it. "I have to get back, but I wanted to check on you. How are you feeling?"

I stare at our hands, his umber hue against my sun-kissed tint. Brought together by an unwanted, last-minute rule. "I think my mother—well, our mothers—made the partnership so we would be forced together."

He goes very still. I know, it's a shocking accusation.

I hurry to explain. "Mama's been acting off since..." Since Apollo arrived. "I heard her talking about needing a backup plan on the day you were at El Escape, and after that she practically disappeared. Then your Ma kept popping up like she was checking in, you know? And the partnering was so random. Mama doesn't do random. When she does something, it's for a reason and it's well thought out. Why would they do that?"

He leans against the counter and shoves his hands into the pockets of his chinos. "To give us time together."

I exhale a relieved breath. He's on my team for this. "Exactly. How could they do that? Even Cozette said she wouldn't mess with tradition, and she's new here and doesn't realize how important this event is. For them to add rules, especially on a year I'm trying to take the Moss Boss title, is like...blasphemous." My eyes well up, and I go to rub my nose, but the IV is in. My eyeroll unseats a tear, and it burns hot down my cheek. I use the palm of my untethered hand to swipe it away.

Apollo is oddly silent. Probably having a hard time taking it all in as well.

"This was a really, really important year, and who knows if we're even going to win. I still can't wrap my head around the Ring Retrieval event, and now this?" I signal to my leg. "All because they wanted to try to get us close...and succeeded."

"No regrets," he grumbles. "I know you're mad, but don't regret us."

"I'm not mad, I'm hurt. Confused. Okay, I'm mad too, but I think I have that right. This is...invasive."

He flinches.

"Do you understand how incredibly invasive this is? To me? To you too. Everyone is talking about us. There are pictures and videos. The people in the lobby told me I'm falling all over the place because of you. Mama made it so we'd be stuck together and on display. She knows me better than this."

He squeezes his eyes shut, takes a deep breath, and then blinks at the ceiling. "Xia. I can't even begin to—" His phone buzzes, and his jaw tightens. "There's something I need to—" Another buzz interrupts his words.

"Just take it," I tell him and sniffle. "Go do your thing. We'll talk later, I guess."

"Xia, you are so important to me."

"Thank you. You're important to me too." I swallow hard, vision going rain-on-a-window blurry. "And you're so busy. Just, I can handle this, okay? You've got too much going on, and it's fine. It's all just fine."

"I hate it when you say it's fine, but what you mean is, it's extremely *not* fine."

I open my mouth and shut it.

"Sorry." He shakes his head. "I'm just...there's a lot we—"

Someone knocks on the door.

I swipe my palm under my eyes. "Come in."

"I have arrived." Jamie steps in with a smile that quickly drops. "Need me to come back?"

I shake my head. "No. We're all done."

Apollo picks me up from the hospital an hour after Jamie has finished working out the cramp. He walks beside me, stoic and silent on the way to the truck. My muscles hurt. My soul hurts. I nearly texted Mama five times but decided against it. I'm too angry and defensive to talk. And now I'm feeling vulnerable and guilty for saying so much to Apollo. It's shocking that my upset words came out so easily with him. However, that makes the quiet all the more intense. He said no regrets, but that was before I went off about everything.

When we get in, he drives slower than ever. I can't take the silence. "Did you get done what you needed to?"

He squeezes the wheel. "Almost. Are you okay?"

I want to say fine, but I'm not fine at all. I'm not sure when I was last *fine*. My stupid brain refers to the thousand images of Apollo, starting with being in his arms on the beach, bra full of sand, heart racing because I missed him and he was touching me for the first time in seven years. I've already spewed out a ton of not fine things in front of him, so why not? "I don't really know."

He glances over at me. "That's valid. There's nothing wrong with that."

Really? It doesn't feel that way. I should know, and I should be fine. I'm not a problem when I'm fine—I don't stick out. I'm under the radar, and everything around me is smooth sailing. People like that.

Apollo takes my hand. "I'm glad we're partners, Xi. No matter what, I'm here and I'm yours."

I rub at my scrunched eyebrows. But he's not here for good, so it doesn't exactly matter if he's mine and I'm his. Unless I follow him. And with the way this Mossy was handled, the anger I feel at the residents and my mother, maybe that would be an option. It would be a sacrifice; ocean for the city, warmth for chilly winters, and island of familiar—albeit nosy—people in exchange for Apollo, but...is that something he'd even be interested in?

He pulls up to the curb, comes around the side and helps me out, walks me inside. He sits on the couch, tension making his stance rigid, and he pumps his hands. Now this is a man who's not fine.

"What's wrong?" I sit beside him, wincing at the ache in my thigh.

Elbows on his knees, he rubs his hands over his face. When I put a palm on his back, he stands up like I've burned him. "I have to tell you something. Several things, actually." He starts pacing the living room. "There were a lot of things I thought about before I came here, and I had a plan. But when I got here, I didn't expect seeing you would go like it did."

I have to look away from him for a moment because he's making me dizzy. "Because of how I, um..." I crinkle my nose. "Acted?"

He deflates like my answer released a pressure valve somewhere in him. "Yes." He waves his hands toward me. "It wasn't bad, Xi, just...unexpected, and I didn't know what to do."

Oh, it was so bad. I stop-drop-and-rolled right out of there. My mother had to drag me in. Which, looking back on it now, she did for a reason. But—"Do?"

"I wanted to tell you how I felt, ask you out, but then..."

An icy chill travels down my spine, and the air that had started to ease between us ratches up, pressurized until it's hard to breathe. "But then?"

He halts, linking his fingers behind his neck. "But then our mothers told me to go slow. That you needed time. And—"

I stand up, regretting it because my leg protests, but at least I don't fall like I did earlier. Mr. Walsh isn't here to pick me up. No one is. "And you agreed with them." Because he is the one person who makes me incapable of playing it cool. "Did you know what they were revealing when you showed up with me at the meeting?"

He closes his eyes and nods.

Unbelievable. "Was it your idea?"

"No." He frantically shakes his head, then stares at his shoes. "But I agreed."

My throat knots up, and my lungs sting. "I've been struggling with this from moment one, and you knew what they were doing. It's bad enough that my own mother would do this, but you?" Deception kicks me hard in the stomach.

"It was not the best choice. Xi?" He's made my name into a question, a plea. "I didn't know the Mossy meant this much to you."

"It's everything."

"You're making that abundantly clear. Look, I withheld stuff from you, and I'm so sorry for that, but we wouldn't have gotten this close without it."

"And that's how it should have been." Because I've shown him more of me than I have to anyone, and that has leaked out, all the messy, hidden parts that no one gets. I've exposed my worst side to Simona for him. And he's out of here the moment the Mossy is done, or sooner if we don't run it. I can't imagine being beside him right now, knowing he was deceiving me all along, knowing what people are saying about us.

He taps at his chest as if expecting his heart to tap back. "How can you say that?" The tightness of his voice makes my eyes burn and blur.

I shrug. "Because we're not meant to be and never have been. This isn't how things go in forever relationships."

"You're so wrong." The venom in his tone sends my anger retreating. "You have this idea that a glimpse of someone is real life. It's not. Life and relationships get messy, you should know this."

"I do. But no one wants to live in mess. They want the

comfort of knowing everything is fine, and eventually it will be." He won't have to see the disaster I am, won't field the thousand questions from frowning lips. He'll catch social media posts of happiness and life moving right along the way it should. I swallow back tears, lift my chin, straighten my spine, and put on a smile that hurts to make. "It's okay, Apollo. You will return to your perfect city life and be fine. It was good to see you again. You should go."

His growl of frustration is sharp and echoes through my small house. "It's not fucking *okay*. You think the city was perfect? It took me seven years of arguments, failures, and falling on my face to get back to you. My worst day with you is still better than any day in the city alone." He presses his fingers to his eyes, then drops his hands, shrugs, and strides to the door. "Good relationships have messy, imperfect parts, and I don't give one shit about bad kisses or stumbles or what people think, because you're worth it."

The slamming door makes me jump, and I close my eyes, washing my cheeks with restrained tears.

23

HOME INVASION

There's a clank outside, then a knock. "Xia," my mother calls out, impressively clear considering the walls between us. "Your door is locked."

"That's because I don't want to talk to anyone," I whisper into my pillow. I feel hungover even though all I've been downing for two days are electrolyte powder drinks.

The knocking continues, then falls silent. The back door jiggles, but I locked that one too.

"I'm mad at you. Go away!" I yell, and the jiggling stops. Good riddance.

The slide of my kitchen window makes me sit up. Oh, she is not! I hop up, enter the hall, and step around the corner.

Mama balances, a foot in my sink, halfway inside, and she's holding Apollo's plant. "This is new." She turns the small teal pot this way and that to study the fuzzy, flat leaves. "It's cute. I like it."

And I crumple in a sloppy pile of tears. "Me too." I hiccup. It's all I will have to remember Apollo by. Beyond the thousand memories and the gaping hole in my soul. "I told you not to come."

"Ay, ay, ay." Mama slips through the window, trickling from the counter with agility and grace I hope I have when I'm her age. She puts the plant in its place and crouches to wrap herself around me. "My daughter goes to the clinic, and I hear about it from Kingston? What on Earth happened, Xia?"

"Dehydration."

She squeezes my chin and jiggles my face. "Then you shouldn't cry." I sob-snort, and she strokes my back. "Now, why are you mad at me?"

"You and Vic made the partnership because of me. You took the tradition of the Mossy and altered it so I'd be stuck with Apollo. How exactly did you think that was going to go when the event was over?"

She tugs me close. "I'm sorry. We thought it was best. You two needed a push."

"Some push. Next time just shove me off the cliffs, okay? Or maybe tell me you're trying your hand at matchmaking and then leave me the hell out of it." I shift away from her and stand, checking the cupboards for food and finding crackers.

"What happened? I heard he's holed up at Demi's apartment. Did you two fight?"

"He knew, Mama. He knew and played along with this game you created, so yes, we had a fight. Not that it matters. Nothing should have happened between us anyways." I lean against the counter and fiddle with the crinkly cracker packaging.

"I disagree."

"Well, of course you do. You're the one pulling puppet strings."

She stands, moves a stack of unopened mail after staring at it a long moment, and sits on my kitchen table. "I just...you two. Xia, you're perfect."

My laughter bounces off the kitchen like a rain of broken glass. "We are the least perfect couple—not couple, we're not that. Our first kiss was horrendous. Everyone on Simona knows I'm a klutz around him, and my own mother fabricated a new rule to force us together. What kind of romance is that? It's not."

"But you talk to him."

"I ramble."

She tilts her head, furrowing her eyebrows like she's mentally saying, "Duh, Xia."

We stare at each other so long, I yell, "What?"

"You love him." The twinkle in her eyes dares me to deny it. "You have always loved him. I'm not dumb, Xia. Nor is Vic. Mothers know these things.

The two of us have always seen the spark between you and Apollo, but we didn't talk about it until Cozette came and alleviated my busy schedule. Vic needs someone to start taking over, and Demi can't do it alone. They wanted Apollo here."

"Okay. What does that have to do with me?"

She taps her pursed lips with her electric-pink-painted fingernail. "Well, after the New York trip you and I went on..." She scrunches, and I'm not going to like this. "You were a wreck being in the same area as he was, and I knew you weren't the slightest bit over him."

"Ugh." I groan and drop my head in my hands before looking back up at her.

"So, Vic and I got to talking—"

"About me."

"About you and Apollo, and Vic called him and, uh, told him about our trip."

My head is going to explode. Just, poof, gone. "She told him to come here, because I was a wreck? And he was just like, 'sure'?"

"I don't think he could have been stopped." There's that *duh, Xia* look again. "When you two were ten, he told Vic he wanted to marry you when he grew up."

My eyes go wide. "No, he didn't."

"Oh yes, he did." She nods. "As he got older, she'd ask him why you two didn't date. He'd say he loved you too much to ruin your friendship. You'd echo the same thing." She picks up my stack of mail and starts thumbing through it. "Do you still feel that way?"

We're well and truly past the friendzone. "It doesn't matter what I feel. He worked with you to torture me over the last month, and he lives in New York."

She sets three letters aside and stands, taking the other two across the kitchen, opening the cabinet under my sink, and throwing them in the recycle bin. "That is a challenge, but we were thinking...hoping that maybe he would move back and work with Vic if things worked out between you."

I straighten. "Has he said anything?"

She shakes her head. "No. He changes the subject when it comes up."

"He's really good at that."

"So what are you two going to do?"

"Nothing."

Mama's brows are so scrunched, I want to smooth out the wrinkle with my finger. "It would be a shame to let something so good disappear because you're angry."

"It's not that, Mama. He manipulated me, along with my own mother."

"Ah, actually, he didn't want to. We talked him into it."

An invisible fist lands square in my gut. "Wha...why?"

She takes the crackers from my fidgeting fingers and puts them aside, then grips my shoulders. "When he makes a decision, he roars in like a hurricane until he gets what he wants, and you...you are an orchid."

"Are you calling me fragile?"

"No. I'm saying that you are so afraid people may notice you need water, or humidity, or warmth, that you hold your perfect shape...until your whole head falls off." She pats my cheek when I groan. "Those who are closest to you see when you're wilting though. Apollo sees you. He pays attention. Always has. He just needed to be patient and you needed to realize it was okay to drop a petal or two around him. He'd pick them up for you."

Exhaustion tugs at me, from emotions, from dehydration hangover, from this big conversation. "I think I need to be alone for a while."

The last days have been odd. It's so quiet. Eerily so, as if Apollo's presence was meant to fill the space and now the house is mourning the loss of him. After I found a mysterious bag of runner-fuel food on my porch—coincidentally, I'd eaten my last cracker pouch for lunch—my phone buzzed with a text from Apollo. A simple *I didn't mean to hurt you.*

Not a *I still want to talk* or a *can I come over?* No loves or loathes. It feels like goodbye, and I can't do anything but sit in silence, drink my electrolytes, and massage my leg. This is closure between us. It's what I thought he wanted, and I guess I was right. It's all working out like I expected. I should be relieved.

I'm not.

Mama has texted, and I talked to Jose yesterday but kept it brief. He wasn't thrilled about that, but he knows me. And that's good. Quiet, but good.

I stand on the west beach staring at indents in the sand. Apollo's been here and that aches. How was it, running without me? I'm having a hard time just being here, walking, looking back as if he were following, then wondering if there's still a warrior woman somewhere inside me.

I turn music on my phone and set it in my pocket to interrupt the emptiness while I stretch again. There's no pain, and my body is antsy to burn off energy with a long run. The Mossy is tomorrow, and I still don't know what to do. Is Apollo planning on running it? Am I? The thought of seeing him makes my heart cramp even though I'm fully hydrated.

Sitting on the beach, I pull out my phone and stare at it. I can't keep going on like I do.

So many don't seem to care that others gossip about them. Camila loves it, and there's usually a huddle of whisperers at any given moment. Arguments pop up here and there, but it's rare and they fizzle out with little strife. People know who to give space to and check on each other so often, there's no time for a problem to arise without an army of helpers to assist.

Maybe the way news carries on this island isn't that terrible. I run my fingers over my aching forehead and press my Yintang point.

Roxanne told me last night that small towns are so gossipy because they're craving involvement with the people in their community, and that was a beautiful thing. She's been in her house for six years and only knows the names of her neighbors because she accidently got their mail. Then she asked me, "Why does it bother you so much?"

Isn't that the question.

Mama told me that once I came back from chemo, I retreated. Those memories are as strong as patchouli. I was the subject of everyone's interest for a long while, overhearing them whisper about my health, or if I was going to make it. The personalized comments were the worst: I was so thin, pale, hairless, my hair was growing in patchy, I was eating or not, gagging at smells, quiet, quieter. The only thing they didn't seem to know was that I could hear really well.

Back then, Apollo would crawl in my window with comics, hand one over, sit on my bed, and start reading. His smell never made me nauseous. He never commented on my hair or how and when I ate. He wasn't lying when he said he understood me.

I loved him then.

Now, he's returned to make amends or whatever's going on between us, and I put him in a position where he had to follow my mother's hairbrained scheme because I couldn't simply relax around him. No, that's not it. I knew I couldn't be perfect around him.

Yet that didn't matter to him. *Because you're worth it.*

My god, what am I doing?

I swallow hard and push the button to join the Simona Island Resident group.

I get an approval notification in less than a minute and start scrolling. The high schoolers spotted an ocelot, and everyone is excited. Mr. Walsh's hernia is back? I wasn't aware he had one. Why was he picking me off the floor at the clinic? There are pictures of plants, smiling faces, and items for grab that people don't need anymore. A photo of two kids sitting on the cliffs overlooking the sunset makes my soul feel like it's going to pop. Then there's Apollo and me.

The world halts, wind pausing, ocean holding its breath in an extended lull between waves. Someone took a picture of us at the grocery store. Apollo has me tucked under his arm as he pulls me from hiding behind him, and we're both laughing. I want this stupid photo on my wall. Scrolling, I check who uploaded it. Justin? I didn't even know he was there. The attention vortex of Apollo strikes again. I read Justin's caption out loud—"I think I've lost my girl"—then laugh at his sad face emoji and swipe at my eyes.

For an hour I scour the threads: the Mossy information, the resident updates, and everything I can find on us. It's less than I expected. Besides the few pictures and the video, most just say we're the ones to beat and they're so happy we're partnering.

But are we still partnering? I need a plan or...to put a toe in the water, because the idea of running the Mossy beside him with everyone watching feels like glass in a wound. I text Jose and Mama, asking them to come to the house, then stare at the picture of Apollo and me for a while longer before picking myself up and walking to my cart on antsy legs.

When I pull into my cart-sized parking spot, Walt holds up two bags. "We brought food, dessert, and a little wine." Jose runs to hug me, holding me three seconds past awkward. Mama is already inside, sitting on the counter, Papa across from her at the table.

"Did you come through the window?" I ask.

"Maybe," Mama seems proud of herself, so my guess is yes. "Are you still angry at me?"

The group hops into motion, rooting around in bags, clanking dishes, and opening drawers, pretending they didn't hear that question.

"Look at this itty-bitty preciousness." Walt beams, holding up the plant.

"I'm not mad." I plop into the kitchen chair next to Papa, who reaches over and squeezes my hand, no words necessary.

These people love me. I've shared something deep with each of them, but have I ever let any of them into my mind? Have I ever let anyone in?

I give pretty, surface details—an orchid. I offered my raw and real self to Apollo only until we changed the game, and then I acted as if he was a different person—like he was everyone else—but my body wasn't having it. I wasn't paying attention to what had been there all along. It's going to be scary to correct that.

The blush creeps up my cheeks, and my mouth dries up. My lungs squeeze, and I'll be damned if I don't wish Apollo was here with his honey eyes and warmth.

"But I need to tell you all something."

The crinkling of bags stops, the glug of pouring wine tapers off with a glass-kissing *tink*, and the spotlight shines on me.

"Okay," I whisper, keeping my focus on my hands. "I am in love with Apollo Fischer. As in more than friends, want to see him every day, and talk and touch constantly like—" I wave my hand around to encompass these people who have found their other halves in this large, hard-to-navigate world.

"He is my forever person and I hate that it's hard for me to express that. I hate that my body goes on the fritz when it comes to him."

Yeah," Jose says. "Your mind short-circuits because of his hotness. Not everyone can be as smoothly subtle as I am."

I laugh at that, as does Walt. "Oh love, should we talk about when—"

Jose squeaks, hands flailing in circular punches. "No! Zip, shh—" Then he falls into a stream of Spanish that is of no help to Walt. This is a story I'm going to push to hear. Plus, I've never seen my friend blush.

"Um, no," Jose says. "But really, Xia, darling, it's okay. We get it. It's...a lot to take when you meet the one. Overwhelmingly so." He takes Walt's hand and leans against him.

I ponder the essence of Apollo. He's funny and competitive, a little jealous because he's a lot mine. The energy that floods a room when he walks in is his big, open heart reaching for me. I clutch my shirt and wish it was his so I could smell his scent on it. "We do talk, I swear. Just not about the important things." I wander, opening a box of pasta salad with zucchini and white beans. More perfect pre-race food. My eyes ache again. I take a deep breath to calm them. These people care so much.

"What are you going to do, hija?" Mama watches me, head tilted.

I fill a plate. "He's leaving, and I'm not sure if we'll run tomorrow or not."

Mama stands up from Papa's knee. "Oh, you're running the Mossy." She holds up a finger before I can say that I'm unsure about it all. "You've worked too hard to just bow out. What on Earth, Xiamara? You won last year by fourteen *minutes*. We did not raise you to give up because you're confused over a man." She lifts her finger a second time when I open my mouth. "Or gossip, or me. Don't you dare let me live with the guilt of harming my only child's opportunity to be the Moss Boss. And then I'd have to stare at that trophy on my shelf forever. Are you trying to raise my blood pressure?" She fans her face as she looks to the ceiling.

I grab a rollerball container of Chillax from the fridge, coming over to rub it on her wrists.

She sniffs, and her shoulders sink. "My talented daughter. Run the Mossy, okay?"

"What if he doesn't want to?"

Jose turns his phone to show me the picture of us. The one at the grocery store. The one I'm going to have to ask Justin for so I can print it. "This man would do anything for you. I know that look." He glances at Walt, who gives him the same looney-in-love grin Apollo has in the photo. "I bet my left eyebrow that he'll be there, waiting for you."

After everything that happened, what it would be like to run beside him as we've trained to do. Awkward? Yes. Difficult? Yes. Worth it?

I blow out a long breath.

Guess I'll find out.

24

ONE MOSSTASTIC DAY

*M*y palms are sweating as I pace the parking lot, eyeing the path that leads to the beach and the crowds and maybe Apollo and definitely my fate. I shake out my hands. Just walk over shells in one particular direction. Run it. There it is, and I need to go or I'm going to miss the start of the race, and what if Apollo is there, waiting, as disappointed as I would be if he's not there?

"So...shall I set up here?" Roxanne twirls her cream-colored parasol, her long dress and red hair floating on the gentle breeze. "Where we can stare at everyone headed to where you should be right now."

I laugh and put my hands on my hips. It's nice to have her back on Simona.

She steps beside me, giving my elbow a nudge. "No matter what, it's going to be okay, Xia."

"And if it's not? If he's not here? What if he already went home?"

"Then you win the Moss Monster Meet by yourself, fly to New York tomorrow to call him an ass for abandoning you, and then kiss him hard. That's the plan, right?"

"That's what we decided on."

"You came up with all of it. I just agreed." She knocks into me with her hip. "Go forth, warrior woman. I can't take this step for you."

So I do. I move forward on shaky legs with Roxanne beside me. A few people who didn't set up early walk with their chairs, making lines in the sand with their dragged coolers. They pause to wish me well. I grow a little stronger with each greeting and wave. The Harpers' toddler runs and grabs my hand in both of her teeny ones, jumping up and down saying "motts botts" over and over until her dad scoops her up and over his shoulder and tells me that she's asked every day for a month if it was Mossy day. He's glad it's finally here, for sanity's sake. My sore soul fills up like a balloon.

I love this island and these invasive, wonderful people. And I love Apollo so much. I can't imagine leaving Simona for good, but if there's a chance for us, I don't want a life without Apollo. But that's a problem for tomorrow. I only have today.

The bullhorn calling the racers has me kicking off into a sprint. I'm going to win this, so I shouldn't start out losing.

"Go get 'em!" Roxanne yells after me.

The starting line is hidden behind a couple of hundred onlookers settled into beach chairs, shaded under umbrellas, and sitting on coolers filled with snacks and booze. Blue, cream, or green marks their resort allegiance, and many hold posters, hand fans, and little flags. On the tables twenty feet from the starting line, attendants load silver platters with a variety of different barware, each filled to the top with blue, red, and peach liquids. If they make the trip, the attendees get to enjoy even more drinks.

Down the beach, twenty kayaks face the ocean. People mill about on the decks of three boats floating past the crest line. Our "victims" for the Wave Rescue event are ready to be saved. Recycled streamers strung along poles stuck in the sand disappear around the corner. That's where everyone starts separating. I bet as soon as we hit the forest, the guides for the Lost Tourist Jungle Hunt will give us clues to where we can find our specific missing person, and once we locate them, we'll travel to the waterfall for the Ring Retrieval. Once completed, we'll hop in our fully loaded cart and speed back to the beach, where we have to park and sprint a half-mile to the finish line. That makes the most sense.

The crowd cheers when I jog into the contestant funnel. I grin and slap outstretched hands. The familiar squeal of Jose makes me pause. Walt holds up a neon poster that says *Xia is the Boss of the Moss* in thick, perfect script. I backtrack to hug them over the orange construction fencing, then move to get to the starting line.

The first people I see when I turn the corner are the adventure twins doing synchronized windmills, making their identical hair flop the same way. The sour catering manager glares. "Oh good. She made it."

"Try to sound a little more thrilled, Frank." Monique grins wide. "I am so glad to see you."

I tilt my head. "That's terrible smack talk."

She rubs her hands together. "I'm just getting warmed up."

I bite my lip and try to find the only face I need in this crowd.

"Oh, hon," Monique says, making my heart sink. Her eyebrows are angled in pity, lips tight. Days ago, I would have smiled, said I was fine, showed that I can do this on my own, but I can't.

"He's not here, is he?"

Crossing her arms, she cocks her hip. "Of course, he is. You think he wouldn't show if there was a chance you'd be here? Please. Nah, I was wondering if you're okay. Heard about your clinic visit."

I go on tiptoes and look around. "It's fine. Like, really fine. I wasn't taking care of myself."

"That's not like you."

I grin. "Well, I was distracted by—"

Apollo steps from around the corner, eyes wide, as if in shock that I'm here, and my heart skitters off in a sprint. We both move toward each other quickly, but he stops short, head pivoting to glance at the crowd, who have grown suspiciously quiet.

He takes a small step back, gripping his neck. "I..." His voice is a tired rumble. "How's the leg?"

I have no idea what to say to him either. Well, I do, but not here and he seems uncomfortable. Probably because I'm uncomfortable. "Um, all better."

He opens his mouth, and the horn sounds for lineup. I'm not ready. We dive into action—him jogging back to the registration table to get the grease pen, and me throwing my bag in the runner's cubby and sliding my goggles in place on my head. He grips my arm, making my skin tingle and heat, and draws on a number. I read the numbers to distract myself from his touch. "Eighteen-A, huh? Out of twenty teams."

"Someone waited to ask me," he says, focused on his work. "Wasn't sure you'd be here today."

I bite my lip. "I wasn't sure you'd be here either."

Beside Bodhi, who's looking a bit green like most first-timers, Indigo flexes her barely-there muscles. "Get out of the kitchen, because you all are losing to *The Heat*." Her mini fan club chants a round of "Turn up the Heat" for her, and both Apollo and I catch each other's amused eyes. My mouth dries up, and I want to kiss him now, hard and forever.

Mama jogs over to hug me. "Has he told you yet?" she whispers in my ear.

I sneak a glance at Apollo, but he's shifting on his feet, arms crossed.

"Told me what?"

Reaching out to pat his arm, she huffs, then grips my chin, studying my eyes. "Run well and fast. This is what you want, hija, you take it." She gives a sharp nod and leaves us standing alone in this uncomfortable bubble of unknown. The crowd's chanting and murmurs come to a quick halt when she steps to the line. "Teams get into place."

I glance at Apollo. "Did you hear that?"

Apollo stretches his arms. "Get into place? Yeah, caught that." He's not going to make this easy, is he?

"No. What Mama said?"

"Wishing you good luck?" Apollo says with a smirk. "I caught that too."

In front of the starting line, Mama whistles and then claps her hands five times in rhythm. The crowd claps back twice to say she has their attention.

"Welcome to the thirty-eighth annual Moss Monster Meet!"

The crowd roars, and I'm unable to ask about this thing Apollo hasn't told me yet.

Mama claps again. "The rules are the same, except this year there are partners. Both runners must be over the finish line for the time to be counted. Are you all ready?"

Apollo leans closer. "There is no doubt that you inherited your announcer voice from your mother."

She walks out of the path and picks up the flare gun. Apollo and I drop in starter positions.

"You remember how we do this?" he asks.

"No, I completely forgot over the last three days. Of course, I do."

"How would I know that since you don't talk to me?" His eyes are forward and narrowed, jaw so tight I'm tempted to bite it. "Be careful, Xi. Someone may see you staring at me and start a rumor that we're involved."

"That's not fair, nor is it relevant anymore."

The loud pop and hiss of the flare jolts my muscles into action, and I tear off the line with Apollo right beside me.

"Not relevant?" He picks up the tray at the first table and takes three careful steps to the exchange line. I'm in front of him, and we shift, both turning at the same time to stabilize the drinks. He gently drops his hand away once I'm facing forward. "You really know how to rub it in, don't you?"

"Rub what in?" I move forward, heel toe, heel toe, don't drop the tray, keep it even, don't think about Apollo.

He snatches the tray's edge as I sidestep. "Focus, Xi."

"I was," I say. Then mumble, "Just on the wrong thing." I push the tray over my head. The clink of glassware makes me remember to relax into motion. *Easy.* I speed walk with steady steps and balanced breath.

The twins jog by, too close, drinks sloshing. Refusing to take the bait to move away or faster, I continue the pace that will earn me the most points. I'm the fastest on the island, besides Apollo. I'll catch up.

Apollo switches sides, blocking the twins from moving closer. "Good. That's it."

I ignore a crash of glasses and a female curse behind me, zone out the crowd cheers, shouts, and gasps. But I have to pay attention when Alani, my favorite teenager, yells, "Team two, six points," as the careless turbo twins sprint for the kayaks. That's the lowest score without wrecking the entire tray. "They're going for speed," I say with an even breath.

"And they will lose because of that."

Five more steps to the switch line and we shift again, load up Apollo, rotate.

Now I can think. "What am I rubbing in?"

He sets the drink tray on the unload table, and we slap hands without thinking as the crowd cheers because those are some full glasses. Barely a drop spilled. He starts toward the open beach and kayaks. "That being involved is irrelevant. That's what you said."

I kick off into a sprint as Alani yells, "Team eighteen, nineteen points!"

"Well, it is, right?"

Apollo yells, "Should have kept the points!" when we sprint past the twins. "If you don't want a relationship with me. Which you obviously don't since you're too embarrassed to be seen with me."

"That's not why I act that way, and you know it."

"I do, but that doesn't make it hurt less."

Shit. We get to the first kayak and grab the handles and sprint into the waves. "I'm sorry!" I yell.

"Me too."

I jerk the kayak, and Apollo turns to look at me.

"I am sorry," I say again. "It wasn't about you. I just needed to get over some things."

"And did you?" A wave hits us, sending us backward a few steps, and Monique and Farid sprint past, high-stepping through the surf. Apollo growls and tugs us forward. "Come on."

We pass the break, and our eyes meet as we silently count, then pull ourselves onto the kayak in perfect sync. I roll into the back seat and slam the paddle into the water, aiming for the boats and floating victims.

"Going right," Apollo directs from the front.

I peek around him to see that he's aiming for Camila. "Can we not?" I ask.

Apollo sighs, giving us a hard boost forward with an extra-deep plunge of the paddle. "She's closest and the tide—"

"I know. It was just wishful thinking." I angle my paddle to turn us so we'll arrive on her right because Apollo is stronger getting back in the kayak on the left. Monique and Farid are in the water along with the twins. Three others are lining up.

"Oh, great," Camila says as we approach. "Is this going to be a problem for the two of you?"

My cheeks heat. "We're fine." That was a reflex. We'll win this thing, and everything *will be* fine.

"Truly looks like it, Nena."

I swoop in beside her, slamming the paddle with force it doesn't need to halt the kayak, but it sends a wave over her.

She smacks water back at me. "Rude."

Apollo checks his goggles and slips off the deck. When he wraps an arm around her, she goes slack.

"Just for that..." Wicked intention is all over her face. "I'm going to enjoy this. Nice arms, Apollo."

"Not right now." He's breathing heavy as he drags her toward the kayak.

Keeping the kayak on course is difficult, but we're still making good time. I send a glare to smirking Camila. "That was uncalled for."

"Says the woman who's kept Apollo on a leash forever. I thought he'd get over you in New York, but no. Just let the poor man down already so one of the hundred swooning women can have a chance."

"I am literally right here, pushing you into the kayak." Apollo lifts her toward me, and I help drag her in, move to steady us as he pulls himself up, then get my paddle going.

Quiet is not a fun trait on Apollo, and that sends guilt through me because this is what he must experience when I hide how I feel from him. Maybe he's done. I've missed my chance again.

I brace myself as we crash against sand. "I'm not dragging him along. I'm in love with him." Stepping out of the kayak, I push my goggles up and take off for the tree line in squishy triathlon shoes, not bothering to listen to the score.

25

HOMECOMING

*a*pollo grabs my arm, swinging me around. "You can't just say that and run off."

Grinning, I back up from him and turn, kicking into a sprint. "Watch me."

"Dammit, Xi. Why now?"

"Because I'm tired of hiding it, okay?" I round a corner, flying by the lost tourist attendant before I slide to a stop and backtrack.

"Xia!" Stella claps her hands and hugs me, even though I'm soaked with ocean and sweat. Apollo pulls up beside me as Stella looks at her paper. "At the fifth rock of Mount Durazno, a woman started her hike. Unfortunately, she didn't have a plan for the temperature spike. Now she's in trouble and trying to find water. Be quick and fetch her, before it gets hotter."

I bark a laugh and kiss Stella's cheek. "Cozette got a hold of the clues, huh?"

"Yes. Now go. Win." She shakes her fist in the air as we step off to the side.

"Xi," Apollo says.

I listen for the monkeys and face the jungle. "If she's trying to find water, she'd go south. Oh! Unless she found the tiny stream flowing under the moss that funnels into the bog."

"Xia, look at me."

I do. "Bog? That has to be it. Do you know how to get there?"

"Yes. Can we—"

"Great, then go that way. Follow the rock turtles, I'll go the moss stream. Meet up at the K-tree, then we'll follow the river back up." I clap twice, taking off down the path, darting into the forest when I see the narrow opening that will lead to the stream, then slow to test the footing, getting into the rhythm of stepping and watching my feet. The monkeys don't disappoint and yell a ruckus at the humans invading their jungle.

There's rustling, and when I glance up, Apollo's ahead, dashing between trees. How did he get in front of me? He trips, and my heart jolts each time I think he's falling.

I can't keep from voicing my concern. "Don't hurt yourself." There are times to go slower to preserve the body. It's hard to sprint a half-mile with a sprained ankle.

"Look, I'm sorry, okay?" he yells, spinning to face me.

It makes me stop for a second before getting back to winning this thing. "Can we talk about this later?"

"Fine," he says, wandering. "No, actually. How can I when you just said you love me?"

"Yeah, I love you. But I don't even know how much that matters because you're gone after this. Let's figure it out at the finish line."

"I'm not leaving!" He throws his hands in the air. "I'm not fucking leaving you again, Xia. I was trying to tell you—"

"So," Monique says, traveling between us on her way south, Farid by her side, dark eyes wide open. "There's this event called the Moss Monster Meet. And you're both like...in it." She shrugs. "Save it for later? Just a caring, well-meaning suggestion." She sneaks on tiptoes. "We're going to win," she singsongs, but in a gentle tone. "Better hurry."

Apollo makes a guttural sound of frustration and heads south, stomping and tripping.

He's not leaving? Ugh, we need to win so we can have this conversation. I refocus and take off, watching my feet. I get close to Monique and Farid, but they're focused as they separate to move east. She's a navigation professional as she does it multiple times daily on horseback. She pauses, studying the thick canopy, and curves south. A moment later, I find the moss-hidden, trickling spring and run it north toward the mountain, sloshy shoes getting muddier with every step. After four minutes, I weave between seven-foot-tall hibiscus bushes, coming face-to-face with my lost tourist. *Oh no.* Like...oh no. We're not going to win. Indigo—The Heat—and Bodhi will be at the finish line by the time we step out of this forest.

"Lovely." Smiling from under a floppy sunhat, lips in her shade of bright fuchsia, Miss Ruth slowly stands from a short camp chair and waves a hand toward it. "Could you get that for me, dear?" When I blink at her, she claps. "Don't look so shell-shocked, Xiamara."

Rushing into action, I collect her chair and give a whistle, hoping Apollo is close enough to hear me. "Sorry." Miss Ruth is agile, energetic for her age. We will move slower than the sprint I was expecting, but we can probably make that work. I should know better than to underestimate people.

"I hope Apollo gets here quick. There's a poker game and bloody Marys waiting for me. If Duchess has a head start on taking all of Jack's shells, I'm blaming you two."

"Mr. Walsh is a lost tourist too?" I ask, tight muscles easing.

"He is. And Angel came as well. We decided that you youthful people were running through the Mossy too fast and that we could help. 'Tis boring when there's no anticipation."

That makes me laugh. "Are you calling the best thing about Simona boring?"

"The best thing about Simona is the people." She looks past me, cloudy blue eyes lighting up. "There's your handsome man."

Apollo steps between the trees, sizing up the situation.

"He's not mine." Looking him over, mesh shorts, athletic shirt, bitable shoulders, lips I really want to kiss again, I sigh. "Not yet."

Miss Ruth rasps a laugh and squeezes my fingers.

Apollo makes his way through the brush and kisses Miss Ruth when she points to her cheek. "How should we proceed?"

I glance at Miss Ruth. "I guess we start..." I point. "Moving. That way then?"

"Was that a question, dear?"

"Let's move that way, toward the main road."

"There we go." Miss Ruth grips Apollo's offered elbow, and I jump in front to navigate the best path.

"So you two are..." Ruth murmurs behind me.

"Uh, yeah," Apollo responds. "Whatever you're thinking, we probably are."

I snort a laugh, moving forward for exactly one minute.

"Uff, this heat," Miss Ruth says. "I think I need a little rest."

I put wide eyes on Apollo, who appears equally terrified.

"You could carry her." He's certainly toted me around enough to prove that.

He nods, turning to Miss Ruth. "Can I?"

She gives a little gasp. "Do you think that's safe? Walking side by side is one thing, but if you trip, we could both be injured. I don't know if that's a good plan. No, stability is key when you're my age. Two sets of legs are always better." She turns mischievous eyes on me, a wicked tilt to her conniving lips.

Apollo snorts. "We should both work together to carry you."

She slaps his chest. "What a smart idea."

I blink and make my way over, handing her the folded chair. Apollo holds his palms out to me, and I settle my arms into them, gripping his forearms, energy sizzling between us even more than usual, like our cells are greeting each other with tight, twirling hugs.

His honey eyes simmer. Miss Ruth clears her throat. I shake my gaze away from Apollo, and we dip, letting Miss Ruth settle into our cradle-hold.

She props the chair against her, then loops her arms around our necks. "There now, that's stable. Onward."

We move forward, carefully navigating the nearly vine-free spring.

"What are your plans for after the Mossy?" Miss Ruth asks.

I glance at Apollo. "I'd like to know that too."

He raises an eyebrow. "You sure? You haven't been interested in talking these last few days. As usual."

"I was thinking through things. Plus, you sent a statement, not a request for conversation."

The path grows narrower. Apollo's grip on my forearms tightens, and he tugs me closer. "I was reaching out, and you ignored me."

"I wasn't sure it mattered. But you said earlier...you're not leaving?"

His lips twitch. "No."

I pause our forward motion to glare at him for ending with that simple word. "Elaborate please."

He glances at Miss Ruth, who is in her element for this front-row show. "Okay then. I'm the owner of Airway Island Tour Company, opening in November here on Simona Island." His grip tightens on my arms. "You okay?"

I open my mouth and squeak when a cacophony of cheers sounds close by.

"Go," Ruth says. "That's coming from the checkpoint. Go, go, go."

We speed walk, nearly jogging up the path in silence, waiting for more cheers to come. As we step out of the jungle onto the soft running trail, Miss Ruth unlatches her arms from us. "Put me down."

We set Miss Ruth down. The seventy-year-old takes off in a run, chair tucked under her arm.

Apollo laughs as we take off after the trickster. We catch up, jogging beside our lost tourist.

"How's that heat treating you?" I ask.

"Much better." Miss Ruth blows out short breaths. "Not sure what came over me back there." She points toward a handful of scorekeepers next to a couple of square tables with cards and drinks set up on them tucked into a cleared-out spot between the trees. "That's the checkpoint. Now go, win this thing."

Apollo and I leap into a sprint past the cheering scorekeepers without slowing down.

"You mad?" he asks.

Our steps are a synchronized, perfect rhythm we've gotten used to over the month. "Only that I knew nothing about it. How long have you been planning this?"

"Since the year I left. I needed a way to return to you, and my parents were fighting over whether I'd work as a transport pilot or at the Cliffs, when all I wanted was to be self-sustaining on this island with you."

I slow. He does too. We face each other, both with our hands on our hips, panting. "Mama mentioned Vic was hoping you'd move back, especially if—" I signal between us.

"I was always trying to return, but on my terms instead of my parents'." He shrugs. "My terms needed funding, a business plan, and training. It took longer than I wanted."

"And you did it. You're here. For good?"

"Yeah," he says with a breathy laugh. "I wasn't sure contracts were going to happen, and I didn't want anyone to be disappointed if they fell through." He glances past me. "Not that you would have been. Others are close. We gotta go."

"Ass," I murmur, starting back on the path and flipping my goggles down.

We pass over the bridge, seconds from the next event. I'm going to the top of the cliff while Apollo directs. Nerves tighten my chest because I'm terrible at this.

"And now we're name calling? I thought maybe you'd be happy."

"I am." I surge toward the upper path. "I've been disappointed since day one because I knew you'd leave again."

"Xia." He exhales my name in either relief or exasperation. Could be both. That would track considering it's us.

The terrain is clear besides the onlookers below, cheering behind a roped section, attention flitting between me and Monique, who's already in the main pond. Let's see if I can catch up. Farid yells directions from a rock outcrop, and Apollo races to the one next to him. Monique is in the lagoon first. I pause and look to Apollo. He beams warm, sweet hopefulness, then cups his hands around his mouth. "I'm told it's near a bush, but you know what you're doing. The rings are in there somewhere. Get one."

I laugh and leap into a swan dive, slipping into the water. I'm at the bottom with ease, ears angry at the pressure of being plummeted thirteen feet underwater as I search in the locations where rings love to hide: tall grass, between rocks, blending in with roots. There are two per contestant scattered below, but in the past they only threw them when another runner got close.

I come up for air twice, but Monique is still in the water, yelling back and forth with Farid. Nerves start hitting hard when I dive a third time, and just when panic settles in, I see a glint next to a green-leafy bush-like plant. Sinking my fingers into the silty bottom, I scoop up a fist of what I hope contains my goal, because my lungs are burning.

Breaking through the water's surface, I sort through the contents in my hand. Sand, dirt, a dead leaf, two tiny spiral-shelled snails, and one thin, silver ring. I whoop and jam it on my right middle finger for safe keeping as I swim toward the edge of the pond, where Apollo is clapping and pacing. He hauls me onto the rocky bank.

More cheers have me checking over my shoulder. Bodhi hits the water with barely a splash. It won't be long until he's out. Apollo drags me toward the grinning older man who takes the ring from me. "Team eighteen, twenty points."

Apollo and I sprint toward the path, flying past cheering attendants, who signal directions.

"I didn't realize you felt that way," Apollo says. "That you were disappointed because you thought this was temporary. You are the most hard to read person I know, Xi."

"And yet you know me."

"I do. There has always been a hope that we could be together. But you crush that sometimes because you act like I'm a dirty little secret."

I could see how hiding from the prying eyes of Simona residents would make him feel like that, especially when I should be strutting around with him as if he's a perfect lavender concoction in my consultation room.

The thinning trees tell me we're close, and as soon as packed dirt loosens into sand, the line of carts comes into view. They've decorated ours with streamers, a light fastened on the top and a poster hanging from the roof that spells out *The Boss-wagon* in glitter.

I trip as I laugh, but Apollo catches me and we pick up the pace. Cozette squeals loud when she sees me, claps, and leaps into the back seat with Jamie, cupping her hands around her mouth. "Get ready, my people! Our champions have arrived."

She leans forward to slap a button on the dash. The light on top flashes blue and spins.

"I hope that's staying there." I wave at the other waiting tourists in the lined-up carts. I high-five Cozette and Jamie as I pass by and plop into the passenger's seat, clearing my throat to prepare for my tour guide voice. "Welcome to Simona Island, everyone. I'm Xiamara, your tour guide. Driving is Apollo. Today we will take you to the Moss Monster Meet. Please keep your hands and feet inside the vehicle at all times. Feel free to heckle any other vehicles, if any come close to catching us."

Apollo stretches his neck. "Which they won't."

I hold onto the roof's *oh shit* handle as Apollo steps on the gas slowly. Rule one of carts: Don't sink in or it's over before it begins.

My passengers taunt the other tourists as we drift into motion, and once we're steady on the loose sand, we pick up the pace.

"Monique and Farid are at their cart!" Jamie yells. "They're taking off. Whoops, too fast. They spun out."

Apollo and I share a *See?* glance.

"Okay, she's going."

Shit. We speed up, and Cozette cackles as we bump over the sand. It's the same motion as sitting on a wave, if that wave were hard plastic that smacks your spine and steals your breath.

"Tell me about the island," Cozette says, voice wobbly from the bumpy ride.

"Well, thank you for ask—" My words are cut off by a particularly vicious bounce as we get to the wet, packed part of the beach. "Simona Island is nearly fourteen square miles of Caribbean paradise. It's home to three-thousand, forty-two— oh!" I turn toward Apollo. "It's official?"

The corner of his lips twitch. "Yes."

"Now, three-thousand forty-*three* residents."

Cozette gasps. "Seriously?"

Jamie claps twice, then grips the armrest bar again. "Happy for you. Look. There's the end."

The stretch of beach curves around to show a sea of people holding up neon signs. My breathing increases as if I'm running. Everyone cheers. This moment should elate me, but there's a restlessness no win will curb. I'm in the lead, things have changed, but I still feel hollow.

"They're gaining," Jamie says.

"You can do it." I put my hand on Apollo's thigh, and he nods, focused on the terrain. He pulls his foot from the pedal as we drift through the checkpoint.

"Thank you for being incredible guests on this tour of beautiful Simona Island." I leap from the cart, sidling up to Apollo for this half-mile stretch, ignoring the well-wishes, cheers, and sounds, instead focusing on the finish line. But something is off. For a second, I believe it's because I'm running with a partner for the first time, but that's not it. I'm running next to Apollo and don't feel like we're truly what we should be. This isn't the right race, because the most important trophy isn't ahead. It's the man beside me who's been doing everything he can to set up a future on this island. He was trying to win *me,* and what have I done? Hidden from him, from everyone, like I always do. I haven't proven to him that he's worth it too.

The cheers grow louder when I tear into the streamer-marked bottleneck, surrounded by Simona Island residents and their families. Someone holds up a poster that says *The new Moss Boss has arrived*. That title doesn't hold the power it used to. My goal has shifted. My feet slow as I ponder, and my lungs burn, not entirely from exercise. The finish is ahead, but all I want to do is tell Apollo how much I love him.

Mama's words drift through my head: *This is what you want, hija. You take it.*

I stop. The buzz of the crowd stumbles like it's tripping

down a short staircase: roar, confusion, cheer, more confusion, murmurs, quiet.

"Xia?" Apollo turns, jogging back to me. "What's wrong? Your leg okay?"

His brows are scrunched tight as he eyes me, the finish line, then me again.

I harness my announcer voice again, loud enough to be heard over the breeze, the whispering hum, and the whir of golf carts in the distance. "You are what I want."

Apollo wipes the sweat from his brow and licks his panting lips as he points a thumb behind him. "The finish line is right there. We should go."

"I can't. Not when you think winning a competition or keeping my life private is more important to me than you are. You thought I didn't love you, but I do."

He dips his head as he eyes the surrounding crowd and peers over my shoulder. "We can discuss this in, like, twenty seconds. You understand that, right?"

"But you need to know now. You needed to know seven years ago, and I couldn't give that to you. You think I'm ashamed of you, but I'm actually a disaster over you. A hot mess, stumbling fool of a mooning woman, and I will do anything to stay that way for the rest of my life if it means you're near me."

The onlookers blink as I step back, take a deep breath, and signal to the man beside me. "Do you all hear me? I love Apollo. I don't care if everyone knows it and sees me falling all over myself around him. Which I'm sure you already did. He's so much more than my Mossy partner, and I love kissing him more than winning. We had sex, and it was leagues above any marathon." With my face burning hot, I wince at Apollo. "And that was too much."

He covers a laugh with his fist and shrugs a shoulder,

appearing smug. "Works for me. It is indeed the best. You mean all that?"

"I do."

A runner flies by me—Bodhi, but Monique is one step behind him and tackles him around the waist. "No, sir."

He yelps from the sand. "What the hell?"

Monique leaps up, blocking him from passing. "We do not go for the win when mental breakthroughs are happening. Get your ass back in line with your partner."

She points, and sure enough, contestants are lining up behind me, including Indigo—The Heat. She's grinning wide, her chin on her clasped hands. Oh my god, these people. As Bodhi hangs his head and trudges toward the others, she follows, clapping him on the shoulder. "And welcome to Simona Island. You'll love it here."

I choke out a teary laugh. It is Simona Island—one big wacky family who shouldn't talk so much about each other but can't help it because it's out of love. Some of us are difficult, some anxious, some are seemingly perfect, and we're all entwined within this small town in paradise.

"Good work, baby," Demi yells from the sidelines next to Vic, who's locked arms with Mama. I think they're crossing their fingers.

"Love you, boo," Monique says, blowing her a kiss.

I swipe at my cheeks. "Okay. So that's that."

"YES, IT IS!" Jose uses his most megaphone voice, pumping his arm into the air—and Walt's, since they're holding hands.

Roxanne pops up beside him. "Claim him, woman!"

Oh, is that a thing? "Um, and everyone who wants Apollo can back off because he's taken. Right? I mean..."

Apollo steps into me and lifts my chin with a finger. "Yes, Xiamara, I am solidly taken." His perfect lips press to mine in a fairytale kiss that has me swooning and wrapping my arms around him. The crowd resumes their cheers, loud as usual. A chant starts: "Moss Boss. Moss Boss. Moss Boss."

I stare into the sweetest honey eyes for one more second before turning and, hand in Apollo's, taking off toward the finish line. Kingston has his phone up, and I smile from my soul for the photo or video that is sure to be on the social media group in the next ten minutes. Mama and Vic bounce as they hold each other. Streamers fly, and posters dance on extended arms. It's another moment that bonds us, just like welcome home celebrations, illness, births, and love that must be shared.

We're not going anywhere.

As soon as I break the streamer for the win, Apollo scoops me off my feet. I wrap myself around him, and he holds me tight, kissing me with ferocious love. How lucky am I to have Simona Island and him? It's lavender and vanilla, dark cherry and cedarwood.

It's our home.

EPILOGUE

ROXANNE HARTFORD

I have been bonfired, rum-punched, salsaed, and hugged by half of Simona Island. The saddest part of this delightful trip is that my bad-girl bra has gone unseen by anyone other than Xia, and though I adore her, she doesn't count.

Tomorrow, I return to my reality: a job I loathe, an ex I tolerate, and a daughter who warms my heart as much as she raises my blood pressure.

My only remaining wish list check mark is to be coveted like I'm a sexpot so I can forget I have to willingly get on a plane back to Florida. I need to get laid.

I lean against the headrest, sighing out my frustrations.

In true Xia fashion, she laughs. "What's wrong?"

"Will there be men at this ceremony?"

"It's not a ceremony." She turns on her parents' street of bright toy-box houses, and I nearly squeal. Simona Island is just the cutest.

"Mama Nivar is handing over the pearl trophy after thirty years, Xia. It's going to be a ceremony with food and words and tears. Now, men. Yay?" I pitch my voice high, then drop low for "Or nay?"

She taps the peeling steering wheel. "Apollo."

I make a gameshow wrong-answer buzz sound.

"My dad."

"Xia, no, no, no. I'm talking available, bed-able men. I'm sure Papa Nivar is a delight in the sack, but your mother would stab a bitch."

"Ew, Rox." She laughs with the greatest, most boisterous ricocheting giggles. "But yes, she really would." We pull into the driveway, and she shakes out her hands. "I'm nervous. Why am I nervous?"

I lean to hug her, jiggling the love right into her. "Because this is a new era and the iconic statue you grew up with is now going to be in your house. When you and Apollo have itty-bitty competitive babies, they'll feel the same way when they take it from you."

She fans her face. "I can't imagine."

I rub her arm. "It's because you're not having enough sex. Don't worry. I'll be gone tomorrow, things will settle down, and you can get totally freaky with your man. Then it's all you will think about."

She's a smitten kitten, and I'm thrilled for her. "Okay. I need to see him now."

"Obviously."

We head over stepping stones to the sunshine-yellow front door. Barging inside, we're greeted with hoots and clapping as if we haven't seen each other for months. It's been literal hours. Mama and Papa Nivar smoosh me between them, asking about drinks and food, then tell me what I like and prance off without me having to say a word.

Apollo greets Xia with a kiss of the ages, and that's when I spot a super-hot target—I mean man. He smiles, though it doesn't get rid of the broodiest brow I've ever encountered, the kind that's straight and low. It not only wants to make me pester him to test how furrowed it can get but also catapults heat right between my legs. Broody brows are my favorite. So good I can even get over the manbun of blond hair. Actually, it's kinda cute on him. He's got a lanky, bearded Thor thing going on.

"Ziggy?" Xia hugs him. *Please don't be a relative or ex-lover.* "You're here!"

"For a couple of days only, then back to England for the summer."

He doesn't sound British. Actually, his accent is closer to Xia's. I step forward and offer a hand. "Hi. I'm Roxanne, Xia's bestie. You two know each other?"

Straight teeth, nice lips, a light panty-dropping stare, and a handshake that makes me want to reel him in. "Sigmund, though my friends call me Ziggy. Xia, Apollo, and I grew up here together."

"Ah. Delightful." I turn wide-hopeful eyes on Xia. She gives me the go-ahead nod. Goody goody.

And then Mama Nivar pushes a drink in my face, grabs my arm, and drags me to the kitchen. I glance back in time to see Ziggy eyeing my ass and, yeah, that's a nice boost for the confidence. Maybe my bad-girl bra will finally get its fifteen minutes in the spotlight.

After taste testing everything in the kitchen and draining my drink, I go to find Xia, moving around the couch, but a tug on my elbow stops me.

Ziggy holds his long finger to his lips.

I lean toward him and whisper, "Why are we being quiet?" Xia must not have gotten a hold of him yet for an essential oil blend. He smells like bar soap and wood shavings, which is nice, but it's not cedarblock baywood or whatever Xia would make him wear. I have on the most incredible of her concoctions, a blend of eight ingredients, though I only remember three. Black tea, ginger, and...okay, two. I remember two.

He points over to Apollo and Xia.

"Where are you going to put it?" Apollo asks as they look at the Moss Boss trophy on the corner shelf. It's a hand-sized half of a mother of pearl shell. The inside is carved into a map of Simona Island, and the work of art is mounted on a wood block. It really is gorgeous.

"I think in the display with my favorite oil vials."

Mama Nivar slides up next to us, and Ziggy reaches across me to cover her mouth. An array of emotions goes through her brown eyes: confusion leads to irritation, then blinks back to confusion, then interest and excitement. *There.* We're all on the same page.

Ziggy drops his hand, tipping his head toward the newest Moss Boss.

"Makes sense," Apollo says, reaching out to run a finger over the right section of the carved map. "I always thought this part of the island looked like a ring."

Xia leans closer. "What? It does not. Where?"

When Apollo pulls something from his pocket, I grip Ziggy's arm. Oh, that's a strong forearm. Nice.

Apollo moves behind Xia, and we all lean to watch as he holds a diamond ring in front of her. "Right here."

I bite my lips closed to tamp down the squeal in my throat because the room is pin-drop silent as Xia stares. She glances back at him, big, pretty eyes full-moon wide. "Urm, ah."

"Yeah, wild, right?" Apollo nods. "I love you, Xiamara Nivar. Will you finally be mine?"

I want this so much for her, and one day for me. When Hadley leaves for college, I will date again, love again, marry again...for good this time.

"Oh my god," Xia says. "Seriously?" The word comes out riding a sob, and my throat goes tight and itchy.

"No," Apollo says, kissing her forehead. "This ring I got my first year of college so I'd remember what I was working toward is just a huge ruse to make you speechless."

"Aw," I say, unable to contain it. I lean against Mama Nivar. "He's good."

She swipes at tears and nods.

"It worked." Xia hiccups. "Yes. I will. We will. I love you too. I do. So much."

"And she's rambling," I say, letting Ziggy's arm go. "Kiss him, Xia."

She does, and we all approach for hugs—and to see this sweet little diamond Apollo adorned my bestie with. Everyone does the *what are the wedding plans?* interrogation that there are no answers to since they're one-minute engaged, but it's fun to think about anyway.

After an hour of talk and tears, Ziggy sidles up to me at the guacamole pot. "I hear you're single."

Oh, are we going there? "I am. And you?"

"Uh huh. Just in for a visit?"

I turn toward him, leaning against the counter. We've entered the pre-foreplay questioning stage of our evening. Splendid. "I am. But back to the States at eight in the morning. You?"

"I only visit for two days, twice a year at the most, unless I can avoid more."

Who would avoid Simona Island? It doesn't matter—he's temporary and safe. I'm in. "Well, wasn't it serendipitous that we're both here at the same time then. Probably won't see each other again."

"Not until the wedding." For as light as his eyes are, they smolder hot and sexy fire. "I assume."

Possibly an issue if this evening goes how I think it will. "Yeah. I won't visit again until then."

"Did you get to do everything you wanted to while you were here?"

"Mostly. I mean, I didn't get laid, so that's a bit of a disappointment, but it's been a great trip."

"How sad." He bites his lower lip, eyes trailing over me in a way that would make me blush if I did that sort of thing. "Maybe I can help you out."

Bingo, baby. That's a wrap. Bad-girl bra perks up. "Aw, how kind. Look at you, saving my vacation."

Thank you for reading! Did you enjoy? Please add your review because nothing helps an author more and encourages readers to take a chance on a book than a review.

Don't miss more from Poppy Minnix with the next book in the Simona Island series coming soon, and discover her paranormal stories at www.poppyminnix.com

Want more holiday goodness? Check out CHRISTMAS ISLAND, by City Owl Author, Mary Shotwell. Turn the page for a sneak peek!

You can also sign up for the City Owl Press newsletter to receive notice of all book releases!

SNEAK PEEK OF CHRISTMAS ISLAND

BY MARY SHOTWELL

Thursday, December 15

Laura Crawford stepped onto the sidewalk in front of her apartment in South End, a tidy, chic two-bedroom in a comfortable nook of Charlotte, North Carolina. Technically, it wasn't her apartment, but rather *their* apartment. Hers and Logan's. The harder she tried not to think about Logan Ainsworth and his misdeeds, the more he popped up in her thoughts.

Just move on. He's never coming back.

He'll come crawling back, begging for forgiveness.

Once a cheater, always a cheater.

He'll see the error of his ways.

Everyone had something to say about her fiancé leaving her for another woman. The cheating itself was terrible enough. Not knowing where to go and what to do about their shared apartment was almost as bad.

She grazed her thumb over her ring finger. The diamond adorned on the gold ring had been a staple of her wardrobe, a part of her hand, that she continued to forget she no longer wore it. She kept it in her purse, not quite ready to lock it away. For whatever reason, keeping it with her, but not on her, felt right.

She walked in her comfortable flats, her stretchy, gray work pants, and a pink blouse under her knee-length wool coat, the dressiest she'd get for her job. Heels were not an option, even though the non-profit office was one neighborhood away in Dilworth. Who really enjoyed wearing heels all day? If Laura had to describe herself in one word, it would be practical. Practicality saved money, time, and like flats, provided the more comfortable choice.

If anything, she wished she had added her knit headband—her pulled back, highlighted hair doing nothing to shield her ears from the stiff morning breeze. She raised her shoulders and clenched her coat, passing by the second of three murals on the workday walk. More than half of the nearly dozen murals along these brick facades were likely there purely for social media attention. Now that Christmas swiftly approached, lighted metal ornaments of candy canes and snowflakes hung off lampposts and facades of businesses willing to participate in the ambiance. The neighborhood was Instagram-worthy; a menagerie of coffee shops, art studios, craft breweries, and modern apartments.

Ugh. That shared apartment. What was she going to do? She couldn't afford the rent so close to work on her own. If Logan didn't have a problem with her staying there—why should he, considering he was nowhere to be found and had cut off communication some three weeks ago—then was it necessary to go through moving stress?

Practicality, Laura.

The Learning Center for Autism Spectrum Disorder sat wedged between a children's boutique and cafe, a first-floor, twelve hundred square-foot space with a classroom, three offices, and front desk. The naming wasn't coincidental. The founder came up with the acronym before the full title—TLC for ASD. Laura and all the employees called it TLC for short.

Laura stepped inside and found the front desk unoccupied. Generally, they left it that way until after school when the majority of clients came by. She walked past the desk and the sign on the wall displaying the logo—a hand lifting an infinity symbol.

"There she is." Cindy stood next to a familiar mother with her son.

"Good morning, Cindy." Laura smiled back, wishing it came as effortless as Cindy's cheerfulness. Not that it pained her to smile. It was just that Cindy became an orientation leader fresh out of college, and her small frame, short, fun bob and undying positivity made Laura's twenty-six years of age seem two generations older. Less peppy.

"I didn't expect to see you here, Ryan. Mrs. Faye."

"We wanted to stop by this morning, since it's a Power Monday for the school. I don't really understand how much an extra hour or two for the kids once a month helps them in any way, but what do I know?"

"Mom." Ryan, wearing a faded Nirvana T-shirt, nudged his mother's shoulder. He held a jacket in one hand, and hid his other hand behind his back.

"Sorry. Show her, honey."

He proudly revealed his secret—a printed book report clearly showing a grade of 'A' on the front.

"That's amazing!" Laura high-fived the teenager. Such a success was the reason she had taken the job in the first place at TLC.

"It's a testament to the work you all do here," Mrs. Faye said.

Laura took the compliment in stride, reaching to tuck her hair behind her ear before remembering it was pulled back in a ponytail. "It's also because of the hard work Ryan has put in."

Ryan had been her first consultation since starting the position as community and regional outreach planner at TLC. A year ago, she'd held a community information night at his high school, one of many schools she visited throughout the greater Charlotte area. He and his mother came in the following morning. Ryan wasn't too keen on being there and kept staring at the door and standing, only for Mrs. Faye to sit him down again. He wore that same Nirvana T-shirt and Laura quoted Kurt Cobain, which promptly won not only his attention but his willingness to participate. Laura came up with a plan that included after-school sessions for academics along with hands-on simulations and field trips to alleviate his social discomfort.

Now here were Ryan and Mrs. Faye a year down the road, showing tangible results. TLC had doubled its employees in that time, and Laura no longer focused on creating and implementing personal plans of action. She didn't miss wearing several hats at once but missed the deeper connections with the students.

"Keep that up and I'm going to have to attend your graduation."

"Mom said I don't have to walk in one of those stupid dresses and hats."

"We're working on it." Mrs. Faye winked.

Ryan turned to his mother. "We'll be late."

"That's my cue." Mrs. Faye led her son towards the front door, and Laura followed.

"Don't take 160," Ryan said. "We have to go to Clanton Road, then right on—"

"I know, I know." Mrs. Faye patted his shoulder as Laura held the door for them.

"Have a great day at school, Ryan."

He walked out to the sidewalk and his mother looked back.

Laura lowered her voice. "Sounds like you'd better take Clanton."

Mrs. Faye smiled. "Who needs a GPS? I keep telling him he needs to be a traffic reporter."

"No cameras." Ryan shook his head.

The two left, and Laura held the door as a young man

carrying a package approached. He read the label. "For...Pham Kim-Anh."

"I'll take it to Kim."

"You do work here, right?" He couldn't have been a day over twenty.

"I do. Where's Sam? He usually has this route."

His apprehension disappeared. "I'm covering him the rest of the week."

"And your name is?"

"Trey."

"Nice to meet you, Trey. I'm Laura. You'd better get going. Sam sets the bar high for reliable delivery people."

Trey smiled. "Understood."

"I'll see you around, then."

Trey nodded, and Laura went back inside the office.

"Wasn't that amazing?" Cindy leaned on the front desk. "His first A on an essay, can you believe it?"

"It was amazing." The full circle Ryan took hit her again.

"What do you have there?"

Laura looked at the package in her hand. "It's for Kim. I'm assuming she's back there?"

"Yep. She was here on the phone before I got here. I don't even know who she could be talking to so early."

"You know Kim." Laura walked down the hallway. The multimedia classroom took up most of the space to her left, while storage, a restroom, and an office took up the right. The other two offices sat in the back, the right corner office her boss, Kim's, headquarters.

Laura knocked on the frame of the office's open door.. Laura always knocked because Kim could get so focused on a task people suddenly appearing in front of her scared the bejesus out of her.

"Morning." Kim's dark hair curled under at her shoulders and simple diamond studs gleamed on her pierced ears.

Although twenty years older than Laura, hardly a gray streak of hair shone through Kim's black locks. Meanwhile, Laura had been highlighting her hair since twenty-one. Her brunette hair was losing the fight, and the blond streaks disguised the gray and subsequent root growth better than her natural color. It was a little annoying to be sandwiched between two coworkers whose looks defied their ages.

"Got a package for you." Laura set it on her desk.

"Any word from Logan?" Kim had a tendency to ask every Monday, but seeing as she led a three-day short course this week, it was the first chance she'd had to ask.

Laura sighed. "So much for work getting my mind off of him."

"I'm sorry. I just thought he had another week to realize what an idiot he is."

"Unfortunately, he is still unaware of that fact."

Kim's shoulders sagged, clearly disappointed in Logan's lack of self-reflection.

"You know, I don't even know if he's told his friends or family?" Breakups were tough enough. But it thickened the hurt when his work friends, and even his family, had accepted her as one of them. Laura had especially bonded with his mother throughout her battle with cancer. It pained her not knowing how she was doing. "I'm guessing the fact they haven't contacted me means they do know."

"They're probably wincing at his behavior, too embarrassed to admit their poor choice in friends." Kim winked. "If it makes you feel better, I do have something to keep your mind off of Buttface McGee."

Laura half chuckled. Kim's straightforward attitude could be a shocker at times. But Laura also worried what could be up her sleeve.

Kim gestured to take a seat.

Laura obliged, bracing for whatever project Kim had on her mind.

"Beverly and James Bennett contacted me. Apparently, they had a chat over Thanksgiving weekend. Long story short, they came up with the idea of a Holiday Fundraiser."

"Oh?"

"To benefit the organization."

"Well, that's good news, right?"

"I believe so. The Bennetts know a lot of families and have really embraced the ASD community the past few months, ever since introducing us to their granddaughter, Hannah."

Laura nodded. Hannah had attended a few regional events with her father and sometimes her grandparents. She was a sweet girl; seven or eight years old.

"They want to have a fundraiser here in Charlotte? Let me guess, you're freaking out because that's incredibly short notice."

Kim's lips curled in a smirk. "*I'm* not freaking out."

Laura jumped from her seat. "You want me to do this? Organize a fundraiser? Isn't that the job of the event manager?"

"You're right, it is. But seeing as Sophie is currently on maternity leave, our community and regional outreach manager is the next best thing."

Laura tipped her head back and closed her eyes. It would be short notice, and to get a venue in Charlotte—

"Wait. The Bennetts aren't from Charlotte. They do mean to have it here, though, right?"

Kim grabbed a folder off her desk and handed it over. "If you head out of here early tomorrow, you should miss the city traffic and get to Waverly Lake in three hours."

"Are you serious? You're giving me a day's notice on this?" Technically, not even a day if she had to leave early tomorrow morning.

"Did you have plans for this weekend?" Kim blinked, hand on her hip.

Laura's mind reeled. Did Kim even care whether Logan called, or was she just asking to know if Laura's weekend would be open? No, Kim cared. And she'd also known no plans existed before asking. That was what happened when the boss-employee relationship crossed into friendship.

Laura groaned, flipping through the file folder.

"They're expecting you tomorrow. The address is in there, as well as your hotel info, along with the groups Beverly Bennett suggested contacting for attendance and spreading the word."

"Hotel? I can't drive out and drive back?"

"I have you staying the night. You'll have to discuss scope and logistics with them so you can help find a venue. Plus, I figured you could use a night away from that apartment. I mean, aren't you reminded of him with every piece of furniture, every decoration?"

"Of course, I am. It's just that I don't have an alternative yet."

"You do now. At least for one night." Kim raised her eyebrows.

Laura nodded. "I didn't get a chance to tell Trey goodbye."

"Trey? Who is Trey?"

"Sam's replacement for this week."

"Who is Sam?"

Laura rolled her eyes. "Our delivery guy. Trey is covering him this week. Poor kid was nervous I didn't work here and was going to steal your package, but we sorted it out."

"Your fiancé is nowhere to be found with his lover, you're still living in his apartment, and you're worried about not saying goodbye to the temporary delivery boy." Kim chuckled and shook her head. "You definitely need a night away."

"Fine, fine." Laura walked to the door and turned around.

"I'll have you know that befriending people you see in your neighborhood every day is a good trait to have."

"Go." Kim waved her out. "Before I make it two nights away."

Don't stop now. Keep reading with your copy of CHRISTMAS ISLAND, by City Owl Author, Mary Shotwell

And find more from Poppy Minnix at www.poppyminnix.com

Don't miss more from Poppy Minnix with the next book in the Simona Island series coming soon, and discover her paranormal stories at www.poppyminnix.com

Want more holiday goodness? Check out CHRISTMAS ISLAND, by City Owl Author, Mary Shotwell!

Twenty-six-year-old Laura Crawford loves her job at The Learning Center for ASD. If only she could get her love-life in order. After her fiancé, Logan, leaves her for another woman, Laura throws herself into her work, helping kids and teenagers with ASD. But the heartbreak bleeds through her work, and her boss sends her on a special assignment—to help the Bennetts with a fundraiser in Waverly Lake. It's a chance to get out of town for a change of scenery, and with a fast-approaching deadline, Laura puts her all behind it.

Hometown attorney Steve Albertson has had it with feuding citizens, and the nearing holidays only magnify the tension. He plans on getting out of Waverly Lake, spending Christmas at a condo on the Gulf Coast. When Beverly Bennett asks him to help with her fundraiser, how could he say no? He only wishes he had when he meets the organizer, Laura, who immediately pegs him as too high maintenance and self-absorbed to care about the task at hand.

As the two work together to hammer down a fundraiser theme and venue, they discover that first impressions aren't always accurate. Between tree farms and Winter Fest, sailing and uncovering an old island mystery, the two are drawn to each other. As a bah humbug citizen threatens to shut down their fundraiser, Laura's past threatens to pull them apart. Can Waverly Lake's holiday magic pull off a Christmas miracle?

Please sign up for the City Owl Press newsletter for chances to win special subscriber-only contests and giveaways as well as receiving information on upcoming releases and special excerpts.

All reviews are **welcome** and **appreciated**. Please consider leaving one on your favorite social media and book buying sites.

Escape Your World. Get Lost in Ours! City Owl Press at www. cityowlpress.com.

ACKNOWLEDGMENTS

Mary! This book wouldn't exist without you. Thank you for asking for more and then honing my words into something I'm really proud of. Your dedication, knowledge, and patience are everything an author could ask for. I am endlessly lucky and appreciative for you. (You just mentally edited this paragraph, didn't you? You're the best!)

My amazing family; thank you for your encouragement and celebration when I finish another manuscript. I couldn't do this without you.

To my writing ladies Cass, Immy, Lori, Rebecca, Linda, Claudia, Carolyn, Jackie, and Annick. Ya'll the best and I lubs you. More sprints and brainstorming tomorrow. Let's do this thing. *insert pumped-up gif*

To my sensitivity readers, Heather and Kelsea; your insight into Caribbean culture, POC and LGBTQ+ characters, and more was beyond helpful. I cannot thank you enough for making sure this book stayed kind, true, and respectful to all.

I'm thrilled to be one of so many amazing City Owl authors and appreciate all the work City Owl Press puts in to make these books and this industry the best it can be for everyone. So many thanks!

ABOUT THE AUTHOR

One bleary winter, Poppy Minnix accidentally wrote a novel—a paranormal romance she obsessively typed out in five weeks. Years later, she still barely sleeps, has nightmares of exploding biscuit cans when she does (it's a valid phobia!), and writes every waking minute.

She lives in Maryland with a husband who is far more romantic than she is and two delightful kids who kindly open the terrifying dough bombs for her. They are all kept busy by the best rescue lab-ish mongrel ever, and two cats who think they are dogs.

Along with authoring, she's also the co-host of Punch Keys Podcast, an encouraging podcast for navigating the writing world.

www.poppyminnix.com

twitter.com/PoppyMinnix

instagram.com/poppyminnix

facebook.com/poppymwrites

goodreads.com/poppyminnix

ABOUT THE PUBLISHER

City Owl Press is a cutting edge indie publishing company, bringing the world of romance and speculative fiction to discerning readers.

Escape Your World. Get Lost in Ours!

www.cityowlpress.com

facebook.com/YourCityOwlPress
twitter.com/cityowlpress
instagram.com/cityowlbooks
pinterest.com/cityowlpress